The Dead Girl Reunion

Amanda's

A Jack McCall Mystery

Best Wishes

P.K. Ross

P.K. Ross

Cover design by Roslyn McFarland

ISBN: 978-0-692-04854-2

Library of Congress Register-1-3166375501

DEDICATION

This book is dedicated to all who teach. There is no greater calling among humankind than to help a young mind grow.

For Lizzie—teacher, wife, and best friend.

And a special dedication to the memory of Jennifer Leigh Schmidt, who watched over the children as they learned and played. A short life, well lived.

ACKNOWLEDGEMENTS

It is no coincidence that the dedication for this book is to "all who teach," and that my first acknowledgement goes to Elizabeth Engstrom, author and teacher. Some people are gifted, or a savant, or a prodigy, or the like, when they start writing. I, however, was not. So, when I was first inspired to write a novel, I took one of Elizabeth's writing courses at Lane Community College in Eugene, Oregon. She taught me how to start, gave me some basic tools of the craft and, most importantly, provided encouragement and guidance that I draw upon daily. I hope that when she reads this story she will recognize her hand in its creation, the true reward for a teacher.

When I finished writing this manuscript, all I really wanted was for someone to read it. Fortunately, I found some exceptional people who were willing to take my story for a test-drive and, more importantly, were willing to tell me what they thought — nothing is more valuable. Thank you Lori Schmidt, Tami Hubert, Connie Hume-Rodman, Kerry Tipton, Tom Catalano, Steve Dixon, George Voss, Mike Bell, and Claranell Hardenburger for your time and your feedback. You helped me become a better writer.

Special thanks to Jim Zeller, Laura Stanfill, and Leigh Goodison. Jim (*an accomplished pilot*) read this story to make sure that the "Hollywood" factor in the aviation scenes did not stray too far from reality. Leigh provided story feedback and coaching during the writing process and reviewed the final manuscript as part of the process for the Northwest Independent Writers Association quality award. Laura provided editing and feedback services on query and synopsis development and offered advice on identifying resource for publishing, as did Leigh. Thank you Jim, Leigh, and Laura.

I would also like to thank the editors who helped me shape this story. Jane Bowyer Stewart (Washington, D.C.), my copy editor and the world's greatest violinist, applied her keen eye and shared her insights, which were instrumental (*pun intended*) in helping me produce a quality manuscript. Aviva Layton (Hollywood, CA), professional story editor, spotted the plot errors that others only sensed. Her experience and coaching helped me create a much better reader experience.

CHAPTER 1

FOR TWENTY YEARS Jack McCall swore he would never return to his hometown in Oregon, but here he was, falling from the sky above Oregon's Willamette Valley as if he had been strapped to his favorite leather easy chair and dropped off a 200-story building. His seat belt and shoulder harness strained to keep him in place as his aircraft plummeted toward the valley floor where he and the dead girl were born—and where, twenty years ago, she was buried.

"Jack—what the hell did you do, Jack?" his wife, and copilot, shouted into her microphone.

A navigational chart rose from the floor on its weightless journey toward the ceiling as the aircraft dropped. The debris brushed the side of his head as it passed. An image of the dead girl flickered into his mind and then vanished, forced into the background by the urgency of the moment.

"I knew I shouldn't have come back, Mollie," he said. "Damned place is still trying to flush me down the toilet."

"Oh, that's a comforting image," Mollie said. "And I'm going to get flushed along with you."

Jack glanced at his copilot, then focused his eyes on the white hands of the altimeter, which measured the alarming descent of the aircraft. "I've lost two already," he said. "I'm not going to lose you."

The aircraft jerked to the right.

"What do you mean, you've 'lost *two*'?" Mollie said.

Jack didn't respond to her question. The sudden movement of the aircraft commanded his attention and provided the perfect escape to avoid explaining his slip-of-the-tongue, or so he hoped.

The aircraft fell for only a few seconds, but to Jack it seemed like an eternity before the wings of his vintage Aero Commander could find enough stable air to halt their downward plunge. When air started to flow over the wings in a normal fashion, the resulting lift drove the couple downward into their seats, trapping them like scrap metal against a huge electromagnet. Several charts and an empty Diet Coke can that were floating around the cabin rained down on the passengers and upholstery. His stomach felt queasy, but he wasn't sure whether it was from the freefall or from the memories of the dead girl that the jolt of the sudden drop seemed to have dislodged.

"Why did you say *two*?" Mollie said, rubbing her stomach as if moving her internal organs back into place. "Were you married to someone else before Janis?"

Jack looked around for air traffic as he gave a slow-motion shake of the head and a barely audible "no."

"Then why did you say two?" Mollie repeated, as she began reorganizing the navigation charts set free during their unplanned descent. "Talk to me, Jack."

Jack didn't answer.

Mollie stared at him for a few moments, then continued to tidy up the cabin. "If you keep it bottled up inside you," she said, as she stowed the last chart in the leather compartment behind the pilot seat, "you're going to start drinking again." She stared at him once more, but he didn't move.

Housekeeping complete, she reached down and freed the thermos bottle secured with an elastic strap to the side of the center console. The large stainless steel thermos was always strapped to the console just to the left of Mollie's legs so she could have easy access to her coffee. Mollie loved her coffee.

Jack never touched the stuff. He watched her pour a large portion of the dark brown liquid into the thermos lid, which doubled as a cup. "Like drinking Drano," he said, shaking his head to feign disapproval.

"Say the word and I'll set up the taste test," Mollie said, punctuated with a chuckle.

An image of the dead girl once again entered Jack's mind, but this time it lingered. "Maybe if I drank some of that magic brew of yours, I'd get sick and wouldn't have to go to this damned reunion."

"High school reunions can be a real bore," Mollie said.

Jack nodded in response to his wife's apparent attempt to dilute the anxiety she knew was building inside his brain. He smiled, pleased by her effort. He closed his eyes and took a deep breath in a futile attempt to suppress the memories of the past.

"Thanks, Mollie," Jack said, as he turned toward his copilot. "You just gave me an excuse to turn this airplane around and head back to Hartford."

Mollie put the coffee cup to her lips and took a drink of the steamy liquid. She looked at the scenery below the airplane and shook her head. "You could go all the way back to when you were sleeping in this airplane on a semi-regular basis—like when I first met you."

Jack groaned at the memory of his struggles following the death of his former wife. "At least the upholstery has been redone," he said. "Upgraded accommodations."

"Jack," Mollie said, "Janis's death wasn't your fault. *She* was driving drunk, not you. But if you let your self-imposed guilt lead you to start drinking and sleeping in this airplane again, you're going to be sleeping alone."

Jack stroked the soft leather seat back behind Mollie's head as he reflected on her words. "Marrying me probably wasn't one of your best decisions."

"At least it's not dull," Mollie said. "I could have married Robert the accountant and spent my life working on tax forms."

"Robert the Accountant," Jack said. "Sounds like one of King Arthur's Merry Men—or knights—or something like that."

"Robin Hood had the 'Merry Band of Men,'" Mollie said, "and don't change the subject." She pointed out the window toward the ground below the aircraft. "That's not Sherwood Forest down there, it's the valley where your drinking started. And Dr. Kemp is not going to be pleased if you don't return to face your demons." She paused and looked at Jack. "You have to go . . ."

"Back so you can go forward," Jack said, finishing her sentence with a grimace and a nod. "Are you going to be the mouthpiece for the good doctor this entire trip?"

"No," Mollie said with a smile, as she rubbed her husband's shoulder. "But I don't think he'd even accept *death* as an excuse for not following through with your commitment to attend this reunion."

"Death," Jack mumbled. "That's the way it all started."

"Whose death?" Mollie said. "The one before Janis? Is that one of the demons?"

Jack took another deep breath. "Demons—yes—can't ignore my demons anymore." An image of the dead girl entered his mind again and morphed from an innocent young face to one cut and bloodied beyond recognition. He felt a nervous shiver travel up his back and out to his fingertips. *Damn. I need a drink.*

Mollie stowed her thermos back in its cradle. "I expect you to tell me about the other person you 'lost' before we land," she said. "You asked me to help you get through this process, but I can't do that if you don't tell me the whole story."

Jack mumbled an acknowledgement of her statement, then contacted the regional air traffic center to give a courtesy report on the turbulence they had encountered.

"Commander Six-two-seven-eight-Bravo, Seattle Center," the voice on the radio replied. "Roger, understand clear air turbulence at one-four-thousand feet over Salem. Thank you for the report."

"You're welcome. Seven-eight-Bravo, out."

"Well done, counselor," Mollie said, offering a hand in the air for a high five. Her eyes squinted just enough for Jack to notice, and then a devilish grin crept onto her face.

"What?" he said, staring at the statuesque pose of his copilot and withholding the celebratory hand-slap.

"You diverted attention away from your sloppy flying by blaming it on an invisible quirk of nature." A sparkle of mischief flashed from her green eyes as she dropped her hand back to her lap. "Too bad you can't do that in court. Otherwise, you could blame a defendant's acquittal on the summer solstice."

Jack hesitated for a moment, contemplating whether he wanted to be drawn into a verbal joust, a contest he would relish under normal circumstances but one he knew he wouldn't win. Mollie's mind worked almost as fast as her computers, and her mouth could spew dialogue faster than the most advanced printer on the market.

"Hand me the Salem section chart," he said. "I want to check our position."

Mollie turned to look at Jack. "What, no snappy comeback?"

"It's been over thirty years since I've flown down this valley," he said, "and Dad was at the controls on that outing. Besides, if I give you something to do, maybe you'll leave me alone."

Mollie's smile in response to her husband's remark was the equivalent of a victory lap after a race. Her green eyes were once again larger than life, and her long red hair was draped across her shoulders. Her hands still trembled a little.

"Drive for a minute, Mollie," Jack said, trying to hold the limp map open with one hand and pilot the aircraft with the other. "I want to look at this chart."

Mollie moved her seat forward, enabling her feet to reach the control pedals in the footwell on her side of the airplane. She adjusted her sunglasses back to their intended position and placed her hands on the control wheel.

"Got it," she said.

Their heading was almost due south, straight down the middle of the Willamette Valley. Mollie checked the compass on the instrument panel in front of her to note the heading, then began looking around for other air traffic. "Can you see Caldwell yet?" she said. "I want to see where you lived."

Jack didn't answer. He looked at the chart for a few more minutes, staring at one spot on its multi-colored surface, then folded and stowed the chart back in the seat pocket.

"Okay," he said, touching Mollie on the arm. "I'll take the controls now." He put his hands back on the controls while moving his feet forward to the foot pedals. As soon as Mollie's hands were clear of the controls, he switched off the autopilot and banked the aircraft to the west.

"Where the hell are we going?" Mollie said.

"You wanted the whole story," he said. " —all the demons?"

"Yes."

"We're going to track down a demon."

As the aircraft made a steady right turn, the sun swept into the cockpit, drenching them in its warmth and brilliance. Jack's eyes struggled to adjust to the intense light flooding through the windshield. The dark green lenses of his sunglasses filtered out enough of the sunlight to allow him to see ahead. Mollie leaned sideways in her seat and began to remove the white cotton jacket she was wearing.

"Let me help you with that, ma'am," the gentleman offered, grabbing the gathered elastic cuff of her sleeve to assist her.

"Thank you, kind sir," was the lady's reply. "But this jacket is the only clothing I'm going to remove, so don't get your hopes up."

Her humor brought a smile back to Jack's face, masking the anxiety of the memory he was about to confront. "What is life without hope?" he said, as he let his hand fall down to a bare spot on her back between her shirt and her pants.

Mollie let his hand linger on her skin for a moment, then nudged his arm away with her shoulder. "Not now," she said, and then finished removing her jacket. She folded it with care and placed it on the seat behind her husband. Her hand, during its journey back to her side of the airplane, stopped to massage his neck and shoulders.

Both of them, for the first time since their abrupt encounter with air turbulence, turned their attention to the countryside below. The tan grass and wheat fields, intermixed with green groves of fir and oak trees, appeared to capture Mollie's full attention. Jack allowed himself to gaze at the scenery as much as was prudent for the pilot-in-command.

Proceeding to the west, the farms, roads, and very small communities gave way to rolling hills covered by an endless patchwork of evergreen tree farms. The only interruption of the green terrain below was an occasional road or riverbed serving as an accent to the dominance of the forest.

Jack pushed the controls forward a little. The aircraft responded by pointing her nose downward just enough to begin a slow descent.

"Dixon State Park was one of my favorite places when I was growing up," he said. "Mom and Dad used to take me there on picnics when I was a kid."

The aircraft circled the west side of the peak and then dropped closer to the terrain as it approached the park area from the south. Small lakes dotted the valleys between the mountain and lower peaks. The bodies of water changed color, from a silver reflection of the sunlight to a deep blue-green, as they passed overhead.

"Blacktail deer," Jack said, pointing toward a small herd grazing on the edge of park. "There are lots of them up here. They have an extended hunting season some years just to keep the population under control."

"It's beautiful," Mollie said.

"There's the park down there," Jack said, pointing ahead and to the right. "In high school this was a favorite destination for couples. We'll go a little lower so you can get a better look."

Jack eased the throttles back and leveled the wings, as the Aero Commander drifted downward, closer to the treetops. The parking lot was on the downhill side of the clearing, at the top edge of a steep incline.

"I can see why it was popular," she said, with a knowing smile. "I'll bet the view from that parking lot is spectacular at night."

Jack banked the airplane to the right again, heading away from the park and away from the mountain peak. "You're right about the view at night," he said, after an exaggerated pause. "But I only saw it once. The Park Service used to keep the gate closed after dark so no one could come up here."

"How'd you get up here to see it that one time?"

Jack took a deep breath; his forearms and hands tightened as though bracing to run head-on into something massive. "The night we graduated from high school, a bunch of us left the all-night party at two in the morning, drove up to the park entrance, and picked the lock on the gate. There were twelve couples in twelve cars." He flexed his hands on the controls as if relieving tension. "We had visions of getting into *The Guinness Book of World Records* or something."

"Why haven't I seen your name in the book?"

"Look down to your right," he said. "Do you see a sharp curve in the road with a guardrail, and a cliff below it?"

Mollie leaned to her right, resting her head against the cold side window as her eyes followed the park access road below. She gathered the waterfall of red hair that complicated her view and brushed it back across her shoulder. She tracked the winding two-lane asphalt road to a curve where the tree-lined corridor was interrupted by a large outcropping of rock on the uphill side. There was a long silver guardrail on the downhill side of the road. Beyond the railing was a forty-five-degree drop-off, lined with rock down to a tree line about a hundred feet below the highway.

"Yes, I see it," she said. "Looks rather treacherous."

"When the twelve couples headed back down the mountain, we found a big hole in the guardrail and one of our classmates in a car at the bottom of the cliff. She was dead."

Mollie glanced in his direction to gauge the sincerity of this unexpected twist. He was not smiling. The tense projection of a bad memory covered his face.

"I can see how that would make you forget about Mr. Guinness," she mumbled, with only halfhearted levity. "How well did you know her?"

Again Jack hesitated before answering. His hands flexed on the aircraft controls, changing color as the blood rushed in and out of his fingers. His head rotated, as if saying no to something, but he did not speak. He didn't want to say the words.

After a long pause, he said, "She'd been my girlfriend, right up until the day before graduation. Her name was Ann Ridgeway."

Mollie's eyes got wider. "Your former girlfriend?" Her head tipped slightly to the left and her eyes squinted a little, suggesting her brain was processing the information.

Jack's whole body started to twitch like it had a mind of its own. His hands shook as he tried to keep the airplane on course.

"Did they ever figure out why she'd gone off the road?" Mollie asked.

Jack gathered some acquired courtroom detachment to block the memory of the dead girl from taking control. "The official verdict was accidental death," he said. "The investigator speculated it was most likely driver error, or she might have swerved to avoid hitting a deer. Suicide was even mentioned as a possibility."

Mollie leaned closer and put her hand on Jack's shoulder. "Was she the first one you lost?"

Jack nodded and turned to face her. "You said earlier that Janis's death wasn't my fault," he said, "and I can rationalize that to a degree. But whatever the cause, Annie's death was my fault."

"What?"

"It was my fault," he said. A single tear started to trickle down his face just below his right eye—and then vanished with a quick swipe of the storyteller's hand.

A few moments passed as Jack squirmed in his seat and swallowed a big chunk of emotion that was trying to escape.

"Why was it your fault?" Mollie said.

"I picked the lock to open the gate. I made it possible for her to be up here, and she was obviously up here to find me because we'd just broken up."

Mollie turned away from her husband and looked at the scenery while digesting this new information. "Ann was number one and Janis was number two—and you aren't going to let me be number three."

Jack grimaced and let out a barely audible groan.

"Is her death the demon that's kept you away for twenty years?" Mollie said, staring at the landscape below.

"Demons," he mumbled. "Yes, that's one of them."

"One of them?" Mollie said.

Jack unbuckled his seat belt and shoulder harness. "Drive for a while, Mollie," he said, rubbing his right knee through his denim jeans. "I need to move around a little."

As his copilot took control, Jack moved his seat as far back as it would go, tilting the seat back a couple of notches in the process. He was a large man, which made stretching within the confines of the cockpit a challenging maneuver. Raising his hands over his head and extending his legs in the footwell, he allowed his frame to consume as much of the cockpit as possible and then settled back into a relaxed, lounging position. He stared out the window for a short time, looking down at the trees and ahead to the valley.

"I don't know if I can do this, Mollie," he confessed, without lifting his gaze from the fields below.

"How did you deal with Ann's death when it happened?" she said.

"The easy way," he said. "Jack Daniels—anesthesia in a bottle. You don't feel a thing."

"So you *didn't* deal with it when it happened," Mollie said.

Jack shook his head. "Nope," he said. "If it hadn't been for Coach Grady, I'd probably be dead and buried in the same cemetery as Annie."

"You've mentioned Coach Grady before," Mollie said, as she reached out and adjusted the cabin temperature gauge.

"Whenever I fell flat on my face," Jack said, with a smile and a shake of the head at the recollection, "he'd pick me up, set me straight, and give me a push in the right direction."

"Well, you're not lying in the cemetery with the dead girl," Mollie said. "You survived the car crash that killed Janis, and now you've got your brilliant, beautiful, and talented new wife by your side. So you'll get through this reunion just fine."

Jack raised his head and looked at her. A suggestion of a smile crept onto his face. He had suppressed the memories of the dead girl for decades and hidden the incident from his wife as well. Now that he had summoned the courage to tell her the story, to say the words, the energy was rushing out of his body. He put his left elbow on the armrest and tried to sit up straight, but his arm just quivered under the weight of his body and his legs didn't want to move. He slumped back into his seat.

Jack sat motionless for a while, trying to recharge. The long hours in the airplane and the gentle, tranquilizing vibration of the engines drained him of the energy required for conversation.

As they approached the valley again, Jack made another attempt to straighten his posture. This time his body responded, so he reached out and put his hands back on the control yoke. "I've got it," he said.

Mollie retracted her hands and feet away from the controls and moved her seat back a notch. "Your reunion will be a lot more interesting than mine was," she said. "Especially if Dakota Douglas shows up."

"Yeah, big Hollywood star," Jack said. "I knew him when he couldn't stand in front of the class without peeing in his pants."

"Really?" Mollie responded. "He did that?"

Jack emitted a low volume chuckle and nodded, "First grade." He pressed the microphone switch on his control yoke and contacted the control tower at Caldwell airport for landing instructions.

"Caldwell Tower, Seven-eight-Bravo, roger. Report two miles out for a right-hand base approach to runway one-seven. Seven-eight-Bravo out."

"I'm surprised that he's even coming," Mollie said.

"Who?"

"Dakota Douglas," Mollie said. "He's driving racecars, he's got that big remake of *Murder on the Orient Express* that he's working on, and he's been in the middle of that water rights mess at his ranch north of Bakersfield."

"How do you know so much about his business?" Jack said.

Mollie reached into her flight bag and pulled out a *People* magazine. "How do you think?" she said, waving it in the air like a street-corner vendor.

"I might have known," Jack said. He nudged the control yoke forward, and the Commander descended to begin their approach to land.

"How many times have you landed an airplane at this place?" Mollie said.

Jack looked around for other aircraft for a few seconds, delaying the answer to her question. He pushed his sunglasses up the bridge of his nose. "Well," he finally said, with an exaggerated grimace and a head movement that suggested he was looking around for explanations as well as air traffic, "that's an interesting question. You see, I've never really landed an airplane here."

Mollie swiveled around to the left, as close to sidesaddle as the seat harness would allow, and leaned forward, watching his body language for a clue to his uncharacteristic evasiveness. "Jack, you're squirming like a puppy that's got to pee. What's wrong? Didn't your dad ever let you land his airplane?"

"Yeah, he let me try to land it—once. I messed up, big-time. I almost wrecked the airplane. Bounced that sucker a good ten feet in the air," he said, raising his hand to demonstrate. "Then it rolled left like it was going to come down on the wing." The hand continued the aerial maneuver.

"What'd your dad do?" Mollie said.

Jack smiled, remembering the moment. "He hit the power and leveled the wings, overpowering my arms and hands and overpowering Mother Earth, who was trying to suck us into the ground."

"How old were you?"

"Thirteen," he said. "Never got another chance after that."

Jack knew that under normal circumstances he could set this sleek, white, aerodynamic sweetheart down with such precision and grace that the tires wouldn't know when to start rolling. But his arms and legs felt weak, and this place was different.

"Caldwell Tower, Seven-eight-Bravo is entering right-hand base to runway one-seven, over."

"Seven-eight-Bravo, Caldwell Tower. You are cleared for a right-hand base approach to runway one-seven, no traffic in the pattern. Report turning final for landing clearance, over."

"Seven-eight-Bravo, roger, report turning final."

"Didn't your dad die when you were thirteen?" Mollie said.

"Yes. He had his heart attack while he was driving to work, about three weeks after I tried dribbling his airplane down this very runway."

"That's why you never got a second chance then?"

"Yeah, that's why." An image of his father in the copilot seat flashed into Jack's mind.

"Caldwell Tower, Seven-eight-Bravo is one mile out on final approach for runway one-seven requesting clearance to land, over."

"Seven-eight-Bravo, Caldwell Tower, wind calm, cleared to land runway one-seven."

"Seven-eight-Bravo, roger, cleared to land runway one-seven."

"Put the flaps down, Mollie."

"Flaps down. Landing gear?" Mollie said.

> *More power, Son, and keep that nose pointed down. That's it.*

"Jack, do you want the landing gear down now?"

> *Now when you get over the runway, just keep her flying and let her settle to the runway.*

"Jack—I'm putting the landing gear down."

"Uh—yeah, landing gear down."

> *Your line is good, just keep her level. When you touch down, cut the power and just let her roll.*

"Gear down, three in the green."

> *You're over the runway, close to touchdown. Bring the nose up a little. That's it. Good line. Just let her settle down to the runway, then cut the power. Don't cut the power yet, Son, you're not down. Oh, shit.*

"Nice landing, Jack. Your dad would have been proud of you. I don't think you've ever made a better landing than that one."

"Seven-eight-Bravo, Tower, report clear of the runway then contact Caldwell ground control on one-one-eight-point-five, over."

"Two-five-Sierra, roger, contact Caldwell Ground on one-one-eight-point-five."

"Jack, you gave him the wrong call sign."

"What? . . . Oh. Tower, Seven-eight-Bravo, roger, report clear and contact ground control."

"Well," Mollie said, "you're home, safe and sound."

Jack guided the Commander off the runway and onto the taxiway leading to the terminal. "Safe?" he said.

CHAPTER 2

THE AERO COMMANDER spun around as if the right main wheel were nailed to the parking apron. Dust and grass on the 100-year-old concrete surface flew in retreat from the propeller blades driven by the roaring engines mounted on the overhead wings. Jack brought the aircraft out of its turn and rolled to a gentle stop over the tie-downs where World War II Army Air Corps pilots had parked their aircraft. He shut the engines down and moved his seat back as far as it would go.

Mollie unbuckled her seat belt and shoulder harness. "I hope that car-dealer classmate of yours hasn't forgotten about our rental car," she said. "I'd hate for you to make your triumphant return to Caldwell riding in the back of some farmer's '53 Ford pickup, with a black Lab named Bob sitting on your lap."

"You worry too much." Jack said. "Stewart Ramsey never forgets—especially when he can make a buck."

A cool coastal breeze coming from the mountain pass to the west welcomed Jack as he opened the pilot's door on the left side of the aircraft. He strained to straighten the kinks out of his body as he put his left foot on the concrete surface.

"Aaaaggghh." His body flew upward, landing back in the pilot seat.

Mollie spun her head around and grabbed his arm. "What's wrong?"

Jack had landed as far away from the door as possible without sitting in the copilot's lap. "*Snake*," he said.

Mollie choked back a chuckle and exited the airplane through the cabin door, also on the left side of the aircraft. She peered at the parking apron. "It's dead," she said. "Looks like it was run over by a fuel truck or something."

Jack leaned to the left and looked over the bottom edge of the door. The head of the rather large bull snake was crushed. "Can you move it so I can get out?" he asked.

Mollie didn't suppress her amusement this time and let an all-out belly laugh escape as she picked up the dead reptile by the tail and flung it into the grass behind the airplane.

"You can come out now, Tarzan," she said. "It's safe."

Jack was used to her teasing him about his fear of snakes, so he ignored her comment as he stepped out of the airplane, trying to act casual by brushing his hair back and stretching. The wind drifted across his face and through his hair as he took a few deep breaths to turn off the flow of adrenaline and to refocus on being home. Airborne scents of a host of different grasses, trees, and flowers found their way to brain cells that had been dormant for two decades. He looked out across the parking apron and saw tufts of grass growing in the cracks between the forty-foot-square concrete pads. As a boy, he had thought they looked like porcupines, huddled down, trying to hide from the wind. The childhood memories were still there.

Jack's reflection on the past was interrupted by the sound of music. Loud, obnoxious, electric guitar music, and a bass so deep it rattled the metal cowling on the airplane. It was getting louder by the second. A shiny black Ford Mustang convertible poked its nose around the Beechcraft Queen Air parked next to the Aero Commander. A skinny face, shrouded in black-framed sun-glasses, bobbed up and down behind the steering wheel as the car rolled to a stop in front of the travel-weary couple. The young driver jabbed the power button on the stereo, bringing instant relief to the ears of all living beings for miles.

"Mr. McCall?" the boy said, opening the car door and climbing out.

"That's me," Jack said.

"I'm Joe Ramsey," the boy said, rounding the back corner of the car. "My dad told me to bring this car out here for you."

"Well it's nice to meet you, Joe," Jack said, extending his hand in greeting. "And thanks for delivering the car." He turned to his wife. "Joe, this is my wife, Mollie."

"How do you do, Mrs. McCall?" Joe said.

"I like this young man, Jack," Mollie said, shaking Joe's hand. "He's polite." The boy's blemished face blushed to a monotone red. "It's nice to meet you, Joe."

"How's your dad?" Jack said.

"He's great," Joe said. "He said to say hello and to invite you to the house for a drink after you get settled. He's having a reception for classmates and his campaign staff."

"Campaign?" Jack said.

"Yes, sir," the boy replied. "He's going all-in for a state senate seat. He's even got some big-wig US senator coming here this weekend to campaign for him."

"Well, thank him for the invitation," Jack said. "But we'd better take a rain check. Mollie and I have been flying all day, and we need to check into our hotel, have dinner, and get some rest. Do you have some papers for us to sign for the car rental?"

"No, sir. This is a demonstrator. Dad said you can use it as long as you're here, with his compliments. This model has a Bluetooth feature on the stereo for your cell phone, so you won't get stopped by the cops."

"That's extremely generous of your father," Jack said. "Perhaps Mollie and I will have an opportunity to do something for him while we are here. Does he like to fly?"

"Don't know," Joe said, "but I do."

"Good. Mollie and I are going to do a little aerial sightseeing within the next couple of days. Perhaps you can join us."

"That would be great," Joe said. "Would it be okay if my girlfriend, Carrie, came along? I mean, would there be enough room in the plane?"

"Plenty of room," Mollie said. "We would love to have both of you join us. In fact, there's room for four of you if you want to invite a couple more friends."

"Thanks, Mrs. McCall," Joe said. "That would be excellent."

"I'll get the luggage from the plane," Jack said, strolling toward the cargo hatch. "Where do we need to drop you, Joe?"

"Let me help you, sir," the boy said, heeling behind Jack. "You don't need to drop me anywhere. My girlfriend should be here any minute to pick me up." Joe put his hand on the fuselage of the Commander as he waited for Jack to open the luggage compartment. "Nice airplane. Is it new?"

Jack chuckled. "I wish," he said. "It's a 1975 Shrike Aero Commander, Model 500S. It's been completely redone."

Joe petted the aircraft again. "You must be rich," he said.

"Not me," Jack said, "my wife."

Joe looked at Mollie who was reaching into the cabin to retrieve her backpack.

"Not that wife," Jack said, "my first wife."

Joe opened his mouth as if he wanted to ask more questions, but then smiled, nodded, and picked up two of the suitcases Jack had extracted from the cargo area. The two men carried the suitcases and Jack's golf clubs to the rear of the Mustang, and then tried for several minutes to fit them into the microscopic trunk of the sporty car. Mollie gathered her travel bag and Jack's briefcase from the inside of the airplane. The briefcase was open, so she set it down on the tarmac, and as she reached for the latch to close it, the case tipped over and a pistol fell out, making a clatter that drew the attention of Jack and Joe. Joe's eyes doubled in size.

Mollie picked up the weapon and placed it back in the briefcase. She closed the latch and picked up the briefcase, giving Jack a disapproving glare as she walked toward the car.

"I thought you were going to leave that at home," she said, as she arrived at the car and nudged the men out of the way so she could put the smaller items in the trunk.

"Changed my mind," Jack said, offering no apology for the presence of the gun.

Mollie rolled her eyes. "Is there more than a guilty conscience waiting for you this weekend?" she said. "Some demons that shoot back, maybe?"

Jack gave her his patented "very funny" grin in response to her question.

Mollie returned his patented grin and then looked down at the remaining baggage. She instructed the men to put two of the suitcases and the golf clubs in the back seat, then headed back to the airplane to clean the trash out of the cabin area and lock the door. The men did as they were told.

"We're all set," Jack said, taking Mollie's hand as she arrived back at the car. He turned his attention to Joe. "You sure your girlfriend will pick you up, Joe? Be happy to drop you off someplace."

"She'll be here," Joe said. "I promised to buy her dinner at The Shed."

"The O'Toole Shed?" Jack said.

"Yes, sir," Joe said.

"Who's running the place now?" Jack said. "Spike?"

"Yes, sir," Joe said. "His grandfather passed away ten years ago and his dad plays golf most days, so Spike has pretty much taken over."

"Well, thanks again for bringing the car out," Mollie said. "We'll be at the Caldwell Inn. One of us will call your house and let you know when we can go sightseeing."

Jack and Mollie slid into the black leather seats of the Mustang.

"The O'Toole Shed?" Mollie said, fastening her seat belt. "Really, the O'Toole Shed? Where do you people come up with these names?"

Jack laughed and turned the ignition key, bringing the 5.0-liter engine to life. The Mustang was light, with a large engine, and when a mistimed clutch release spun the rear tires, they responded with a chirp to let the world know a driver error had occurred.

"Awfully nice of Stewart Ramsey to let us use this car, wasn't it?" Mollie said. "Kind of blows the hell out of your 'anything to make a buck' assessment."

"I guess it was short-sighted of me to assume that I was the only one who might change in twenty years," Jack said.

Mollie ended the conversation with "Yup."

Jack piloted the convertible down the parking apron.

"Stop at the hangar a minute," Mollie instructed.

"Girls' room?" Jack said.

He received only what he interpreted as a "stupid question" look from his wife in response. She exited the car before it stopped moving, leaving Jack sitting alone, staring into the large aircraft hangar he had roamed as a boy. The airplanes huddled inside were newer, but the age of the World War II–vintage building showed through the multiple layers of paint that tried in vain to preserve its youth. His recollection was of a cavernous structure that dwarfed him as a small boy, but now it seemed unimpressive and feeble.

Mollie interrupted his time traveling by climbing over the closed car door and sliding into the passenger seat. "Home, Jack," she ordered.

Jack put the Mustang into first gear and chirped the tires again as the car left the parking apron and turned onto the access road leading to the main street. He had traveled this route before, but it felt much different this day. Mollie was with him now, her hair whipping in the wind as they turned onto the tree-lined main road into Caldwell.

The Caldwell Inn had been on the outskirts of town when Jack left for college. His memory of the place was of a single-story deluxe motel, restaurant, and bar, originally built by Cyrus Hackett. The Mustang cruised past the green-and-white city limits sign and several brick-fenced residential developments before arriving at the main drive that led to the inn, now surrounded by restaurants, shops, and an office complex. The tall fir trees and expansive lawns on the hotel grounds still gave the place a rural feeling, but time and suburban sprawl had caught up with the community landmark, even passed it by. The place was manicured to perfection, not a blade of grass out of place. The landscaping was the same, he thought. It had not been allowed to change. The walkways and driveway were the same. Jack stared at the white-stucco-and-red-tile Spanish-style four-story structure at the end of the drive that now stood where the motel had once been. The building had definitely changed.

The sleek Mustang with the big engine rolled down the drive at a slow pace, more like a Cadillac carrying mourners than a hotrod convertible transporting a middle-aged man recapturing his youth. As they approached the drive-through carport in front of the main building, several groundskeepers crossed in front of them, pushing a cart and being herded by a very large man in a denim leisure suit.

Jack's face cracked a broad smile and then dropped to a menacing frown. "Hey," he shouted, bringing the car to a halt in the driveway, next to the entrance. "Somebody call animal control. A hippo has escaped from the zoo."

The large mass of a man turned and advanced toward the couple, a tense smile leading the way. As he reached the car, the smile relaxed and the man raked his salt-and-pepper hair backward with a massive palm. "I ought to kick your ass, McCall, just for old times' sake," he said, wrapping both hands over the top of the driver's-side car door.

"Hackett," Jack said, looking him square in the eye, "you couldn't whip my grandmother—and she's dead."

Mollie's hand slid onto the door handle and her body tensed, pushing her shoulder against the door. Her posture suggested escape was her foremost thought until both men erupted in laughter and clasped hands. "I take it this is one of your friends, Jack," she said, sliding her right elbow up over the top of the door and striking a casual pose.

"Mollie, this behemoth is Bruno Hackett, the largest offensive guard to ever put on a Caldwell High School football uniform."

"Thanks, Jack," Bruno said, "You could have at least introduced me as the 'Best Offensive Guard', or the 'Most Skillful Lineman,' or . . ."

"Like I said," Jack interrupted, "the largest ego on the offensive line. Bruno, this is my wife, Mollie."

"It's a pleasure to meet you, Bruno," Mollie said, giving a brief wave to prevent Jack from being crushed in the path of a formal handshake.

"Mollie, it's a real pleasure to meet you," Bruno said, backing away from the car door. "Your room is ready and waiting for you." Bruno looked around, then pointed toward a red-white-and-blue tow truck that was backed up to a car, blocking the entrance to the parking lot. "I'll have Billy move your car as soon as Earl Cramer gets that car on the hook and towed away," he said, as he opened the door for Mollie.

Jack got out of the car and stared at the tow truck.

"Is that Lamont Cramer's boy?" he said.

"Yes," Bruno said. "He took over driving the truck after Lamont's accident. Lamont got hurt bad. A Caddy got loose under tow and pulled the truck off the road into a bridge abutment. He doesn't walk too well now." Bruno raised his hand and summoned a valet stationed just inside the glass front doors of the inn. The boy quick-stepped his way out the door and headed toward the Mustang. Jack tossed the uniformed boy the car keys and followed his host into the building with Mollie on his arm.

The lobby area was decorated with crushed-velvet Mediterranean furniture, an abundance of wrought-iron lamps and accessories, and, for accent, a huge conquistador's helmet with crossed swords above the brick fireplace.

"This furniture is in great shape," Mollie said to her host, as they followed him toward the front desk.

"Thanks," Bruno said. "Just had it all reupholstered again this year. Had to order the fabric from South Carolina, but we got the best."

"I don't believe this place," Mollie mumbled into the shoulder of Jack's shirt.

Jack responded with a barely audible "Be nice" out of the side of his mouth as he strolled up to the front desk, where Bruno grabbed a pen.

"Just sign here, Jack," Bruno said, thrusting the pen at Jack. "No need for a card imprint. You always were the most honest man I ever met."

Jack chuckled at the compliment and signed the registration card. "Where's the boys' room, Bruno?" he inquired.

"Down that hallway, second door on your right," the host said, pointing toward the far side of the lobby.

"How about a Coke machine?" Jack said.

"Same hallway, on the left," their host said. "And while you're in there, I'll give the little lady here a tour of the main floor."

"Lead the way," Mollie said.

Jack headed across the lobby, and Bruno motioned for Mollie to follow him as he headed toward another hallway, just beyond the elevator door at the end of the registration desk. As they reached the first doorway on the right, Bruno grabbed Mollie by the elbow and redirected her into the room.

"I'll show you the bar first," he said. "It's right in here. We've been waiting for Jack to show up. We haven't had a good party since he left for college."

"I appreciate the offer, Bruno," Mollie said, "but Jack and I haven't eaten yet, and we've been flying all day."

"Oh, nonsense, Mollie," he said. "There's a bunch of Jack's classmates right back there at the end of the bar just dying to say hello."

"Well, I guess I can't disappoint my husband's classmates, now can I?" Mollie said, giving in to her host's determination.

Bruno waddled between and around the first wave of low-backed red vinyl lounge chairs, arranged neatly throughout the long, narrow room. White macramé plant hangers, full-length self-adoration mirrors, and spotlighted disco posters lined the elongated time capsule, which had ceased to evolve on March 17, 1973, the date on the faded "Grand Opening" banner still hanging in the far left-hand corner of the room. A long belly-high bar dominated the left wall, with liquor-bottle-lined glass shelves attached to mirrored wall panels, and bar glasses hanging down like crystal stalactites. Red vinyl trim stools and an abundance of brass accessories made the bar area blend with the rest of the room.

"Where's the mirrored ball thing that's supposed to be hanging above the dance floor?" Mollie said to her gigantic host.

"Fell down and broke four weeks ago," Bruno said, continuing toward the rear of the room with the inquisitor in tow. "The new one will be here in three days. Can't wait 'til it gets here. Our Saturday night disco contests just haven't been the same since the damn thing broke."

"You just answered my next question," Mollie said.

She followed Bruno through the maze of chairs and tables, a few of which were occupied by a variety of characters clad in everything from shorts and T-shirts to suits and dresses. The variety of people seemed consistent with the variety of odors, ranging from powerful sweet perfume to stale beer and twenty-year-old cigar smoke, stagnating in little air pockets the entire length of the room. Weaving their way through the final row of chairs, the pair arrived at the end of the bar to join three men who were huddled around a large pitcher of beer.

"Hey, guys, guess who this is?" Bruno said. "This here's McCall's wife, Mollie."

One of the men, who was sitting directly under the overhead recessed light, stood and offered a weathered and calloused hand in greeting.

"Hi, Mollie," the tall, sandy-haired man said, "I'm Henry Coleman."

Mollie, Bruno, and Henry were standing directly under the light, making the other two figures difficult to see. Time and sun had etched lines in Henry's face, and their general shape confirmed that the smile he flashed was one of his most frequent facial expressions. Their prominence was amplified by the aftermath of an only semi-efficient removal of dirt from the crevices in the skin down each side of his face. His once-white T-shirt was a grayish brown, with darker brown circles where sweat and dirt from the day's work merged beneath his arms and around his neck.

"Excuse my appearance, Mollie," Henry said, "I've been harvesting grass seed since sunup, and I just stopped in for a cold one on my way back to the farm. Where's Jack?"

"He'll be along in a minute," she said. "He stopped to use the men's room and to get a Diet Coke from the vending machine."

Bruno poured himself a beer and then raised his glass in the direction of one of the other men. "Mollie, this is Frank Kirby," he said.

A hand stretched out into the light, followed by an arm covered in light-gray tweed, then a rounded face, a crop of whitish-gray hair, and the rest of the sport coat. "Welcome to Caldwell, Mrs. McCall," he said, shaking Mollie's hand one cycle, then withdrawing. A shoulder holster and pistol peeked out of the sports coat as Frank straightened and leaned back away from the light.

"Frank," Mollie said, with a cautious smile.

"Mrs. McCall," the third man said, extending his hand out into the light. "My name is Joshua Pitts. I'm another of your husband's classmates."

Joshua stood his ground out of the light, requiring Mollie to nudge Bruno out of the way to position herself to shake the man's hand. His face was not well illuminated, but two features were evident: a severe case of male-pattern baldness, and thin, sharp features dominated by large, close-set eyes.

"Hey, Jack," Bruno shouted toward the main entrance, waving his large hand over his head, "we're back here."

Jack stood at the doorway, his shoulders square to the room, his back straight, and a Diet Coke in his right hand. He could see Mollie at the back of the room. Her shining red hair and the presence of her large tour guide were unmistakable. He hesitated a few moments at the entrance to see whether Mollie would excuse herself and join him in the hallway. No such luck. He wasn't quite ready to start this reunion, but social etiquette was not giving him a choice.

The room smelled like stale beer and popcorn. Glasses tinkled as the bartender triple-rinsed them and hung them overhead to dry. Jack moved across the oak floor planks that led him further into the room, through a minefield of low-backed red vinyl chairs. The drink blender at the bar crunched and screamed in an attempt to digest ice for some sort of frozen concoction for a man with that "traveling salesman" look, who was supervising the mixing process from a barstool right in front of the machine.

"Come on, Jack," Bruno shouted. "No need to buy. We've got a full pitcher back here."

Jack quickened his pace and arrived at the gathering with his courtroom smile hiding the butterflies in his stomach. Mollie took his arm and moved close to him.

"Pour the man a beer, Henry," Bruno insisted, sliding a fresh glass toward the pitcher.

Jack and Henry both moved a hand toward the glass, with Jack's arriving first, palm-down over the top with an aggressive and firm "No, thank you."

Henry drew his hand back, his mouth open in confusion over his old friend's unexpected reaction.

"Don't drink anymore," Jack announced, removing his hand from the glass and placing it on Henry's shoulder, "but thanks for the offer anyway."

"Welcome home, Jack," Henry said, nodding his head in approval. The two men locked right hands.

"I'd like to second that welcome, Jack," Joshua said, stepping full into the light. "In case you don't recognize me, I'm Joshua Pitts."

Jack extended his hand with a noticeable hesitation. "Pitts, yes," he said. "Nice to see you again." He looked at the fourth man. "Kirby?"

"Hello, McCall."

Jack hesitated, then offered his right hand in greeting. Frank's grip was firm and the pressure squeezing Jack's fingers together increased, causing him pain as the two men progressed through the formal greeting.

"You're still in good shape, I see," Jack said, as Frank release his hold on Jack's hand.

Frank smiled and let out a low-volume chuckle, seeming to be pleased with the exchange.

"You'll have to excuse me," Frank said, taking a step toward the dance floor. "I'm still on duty and I need to get back to the station."

Jack flexed his fingers as he watched Kirby walk away. "Well, he hasn't changed much in twenty years," he said. "Is he still pissed that I beat him out for first-string quarterback?"

"Ignore him, Jack," Bruno said. "He's been a jerk since he first moved to town, and when he became chief of police he got even worse." Bruno put an arm around Jack. "No sense in spending this week worrying about Frank. Let's celebrate." He wrapped his hand around one of the beer pitchers, ignoring the handle, and filled the glasses of the remaining group.

"You'll never guess what Pitts here does for a living these days, Jack," Bruno said. "He's a freelance photographer, just like his parents. Right, Josh?"

"Actually, I get paid much more than my parents ever did," Joshua said, fidgeting with a huge diamond ring on his right hand. "I travel all over the world and have covered just about every major event in the last fifteen years."

"Do you still live here in Caldwell?" Mollie said.

"No," Joshua said. "I have a very nice condominium in the River Plaza development in Chicago. My office and studio adjoin my condo."

"High rent district," Mollie said, raising her glass to toast the achievement.

Joshua sighed and fondled his ring again. "Like I said, I'm well paid for my work. How about you, Jack? What keeps you busy these days, besides keeping up with your lovely wife?"

"Law," Jack said. "I work for the feds, putting bad guys behind bars."

"FBI?" Joshua said.

"DOJ," Jack said.

Bruno looked at Jack. "DOJ?"

"Department of Justice," Joshua said. "He's a federal prosecutor, probably?"

Jack nodded, his response punctuated with a yawn, the result of both fatigue and anxiety. "Listen," he said, "Mollie and I are going to grab a bite to eat. You guys want to join us for dinner?"

Henry took a handkerchief out of his pocket and wiped his forehead. "Jack, I'm lucky Bruno lets me sneak in the back door for a beer. If I tried to set foot in the dining room, I'm afraid it would tax our friendship."

"I have a previous engagement," Joshua said.

The small group went through the football coin-toss handshake routine, ending with Joshua departing toward the lobby and Henry through a back door that led to the alley.

"I'll take you to the dining room, Jack," Bruno said, "but I can't join you for dinner. I have a staff meeting with the night crew in fifteen minutes."

Mollie and Jack followed Bruno back through the maze of seats. "What was that all about with Frank?" Mollie said, in a quiet voice.

"Tell you later," Jack whispered.

"We're pretty busy tonight," Bruno said, as they entered the dining area. He walked the couple to a table for four near the middle of the room. "Lots of our classmates from out of town are staying here." Jack tended Mollie's chair as she slid into the red vinyl seat that matched the bar decor. The subtle screech of her chair sliding on the floor was accompanied by a variety of dining room clangs, tinkles, and clunks. The whole scene was accented by the distinct odor of garlic and oregano that filled the room. Even to a novice cook it would have been apparent that pasta was piled somewhere nearby.

"Who's going to win the prize for traveling the furthest for the reunion, Bruno?" Mollie said, fidgeting with the dining utensils atop the starched white tablecloth.

"Rosemary Poole," Bruno said without hesitation. "She came all the way from Africa."

"Rosemary Poole," Jack said, squinting his eyes and rippling his mouth as his brain strained to recall the girl. "Don't seem to remember her."

Mollie patted Jack's hand. "That's odd," she said. "From all those stories you've told me, I thought you knew every girl in your class and at least one class ahead and behind you—intimately."

"You probably don't remember her, Jack," Bruno said. "She was only here for one year while her folks were overseas setting up a village hospital in Kenya. On top of that, she left to be with her parents the morning after the graduation party."

"You're a regular *Who's Who* of Caldwell High School, Bruno," Jack said. "How do you keep all this information straight?"

A shadow engulfed Jack as Bruno leaned down close to disclose his secrets. The garlic aroma grew stronger as well. "Actually, she's staying here, and I spent about half an hour talking with her yesterday," he revealed. "The girl was dying to hear as much gossip as possible. She didn't even know that Annie Ridgeway died in a car wreck the night of the graduation party."

Jack got a knot in his stomach at the mention of Annie's name. He reached out to pick up the water glass in front of his place setting but knocked it over instead, drenching the tablecloth and an assortment of sugar substitutes at the center of the table.

"Damn, I'm sorry, Bruno," he said, his hand darting to the tablecloth in front of Mollie and lifting it to stem the tidal wave heading toward her lap. "I guess I'm a little tired. Can't even make my hands work right."

"No problem," Bruno said. He raised his hand, and two busboys magically appeared and began to repair the damage. A waiter, near the service prep area, tucked his order book into his starched white apron and grabbed a new tablecloth and two setups. He traversed the tables at a dignified jog and began resetting the table. Bruno's eyes watched every move the trio made. His face was rigid during the entire process. Only when the two busboys finished setting the table and replacement drinks arrived did he smile and thank his staff.

"You'll have to excuse me," Bruno said. "Duty calls." He rose from his chair to leave.

"Wait," Jack said. "Where is Coach Grady living now?"

"He's in the assisted living facility a couple of blocks from here," Bruno said.

"I want to visit him tomorrow," Jack said.

"Better call first, Jack," Bruno said. "He's not doing too well these days."

"Is Dakota coming to the reunion?" Jack said.

Bruno nodded. "I talked with him last week and he said he'll try his best to be here. He's hassling with the producers of his new movie—something about a big life insurance policy—and with some big corporate farm near his ranch in California. The film company doesn't want him to do any racing, and the corporation wants his water."

"Bet he loves that," Mollie said. "The *People* article I read said that he'd rather race Porsches than act."

"Oh, yeah," Bruno said. He turned and started off toward the kitchen.

"Do you think Virgil will make an appearance?" Jack shouted at Bruno as he walked away.

Bruno turned his head and smiled as he continued walking. "Hope so," he said.

Mollie buried her face in the menu as though searching for treasure. "Okay," she said, without lifting her eyes from her search. "So tell me about these three characters I just met. And who's Virgil?"

"Long story," Jack said, surveying the occupants of the dining room. "And as for the guys in the bar, well, I've known Henry the longest." He glanced at the menu.

"And . . . ," Mollie said, twirling her hand to prompt a continuation of the story.

"We grew up together," Jack said. "Grade school—junior high—but in high school we didn't hang out together much. I guess it was because he always had to work with his dad and his grandfather on the family farm. Looking back on it now, though, it seems odd," he said, staring at the candle flickering in the middle of the table. "We were such good friends."

"Why were you such good friends?" she asked Jack.

Jack's eyes continued to fixate on the candle. "When we were in grade school, second grade, I think, I got into a fight with the Jimmerson brothers. There were three of them: two older than me, one younger. They were beating the crap out of me." A smile crept onto his face. "I was lying on my back on the ground when I saw this hand grab Sammy Jimmerson's hair and pull him off me. It was Henry."

"Then what happened?" Mollie said, sipping her coffee and watching his face.

"Henry kicked the shit out of all three of them," Jack said, his grin even wider than before. "He saved my butt and got expelled from school for it. We were best friends after that—did everything together. I even wanted to be a farmer when I grew up."

"What about this Pitts guy?" Mollie inquired. "He looks like a character straight out of *The Godfather*."

"He was okay in grade school and junior high, but he got kind of weird in high school," Jack said, with a slight grimace. "Weird family, too. Everyone speculated his parents were hiding out from the Mafia, or at least it was entertaining to think so. They had a business sign in front of their house that said 'Pitts Photography' but not very many customers going in and out of the place."

"He's well-spoken now," Mollie said. "Seems to have acquired some sophistication."

A busboy brought Jack's salad.

"He had a little sister too," Jack said. He paused for a long time to poke at his salad with a fork. "Kind of cute, brunette."

"How little?" Mollie said.

"Six, seven years younger," he said. "She always hung around him when he was taking pictures after school for the student newspaper and yearbook. That was the only thing he was really noted for, and that was about the only time you'd see his sister."

"Does sound like a weird family," Mollie said. "You want to tell me about Constable Kirby? You two seemed to have been arm-wrestling in the bar."

Jack was quiet for a few moments, slowly shaking his head. "I can't help it," he said. "He moved to town when we were in the seventh grade, and he and I have competed for everything since then."

"Are we talking cage-fighting or dogs peeing on fire hydrants?" Mollie said with a grin.

"More the hydrant type of competition. We both played the same position in football, from middle school until our senior year in high school."

"Quarterback?"

Jack nodded. "He was always first string until our sophomore year, but then I had a growth spurt and played ahead of him after that."

"So you just competed in football?"

"No," Jack said. "Everything: sports, student government, dishwashing — everything."

"Girls?"

Jack smiled. "Yeah, he dated Annie before I did. After she started going out with me, Frank went out of his way to make me look stupid, when he got the chance."

"And what did you do to him?" Mollie said.

"Nothing," Jack said. "I felt sorry for him."

"So you only peed on his hydrant in self-defense, then," Mollie said.

Jack picked up his fork and pushed around some lettuce on his salad plate. "Something like that," he said.

Mollie downed a few fork-loads of salad. "You still haven't told me why you broke up with Annie the day before you graduated."

Jack looked around the room again and raised his hand to acknowledge a classmate who was staring back at him. The process gave him time to decide how to answer her question. "What makes you think *I* broke up with *her*?" he said. "Maybe *she* broke up with *me*."

Mollie looked up at him. "Did *she* break up with *you*?" she said, mocking his emphasis.

"Can we talk about something else?" Jack said. "I'm tired."

Mollie was quiet for a few moments. Jack knew she wanted more information but was hoping that fatigue and her concern for him would override her curiosity.

"Well, okay then," she said, accommodating her husband's request. "I hope Dakota Douglas shows up. I want to get his autograph."

"Maybe he'll leave his ego in LA," Jack said.

"He's an Academy Award–winning actor," Mollie said, "and all the trade magazines portray him as having an ego the size of Texas. Do you really think he'll show up in his hometown to attend his high school reunion without trying to hog center stage?"

"Good point," Jack said.

"And you promised that I'll get to meet this *Virgil* character," Mollie said.

Jack responded with a smile as a server brought a tray of food, an interruption he welcomed. He was tired of thinking about Frank Kirby and Ann Ridgeway and everything that had happened twenty years ago.

The couple ate their meal without much further conversation and headed upstairs to their room. The rooms at the Caldwell Inn were what Mollie and Jack expected after their tour of the downstairs: Mediterranean décor with red velour, wrought iron, stucco, and all the armor accessories the well-dressed conquistador might require. Jack opened the wrought-iron-framed double doors leading to the balcony of their fourth-floor room. The fresh air that drifted in relieved the institutional smell that was common throughout the building. He closed the curtains just enough to afford them privacy from the adjoining balconies yet still allow the moonlight to settle into the room. Beyond and below the balcony rail were streetlights and the lights from the nearby shops and office buildings.

Jack sat on the edge of the bed, shedding his boots, trousers, and shirt. A day of flying and the anxiety of being in this town had taxed his emotional endurance, leaving him exhausted. His legs and arms felt stiff as he slipped off his boxer shorts and socks, pulled back the covers, and dropped to the sheets like a stuffed toy with no stuffing. Mollie came out of the bathroom and switched off the light, leaving the room dark except for the moonlight shining through the open balcony doors.

"You okay?" she said, walking to the balcony side of the bed.

"Yeah, just tired," he said. He rolled over to make room for her. "I'm going to see Frank tomorrow and sign a peace treaty. I don't want to spend the next week dreading the sight of him."

Mollie stood beside the bed, silhouetted in the moonlight. She brushed her robe back off her shoulders, letting it slide down her bare skin. The silk fabric, black against the whiteness of the curtains, floated downward to her hands, which were drawn behind her to capture the garment before it fell to the floor. She leaned forward to place the robe on a chair beside the bed. Moonlight and shadows moved around her body, creating soft outlines of every shape and contour and illuminating the smooth skin on her back. Each movement she made—placing the garment on the chair, pulling back the sheets, and sitting on the edge of the bed—slowed the rush of unpleasant thoughts through Jack's brain. For two years he had watched her perform the same simple task, night after night. Yet he continued to be captivated by her presence, entranced by her movement.

She was pretty, but her allure went far beyond her outward appearance. He tried to describe to her once how he felt, but it was like trying to tell a story, and no matter where he paused, he realized he was still only halfway through. He often wondered whether other men felt the same fascination for her or it was just his own unique response to being with her. She was his best friend. She lay down next to him.

Jack closed his eyes, allowing his senses to focus on the scent of a fir tree near the balcony. He rotated his head toward Mollie's shoulder, resting his cheek against her skin. This scent was equally familiar and equally cherished. With her beside him, he could sleep.

CHAPTER 3

IN THE SHORT FEW MOMENTS between sleep and consciousness, Jack's brain was sending mixed signals about the condition of his body. His face was being warmed on one side. Probably by the sun, he thought, but his eyes refused to open to validate his theory. The other side of his face was warm, but also felt damp, accompanied by the smell and feel of cotton motel sheets, sanitized in a blend of pine and chlorine. The smell quickened his journey toward consciousness. He wanted to lift his face away from the dampness and the smell, but gravity seemed to be preventing it.

Jack's entire body was pressed face down against the wrinkled white sheets. An ache, flowing up to his brain from his lower back, marked his arrival at being totally awake. A hand settled on the middle of his back and crept downward to his bare buttocks, then back up to his neck. It was Mollie's hand, he assumed, still unable to command his eyes to open. *McCall, you slept on your stomach last night, you dumbass. You know what that does to your back.*

Mollie's hand made its way up and down his back several more times. "You slept on your stomach last night, didn't you?" she said. "Your lower back is tied up in knots."

Jack just moaned and slid his upper body across the sheets in her direction. The pain in his lower back quadrupled. He reversed direction and returned to his original uncomfortable position. *God–am I old?*

Can't be, he concluded, having received no divine response to his question.

Mollie got out of bed and did her usual bouncy birthday-suit quickstep toward the bathroom, closing the door behind her. Jack normally enjoyed the spectacle, but his prone position, and the pain required to change it, prevented him from watching her.

Thank you. Now I can be alone in my agony. He did a slow-motion rollover onto his back and ended up spread-eagle on Mollie's side of the bed. The sun cloaked his entire body, soaking through his bare skin and working its way down to the muscle. The sheets were still damp, but the aroma was sweet and clean, pure Mollie McCall. Jack lay there, eyes half open, letting the sun's energy penetrate down to the bone.

Mollie came out of the bathroom, grabbed some underwear out of a drawer and headed back toward the bathroom door.

"You sure are energetic this morning," he said.

"That's because I'm younger than you," she said, pulling the door closed behind her.

Thank you. Just what I needed to start my day.

Jack rolled out of bed and straightened up in one slow, deliberate motion to avoid damaging his deteriorating frame. Even without Mollie's teasing, he felt old. Part of him hoped this trip would make him feel young again, recapture his youth and all that, but his body hurt. The image he saw in the mirror on the wall verified that his hairline had begun its inevitable journey from the front to the back of his head, and his stomach, also prominently displayed in the mirror, was getting harder to fit inside his size thirty-four jeans. *Journey back to my youth? More like journey forward toward depression and death.*

Jack took a few steps to get his legs working, then made his way out onto the sun-drenched balcony, wrapping a towel around his waist as he went. As he looked out over the city, everything he saw looked different from what he hoped to see. If this town had been the same after twenty years, then logically he could be the same. No older, no younger. Made sense, right?

"Nice towel," said a soft, low voice from his right. "Looks like the mate to one I have."

Jack turned to see a woman reclining in a lounge chair on the adjacent balcony. She wore brown tortoiseshell sunglasses and a white terry cloth robe that was draped open to reveal maximum cleavage at the top and minimum modesty at the bottom. Blonde hair flowed from the top of her head and disappeared at various places behind her shoulders and arms.

36

The ancient man stood up a little straighter and sucked in his gut.

"You like it?" Jack said, making a half turn to model. "I had it flown in from a clothier in Greenland just for wearing at formal occasions."

The woman raised a well-manicured, slender hand to her glasses and slid them down the bridge of her nose, just enough to see over the top. "We don't have to be formal—if you don't want to," she said.

Jack stood for a moment with his mouth half open as Blondie repositioned her sunglasses and half-rolled in his direction, in a manner that was both provocative and inviting.

Jack's brain started sending out a trouble alert, loud and clear. "I have to go inside," Jack said, recognizing the siren calling him toward the shore of disaster. "It's getting hot out here." He turned back toward the patio doors and stepped inside, hearing a faint chuckle from his newfound friend as he closed the door behind him. He closed the curtains. The day wasn't starting well. Maybe some food would help.

******

Breakfast at the Caldwell Inn was served family style. The tables were strung together in long rows, and guests were served from trays and dishes kept full by Bruno Hackett's robotic crew. Mollie and Jack stopped at the entrance to the dining area to survey the choices for table companions.

"Can't we eat somewhere private?" Mollie said.

Jack took her by the hand and headed toward the rear of the room.

"McCall," a voice echoed from an open doorway to their left. Jack looked in the small side room and saw Joshua Pitts seated at a semi-populated table with his arm in the air, inviting them to join the group.

"Give me one minute to be polite, Mollie, and I'll be right back," Jack said. He walked into the small room, which contained one large dining table and a serving station at each end. The back wall was mirrored and revealed the faces of the people seated with their backs toward the door. Frank Kirby was at one end of the table, with his sport coat draped over the back of his chair and his shoulder holster and pistol strapped to his body in plain view. The rest of the group were classmates and several people he didn't recognize.

"Jessie," Jack said, leaning down toward a blonde woman and giving her a kiss on the cheek. "I hoped you'd be here."

Mollie entered the room.

Jessie blushed just bright enough to notice. "I decided to attend at the last minute," she said.

Mollie looped her arm through Jack's and tugged upward, commanding him to straighten up. "Who's your friend, dear?" she said, extending her claws.

"Mollie, you remember me telling you that I'd bumped into Jessie Dalton at that convention in DC? Well, this is Jessie Dalton."

Jessie turned sideways in her chair and stood for the introduction. Her frame unfolded upward for what seemed like a decade and stood a good six feet tall when it reached full extension. Long blonde hair surrounded pale skin that looked starved for sunlight. Her plain clothing understated the well-proportioned figure it covered.

"You didn't tell me she was so pretty, Jack," Mollie said, forcing a polite grin. "Hello, Jessie," she said, "I'm Jack's wife, Mollie."

"Hi, Mollie," Jessie said, taking Mollie's hand and holding it longer than would be normal. "It's nice to meet you."

"Mollie, let me introduce some of these other characters," Jack said, dragging her toward the end of the table and breaking Jessie's grip on her hand. "Constable Kirby you've already met, and this gentleman appears to be the forever youthful Sterling Whitehurst," he said, stopping in front of a tall man wearing a white suit and gray tie. The man's face was handsome, smooth, and noticeably tanned. Not a blemish or mark on it. Blonde hair and blue eyes complemented his tan skin and starched light-gray shirt.

"Still the diplomat, eh, Jack?" Sterling said, with a bit of a southern accent. "Hello, Mollie."

Mollie smiled and mumbled a hello.

"And Joshua you've already met," Jack continued. "And this girl looks familiar, but the name is covered with cobwebs."

The woman he addressed stood and extended a tanned, weathered hand that matched the character of a once-attractive face now wrinkled and reshaped by time and Mother Nature.

"Rosemary Poole, Jack," the woman said. "I would have been astonished if you had remembered me."

"Yes—Rosemary," Jack said. "Bruno said you were here. Good to see you again. Rosemary, this is my wife, Mollie," he said, gesturing toward his spouse.

The two women exchanged greetings, along with another woman who was introduced as Sterling's wife, Victoria. Victoria was short and rounded, with very expensive tailored clothes and a beautiful brunette wig that had been mounted in haste, leaving a telltale list to one side. She seemed a mismatch for the statuesque Sterling.

"Rosemary was just telling us that her husband is in Portland at a medical convention," Joshua said, playing the host.

Rosemary nodded. "I have wanted to visit Caldwell again for a long time, and fortunately the convention and the reunion coincided," she said.

"And you came all the way from Africa, I hear," Jack said.

"Yes," Rosemary said. "This is my first trip back to the States since I left, the day following our graduation."

"Well, at least you didn't miss the party," Victoria said, raising a tumbler full of red liquid in a mock toast, then downing the whole thing.

"Must be good tomato juice," Mollie said.

"Yeah, but the vodka's better," Victoria said, licking her lips.

Rosemary frowned and placed her coffee cup on the table. "From what Bruno tells me, it wasn't all fun and frolic. I was sad to hear that Annie Ridgeway was killed in a car wreck the night of the party."

Jessie reached for a stemmed glass full of orange juice. Her hand, shaking like an earthquake, struck and toppled the glass. Pieces of glass littered the table, and the tablecloth soaked up the orange liquid, leaving tiny pieces of orange pulp resting on the surface like dead fish on a beach.

"Ohhhhh—oh, I, uh—I'm sorry," Jessie stammered. She stood to a slumped posture and jabbed at the wet mess with her napkin. "Ouch." She pulled her hand back and extracted a sizable piece of glass that had pierced the napkin and lodged in her finger. Blood gushed from the cut, changing the orange stains on the tablecloth to bright red.

A chorus of sympathy erupted from the gathering, half of whom immediately huddled around their wounded classmate.

"Let me see that cut," Joshua said, sliding his hand under Jessie's bloody fingers. "My, that's a nasty cut." His eyes seemed to get larger as he stared at the blood flowing from the wound.

Several heads peered in and continued to offer concern and advice. Joshua took the napkin from Jessie's other hand and used it to cradle the injured finger.

"You know how to treat a cut like this, don't you, Jessie?" he said, still staring at her finger. "We have to let it bleed just a little to make sure it doesn't get infected." He squeezed the cut finger, accelerating the flow of blood. The look on his face was more befitting Count Dracula than Florence Nightingale.

Jessie's lungs gulped two quick portions of air, and her face began to turn even whiter.

"That's it," Joshua said. His attention was fixed on the red stream pouring out of the opening and onto the cloth, now saturated with blood. A small pool formed on the fabric and began to drip onto the tablecloth. He never looked up.

"It's not going to get infected," Victoria said, waving her tumbler in Jessie's direction. "That glass had her drink in it."

"Her drink didn't have any vodka in it, dear," Sterling said, grabbing the tumbler and steadying his wife's hand.

"You really don't need to let that bleed, Joshua," Rosemary said. "I'm a nurse, and I have plenty of experience with these sorts of things."

Joshua looked up at Rosemary and nodded, then stood up in slow motion. "Had a friend once who got a bad infection from a cut like that," he said, followed by a deep breath.

Rosemary grabbed a freshly folded napkin and wrapped it tightly around the cut. "That should stop the bleeding in a minute," she said, putting one hand on Jessie's shoulder while holding the napkin with the other. "So, was the other person in Annie's car hurt in the wreck?" she asked Jessie, to distract her from the pain.

Jessie looked up, still a little woozy. "Annie?" she said. She stared at Rosemary for a moment. "Oh, you mean back when we graduated." Another long pause. "What other person?"

"Yes," Jack said. "What other person?"

"The other person that was with her in the car when she headed out of town for Dixon Park," Rosemary said. "Bruno said that's where her car crashed that night."

Jack crouched down beside Rosemary, who was on her knees in front of Jessie. "Do you mean to say there was someone else in the car with Annie that night?" he said.

"Yes," Rosemary said.

"You saw someone else in the car with her, and they were heading toward the park," Jack said.

"Yes," she said.

Sterling Whitehurst walked over and put his hand on Jessie's shoulder. "Probably means nothing, Jack," he said. "You're upsetting Jessie. She needs to calm down so the bleeding will stop." Jessie stared at Jack and then seconded the request with a nod.

"How do you know it was Annie's car?" Jack said, ignoring Sterling's attempt to distract him.

"We had several classes together, and she used to give me a ride occasionally to the Jacobson's farm, where I was living,"

Rosemary said. "I saw her that night from the doorway of Murphy's Market as she was pulling out of the parking lot. I hollered goodbye to her, and she waved at me."

Jack shifted positions so he was eyeball-to-eyeball with Rosemary. "There wasn't anyone else in the car when we found Annie that night," he said. "Tell me exactly what you saw, in detail."

"Oh, for God's sake, Jack," Sterling said. He turned and walked to the other end of the table.

Frank Kirby, who was still seated at the end of the table with his cup of coffee, stood and walked over to Jack. "Give it a rest, McCall," he said. "You sound like you're starting an investigation."

Jack looked up at Frank. "I don't recall any mention of another person being seen in the car with her that night."

"What's the matter, McCall?" Frank said, "Think I can't handle an investigation—hotshot DOJ attorney going to ride into town and save the day?"

"That's a little harsh, Frank," said Joshua. "But, Jack, you really shouldn't give it any more thought. It was a long time ago, and it's best left alone."

Mollie grabbed Jack by the arm and coaxed him up by asking for a cup of coffee. Jack went to the end of the room, retrieved a pot from the warming tray, and brought it over to the table where everyone, except Rosemary, had reseated themselves. He walked around the table filling coffee cups. His curiosity was in overdrive from what Rosemary had said, and his temper was close to the boiling point from Frank's insults. On top of that, everyone was acting strange, and it had all started with the mention of Annie Ridgeway. Sterling, Joshua, Frank, and Jessie all wanted him to totally forget about Annie. Sterling was losing his temper, Joshua was being quietly persistent, and Jessie had started shaking, knocked over a glass, and cut herself badly just at the mention of the girl's name. The one person who Jack thought should logically want to ask more questions was Police Chief Frank Kirby.

Rosemary selected a bandage from a first-aid kit, which had been brought in by an observant waiter, and wrapped Jessie's finger to seal the wound. Having finished her first-aid duties, she sat down again and sipped her coffee.

Mollie, noticing the scowl on Jack's face and the now-empty coffee pot in his hand, felt compelled to cajole him into a better mood. "Jack," she said, "you were so glad to see your friends here that you gave them all the coffee and didn't save any for yourself."

"Oh, yeah, you know how much I love coffee," he said, with a tone of annoyed sarcasm.

Victoria rose from her chair and started for the door. "I'll get some more coffee from one of those damned waiters," she said.

Jack took her by the arm as she passed him and gradually changed her heading 180 degrees. "That's all right, Victoria," he said, guiding her back to her chair. "I'll get by without it for now." He held her arm until she was seated squarely on the chair.

"So you're a coffee connoisseur, are you, Jack?" Joshua said, stirring the liquid in his own cup.

Jack turned to respond. "Well, actually, I . . ."

"McCall," Frank said, stepping in front of Jack, "I don't know why you bothered to come back to Caldwell, but while you're here, don't start playing detective. If there's any investigating to be done or questions to be asked, I'll do it."

Jack's right hand folded up into a fist.

"Come on, Jack," Mollie said, tugging him toward the doorway. "I'm not hungry anymore."

Jack at first resisted her efforts to leave the room but then followed at a reluctant pace. He gave an abbreviated wave in the general direction of the table but kept eye contact with Frank until he exited the room.

They walked out of the restaurant area and caught the elevator back up to the fourth floor. Jack's right hand was still clenched. Probably a dumb move to start a fight with the local police, he thought. Mollie unlocked the door to their room and headed for the bathroom, while Jack got his sunglasses and waited for her to join him at the door.

"Thanks for getting me out of there," he said.

Mollie didn't answer. She came out with her hair tied back in a ponytail and grabbed her handbag. "I didn't bring along enough cash to bail you out of jail for punching out a cop," she said. "In fact, I don't think I have enough in the checking account, either. Let's go."

Mollie went down to the small gift shop, and Jack went to the reunion bulletin board in the lobby to check for messages. He checked the board and then walked away with an easy, confident stride, stumbling and tripping inside from the new information about events the night Annie died. He had managed to push Annie out of his conscious mind years ago, but his sessions with Doctor Kemp had made him aware that she was still very much present in his subconscious. Now he had to deal with the past and the present, a complication he hadn't expected. Mollie was waiting by the gift shop window, near the main entrance. Jack took her hand as he passed by, and the two headed for the parking lot.

"Ready for your car, Mr. McCall?" the young valet said.

"That's okay, son, I'll get it myself," Jack said, taking the keys from the young man's hand and continuing toward the lot. He left the boy standing with a bewildered look on his face. The couple was in the car and heading down the driveway before the boy shrugged his shoulders and returned to his post.

Mollie's ponytail danced around in the wind while the Mustang accelerated toward the main part of town. "You going to show me where you lived?" she said.

"Maybe later," he said.

"Well," Mollie responded, "when you're ready to visit ghosts of the past, I'd like to go with you."

Jack nodded, but it was only an acknowledgment of the request. He wasn't sure about granting it.

"So, where are we headed now?" she said, not wanting to press the point.

"I'm headed for the police station," Jack said. "I think I'll kiss Frank's ass for a while and see if that gets better results."

"They might lock you up for kissing his ass just as quick as for punching him in the face," Mollie said. "Better drop me off at a mall. I feel like spending."

They cruised around for a while to give Frank time to return to his office, and to find a suitable playground for Mollie, who received a kiss and a wink from Jack before she climbed out of the car.

"You got your phone?" Jack said.

Mollie patted her handbag and headed for the entrance to the closest store.

Jack slipped the car into gear and took off toward City Hall.

So far his day wasn't going well. He had retreated back into his room to escape from the overly friendly half-naked blonde on the balcony, and he had nearly gotten into a fistfight with a police officer. He looked around for the Fed Ex courier who was undoubtedly rushing his way to notify him that his dog was dead and his neighbor was suing him for allowing a hundred-foot tree to fall on his prized Edsel station wagon. He didn't have a dog, he lived in a condo, and his neighbor was old and didn't drive, but somehow he half-expected the FedEx courier to appear anyway. The more he thought about it, the more convinced he was that this whole trip was a bad idea. If Dr. Kemp and Mollie hadn't pretty much forced him to come, he would have stayed in Hartford and played golf. Even if it was hot and humid, at least he had friends there. Granted, there were a few people in and around the state of Connecticut who weren't very fond of him. You can't be a federal prosecutor and not step on some toes. But his journey down the road to becoming an alcoholic had started in Caldwell, so logic—and everyone close to him—told him that this was one of the critical stops on his lifelong journey of sobriety.

Jack headed down a side street that skirted the mall's parking lot. Using the Mustang to vent a little frustration, he cranked the steering wheel hard right and floored the gas pedal.

The tires screeched and spewed blue smoke all the way around the corner, leaving a telltale black streak on the pavement for thirty feet heading due south on 49th Street. The street was void of houses or activity, so he left his foot planted hard against the floor until better judgment set in and he backed off the speed. Felt good, though. Even for those few short moments.

The car quieted, and Jack looked at a few street signs, trying to find a name he recognized. He knew the layout of the city well. It was etched into his brain like a road map. He could visualize it clearly, as if he were flying high above the ground looking down. But when he left town twenty years ago, the street numbers in this area only went up to 32. If he could find a cross-street name he recognized, he could find his way back downtown easily. *Dixon Boulevard*. The tires squealed once more, and the Mustang headed east.

City Hall hadn't changed much, Jack observed, pulling into the parking lot. The traditional red-brick construction looked like a Norman Rockwell painting on the outside and a 1950s police movie set on the inside. The floor was covered with dark-brown linoleum tiles, their once-white streaks waxed to a brownish yellow. The woodwork was covered in multiple layers of institutional white paint that made the doors and trim look ancient and had probably sealed or severely restricted the movement of the windows. A reception desk at the rear of the room was staffed by a young female of the Goth persuasion. She had black hair, lips, and nails, a nose ring, and six earrings in her left ear. Her nametag read "Trina."

"Frank Kirby, please," Jack said to the unusual looking receptionist.

"Your name, please, sir?" she said. Her polite manner belied her in-your-face appearance.

"McCall," he said. "Jack McCall."

"Have a seat, Mr. McCall," she said. "I'll let Chief Kirby know you're here."

Jack strolled to the far corner of the reception area, scanning the historic photographs that covered the walls. There were several magazines on the chrome-and-Formica end-table in the seating area where he parked himself, including the obligatory copy of *Police Gazette* and assorted general-interest magazines.

"Mr. McCall," Trina said, "Chief Kirby is busy now. You're welcome to wait, or you can come back later."

Something told Jack that no matter when he came back, Frank would be busy. The guy had a chip on his shoulder the size of a two-by-four, and in order to "make nice" and abate Frank's hostility, Jack was going to have to be patient. "I'll wait, thank you," was his response. He settled in with a copy of *People* magazine and prepared to win what might be a long battle of wills.

Jack finished off the first magazine and six more before Trina's phone rang. She spoke for a moment and then hung up. "Follow me, Mr. McCall," she said. "I'll show you the way to Chief Kirby's office."

Jack stood and fell in step behind his guide as she wandered down several corridors. She opened a door at the end of a hallway and stepped aside to allow Jack to enter. "Chief Kirby will join you in a few minutes, sir," she said, leaving the office door open as she headed back down the hallway. Jack stood just inside the door for a minute and surveyed the room, which smelled of stale cigarettes. It seemed a little cluttered with memorabilia and personal stuff. No files or other official looking things that one would expect. Two walls were sixty percent covered with photographs and plaques. Jack estimated the photos ranged in age from high school to the present. He stepped between two overstuffed cloth chairs to inspect one of the older pictures that caught his eye. It was of Frank, Annie Ridgeway, Candy McConnell (who was two years younger than Jack), a girl who looked like Joshua Pitts's kid sister, and Olivia Rice, another classmate. Candy had died during their senior year in a car crash, and Jack didn't know what had become of Pitts's sister or Olivia Rice. At the bottom of the picture were the words *Knights Weekly*, the name of the Caldwell High School student newspaper, and below that was written, "Photo by Joshua Pitts."

"Interesting picture, isn't it, McCall?" Frank Kirby said as he entered the room.

Jack turned to see Chief Kirby walking toward him. His coat was off, and his shoulder holster and pistol were strapped around his upper body. "All but two of those people are dead: me and Rebekah Pitts," he said, seating himself on the front edge of the desk.

"I didn't know Olivia Rice was dead," Jack said, continuing to look at the picture.

"Died about six months after graduation," Frank said. "An explosion in a silo on her folks' farm."

"How do you know Rebekah Pitts is still alive?" Jack said.

"I asked Joshua about her yesterday at the inn, before you showed up," Frank said. "He said she owns her own photography business in Florida. Another chip off the old block, so to speak."

Jack looked at Frank and then back to the picture. "Do their parents still have the studio in town?"

"No," Frank said. "It closed shortly after we graduated, as I recall. Then the whole family kind of disappeared without any fanfare."

Jack sat down in one of the overstuffed chairs and flopped one leg over the other in what he thought would be a casual and unthreatening posture.

The two men had a short staring contest.

"What the hell do you want, McCall?" Frank said. "I'm busy."

"I don't understand why you're not curious about other person that Rosemary saw in Annie's car the night she died?" Jack said.

Frank moved around the desk and sat down in his chair. He leaned back and clasped his hands behind his head. "McCall," he said, "Everyone knows you have a guilty conscience because of Annie's death. You and your posse were indirectly responsible for her death. And now you're trying to get me to start an investigation based on a minor bit of new information in order to shed some of that guilt."

Jack walked over to Frank's desk. "I'm not . . ."

"Yes, you are," Frank said. He laughed and leaned forward in his chair. "This is my town now. You left. You're not the quarterback anymore—I am.

"And as for your *new information*, I've had several bits of information and evidence pop up over the years relating to Annie's crash."

Jack scooted forward in his chair. "Like what?" he said.

Frank picked up a pack of cigarettes from the credenza next to the window, pulled one out, and lit it with a wooden match he retrieved from a brown ceramic bowl on top of the credenza. "Always the curious lawyer, aren't you, McCall?" He blew a large cloud of smoke into the air, then put the cigarette in an ashtray. He pulled the pistol out of his shoulder holster.

Jack's arms and legs went to red alert.

Frank pulled back the hammer and aimed the weapon at the wall, about halfway between Jack and the window. "Guns make you nervous, McCall?" he said, continuing to look down the sights on the pistol.

"Yes," Jack said.

"Would have thought you'd carry one," Frank said, tipping the barrel of the weapon up toward the ceiling and then releasing the hammer with his thumb to let it ease back to safe position. "All lawyers should carry a weapon. It gives them a sporting chance when their victims—I mean clients—come looking for them." He took a drag on the cigarette and exhaled the foul smoke in Jack's direction.

"Save your sarcasm, Kirby," Jack said. "I'm a prosecutor, not a defense attorney. And as for weapons, I do carry a gun and I've been trained by the FBI on how to use it."

"Smart move, McCall," Frank said. "And as for evidence, when Annie's mom died, she had no family. So, as a duly appointed representative of the people, I saw to the disposition of her things. I found a letter from Annie among her mom's personal papers." He walked to a file cabinet, took out a piece of paper, and set it on the desk in front of Jack. "You might want to read it."

Jack picked up the paper and began to read.

Frank walked to the office door, closed it, and then walked back to the desk, stopping in front of Jack. He began to extinguish his cigarette by grinding it slowly into the bottom of the glass ashtray. As he stared at Jack, his hand drove the paper and tobacco downward until the cigarette spread out and tore apart, leaving only the light-brown paper–wrapped filter in his fingers. He leaned forward until his face was within inches of Jack's face. "That letter," he said, "talks about life and love and forgiving. She said she was looking forward to learning to love her brothers and sisters. You took away her future—her chance to love her fellow man, to love her brothers and sisters . . ."

"No," Jack interrupted, "she said 'brother *and* sisters.'"

"Whatever," Frank said. "The meaning is the same. You and your pals set the entire nightmare in motion, and I have no interest in clearing your conscience."

Jack handed the letter to Frank, then stood up. "I came here to try to understand why you aren't interested in this new information, but I can see nothing I say is going to change your mind." He walked to the office door, grasped the doorknob, and turned back toward Frank. "She also said in the letter that after she graduated, she would be set for life. What did she mean?" Jack turned the knob and opened the door. "Maybe the person in her car that night had something to do with her pending good fortune." He started to walk out the door, then stopped. "I'm going to find out who it was—but that should really be your job. You're the cop." He closed the door and left the building.

Jack's hands were shaking when he grasped the door handle of the Mustang. This reunion was supposed to be a healing opportunity for him, but everything that had happened so far was making things worse. His confrontation with Frank had provoked an emotional response. He felt an urge to have a drink. *Not good.* An image flashed into his mind. It was of Coach Grady, leaning back in his office chair, listening—just listening. He started the car and headed out to find the coach.

Jack thought he remembered seeing the assisted living facility during his journey into town the day before. He wasn't sure, though, so he eased off on the throttle when he got to within a few blocks of the inn so he could check both sides of the street. He passed the inn, then noticed a brick-framed sign identifying the facility as the Premier Living Club. He turned into the driveway. The parking lot was nearly empty, and there were a couple of people in wheelchairs sitting under an awning on the side of the building, smoking cigarettes. Jack remembered that Bruno had told him to call ahead if he wanted to visit with the coach, but he needed to focus on something other than tequila, so he parked the car and went inside.

"Is this where Coach Grady lives?" he asked the attendant at the front desk.

"Yes," she said. "Is he expecting you?"

"No," Jack said.

"Just a minute, please," she said. She went into an office in the back of the room and spoke to a woman seated at a desk that Jack could see through a window in the office wall. After a brief conversation, the attendant returned to the front desk.

"Ms. Bascom will let the nurse know you are coming for a visit," the woman said. "Go to the end of the hallway to your right, then turn left. The nurses' station is at the end of that hallway."

Jack was confused about the need for a nurses' station at an assisted living facility, but he followed the instructions, figuring he would learn more from the nurse. He headed down the hallway as instructed, glancing at rooms and occupants. He didn't like this place. It reminded him of the place where his mother died. His stomach turned a little, but he forced himself to keep walking. He needed to see the coach.

Jack turned left as directed and sped up his pace. Arriving at the nurses' station, he asked to see Coach Grady.

"You're in luck," the duty nurse said. "He's awake."

Jack looked around the area while the nurse finished some paperwork. There were rooms in a circle around the central nurses' station. It looked more like a hospital ward than an assisted living environment. "Is he okay?" he asked the nurse.

"He has stabilized since we moved him to this section of the facility," the nurse said, as she walked out from behind the counter and led Jack to one of the rooms in the ward.

Jack walked in the room and flashed a broad smile when he saw the coach sitting up in bed. "Coach," he said. "It's me, Jack McCall."

The old man didn't move. He just stared straight ahead.

"The doctors are not sure if he understands what's going on," the nurse said. "The stroke has left him unresponsive."

The smile on Jack's face disappeared, and he felt faint. He slumped into a chair next to the coach's bed.

"Are you okay, Mr. McCall?" the nurse said. "Didn't you know about the stroke?"

Jack shook his head. "I came back for the reunion," he said, "and to tell him how much I appreciate what he did for me when my father died."

"I'm sorry," she said. "I'll be at the nurses' station if you need me." She turned and left the room.

Jack didn't know what to do. He had come a long way to say a lot of things that had remained unspoken for way too many years. But now it was too late. He wanted a drink. A nice big margarita, maybe two. But he knew it wouldn't end with one or two. Mollie. He needed Mollie.

He pushed himself up out of the chair and stood next to the coach's bed. *Do you even know I'm here?* He leaned over and kissed the old man on the forehead. "I'm okay, Coach," he said. "You saved my life."

Jack thanked the nurse for her help as he walked past her station on his way out of the building. He got in the Mustang and headed to the mall to pick up Mollie. He needed to be with Mollie.

CHAPTER 4

MOLLIE WAS SITTING on a sunlit bench outside Wagner's department store, waiting for her husband to arrive. There were just a few cars sprinkled throughout the lot. Her stomach growled. She wasn't a voracious eater, but her body always seemed to let her know when it was time to fill up.

"Waiting for Jack?" a voice asked, from somewhere behind her.

Mollie turned and looked up to see Sterling Whitehurst standing next to one of the square stucco columns that decorated the store entrance. "Yes, I am," she said.

"Mind if I sit down for a moment?" he said, walking to the bench and sitting down, not waiting for her permission. "Beautiful day, isn't it?" he said. "I remember how shocked I was the first summer I spent in Louisiana. Thought I would die from the humidity. Growing up here kind of spoiled me."

"Why did you stay in Louisiana, then?" Mollie said.

"My wife's family is very prominent in Louisiana," Sterling said, lifting his chin a little and panning the skyline. His posture was straight and rigid, causing him to look down past his nose at Mollie when his head movement brought his eyes around to her direction. "Victoria's uncle is United States Senator J.W. Wainwright. You've obviously heard of him. And her father owns Wainwright Industries, one of the largest manufacturing firms in the state."

"Impressive," Mollie said. "What do they manufacture?"

"Plumbing fixtures," he said, crossing his left leg over the right and running a hand through his hair.

"Oh, like urinals and toilets?" Mollie said, mocking his air of self-importance.

Sterling put his hands down to the bench and shifted his weight backwards. "They make the highest quality fixtures in the United States," he said, either not noticing her sarcasm or not acknowledging it. He turned his body halfway towards her and slouched just a bit to put himself more on her level. "Speaking of quality, everyone would have a much better reunion if you could convince Jack not to stir up bad memories by talking about Annie Ridgeway so much. It makes a lot of people uncomfortable, and nothing can be gained by dragging up events that happened so long ago."

Mollie looked him in the eye, and he turned away. "Does it upset you, Sterling?" she said.

"No," he said, staring off toward the parking lot and wiping his brow with his handkerchief. "She was only a casual acquaintance. I just know Jack can grab onto something and not let go. It could ruin the weekend for some people if he dwells on such a sad memory. Too many fun times to think back on."

Mollie watched him in silence. The air was dead still. Sunlight sparkled off the drops of sweat that reappeared on his forehead.

"Well, Victoria is probably finished shopping," he said, rising to his feet. "She'll be needing my help to carry her packages. Do talk to Jack," he said, placing a hand on her shoulder. "I'm sure you could help him enjoy this reunion."

"I'll mention it," Mollie said.

Sterling strolled back through the main entrance of the store at a casual pace. Mollie watched him until the glare from the glass doors obscured his movement, then turned toward the store window directly behind her. Moments later, she saw Sterling trotting past a group of women swarming around a bargain table, nearly knocking one of them over in the process.

A car rolled up to the curb in front of Mollie's bench, giving a little squeal as the brakes brought it to a halt. It was Jack in the Mustang.

"Just spent a few peculiar minutes with Mr. Sterling Whitehurst," Mollie said, sliding into the passenger seat. Her rear end no sooner hit the black leather seat than it rocketed upward, wedging its owner between the floorboard and the headrest. "Shit, that's hot!" Mollie exclaimed.

Jack took off his shirt and slid it onto the seat beneath her. "Eloquently stated, my dear," he said. "You've been hanging out at the Navy base again, haven't you?"

Mollie eased her buns back down to the seat and buckled her seat belt.

Jack slipped the car into gear and headed toward the street. His insides were starting to calm down now that he was with Mollie. He focused on her, instead of on the coach and Annie and his dad, and all the other sources of guilt that fueled his need for alcohol.

"What was that comment about Sterling?" he said.

"The guy's a little strange," she said. "He asked me point-blank to talk you out of asking any more questions about Annie what's-her-name's accident."

"How did it seem strange?" Jack said.

Mollie laughed. "The guy was sweating like a toilet tank in mid-winter, and he couldn't sit still," she said.

Jack steered the Mustang onto Caldwell Mall Boulevard and headed toward the inn. "Maybe it's the heat," he said.

"He lives in Louisiana," Mollie said, slapping Jack on the shoulder. "Oregon summer heat at its worst is paradise compared to Louisiana."

"Good point," Jack said, rubbing his wounded shoulder.

Mollie shifted her left knee toward the center console and leaned toward Jack. "Why do you suppose he was so nervous?" she said. "Maybe he was the other person in the car with Annie."

Jack shook his head. "He was in his own car that night, with his girlfriend of the week. They were part of the group that went to the park."

"Did he and Annie ever have a thing going in high school?" Mollie said.

"No," Jack said. "In fact, I don't recall ever seeing them together. Maybe in a group, but never just the two of them. Sterling and Annie were from opposite ends of town, literally and figuratively. The Whitehursts had a big house up on Whitehurst Drive overlooking the city. Lots of money."

"And Annie?" Mollie said.

"Annie lived in a modest subdivision north of town. About the only thing she had remotely in common with Sterling was that her mom worked at the dry cleaners that the Whitehurst family owned."

"That's a connection," Mollie said.

"Not really," Jack said. "The Whitehursts owned several businesses and had managers that ran each of them. They spent most of their time at the country club—left the work to the peons. They weren't known to hang around the cleaners or any of their other companies. And they never mingled with the hired help."

Mollie turned back toward the front of the car and stuck her hands over the top of the windshield, letting the warm air flow between her fingers. "Then why would he be so nervous about someone asking questions about her death?"

"Does seem weird," Jack said. He glanced in the rearview mirror, flipped on the turn signal, and turned the car into the entrance to the Caldwell Inn.

"What about her father?" Mollie said, opening the car door as the Mustang rolled to a stop in the parking lot. "Any connection there to the Whitehursts?"

Jack got out of the car and headed to the front door of the inn, taking Mollie by the arm as he walked past her side of the car. "She didn't have a father," he said.

"Are we talking immaculate conception here, or deadbeat dad?" Mollie said.

"Wasn't around," Jack said. "She told everyone that he was dead."

"I still think he's hiding something," Mollie said.

The couple entered the main lobby, finding a crowd of classmates wearing reunion T-shirts huddled around a bar set up by the lobby fireplace. Jack's pace slowed and then stopped. He scanned the crowd from one end to the other. Glasses and ice cubes clinked and rattled, mixing with the dull roar of storytelling and frequent outbursts of laughter. Twenty years had certainly taken its toll on some of the group, he thought, but hardly laid a glove on others. From a lack of hair to an excess of chin, Father Time had trampled on some of the most prized specimens his graduating class had to offer. It had also taken some half-developed boys and girls and aged them to perfection. Jack just stood and stared. He looked in the mirror on the wall next to where he was standing. His shoulders were drooping a little, so he straightened his posture. He saw Mollie looking at him.

"What's the matter?" she asked his reflection.

"Do I look as old as some of them look?" Jack said, pointing to the reflection of the crowd.

"Thank God it's only vanity that's disturbing your soul," Mollie said, rolling her eyes to exaggerate her artificial sense of relief. "I thought it might be something serious."

"It is serious," a voice echoed from the other side of the entrance.

Henry Coleman, in the company of an attractive brunette, walked up and put his hand on Jack's shoulder. "The first day of our first year in grade school," he said, "this guy was fascinated by the mirror that was hanging by the sink in our classroom. The teacher made him sit in the front of the room so he wouldn't spend all his time admiring himself."

"You have an excellent memory," Mollie said.

"Actually, I was watching Henry here in that mirror," Jack said. "Mama told me it wasn't polite to stare at odd looking people, so I was being covert." Jack looked at the woman with Henry. "Introduce us to this lovely lady, Mr. Coleman."

"Certainly," Henry said. "Jack, Mollie, this is my wife, Jennifer. Jennifer, Jack and Mollie McCall."

Jennifer was a stark contrast to the weathered and rugged Henry. Not your typical farm wife, with her smooth skin, almost pale by comparison, and well-manicured nails that probably had never been near a bale of hay. Her hair was cut short and combed away from a face that was pretty, unpainted, healthy, and at least fifteen years younger than Henry's.

"How'd such an attractive woman as you end up with an ol' hayseed like this?" Jack said, pointing to Henry.

Jennifer smiled and wrapped her hands around Henry's rather impressive bicep.

"Jenny can't speak, Jack," Henry said. "She was in a car accident when she was little. Took a pretty good shot to the throat that permanently damaged her vocal cords."

Jack cast an awkward glance at the floor and then back toward Jenny. "Must be terrible to have Henry here do all your talking for you," he said, in a booming voice that caught the attention of half the people in the room.

Jenny smiled twice as big and uttered a strange, crippled sounding laugh. Henry laughed as well while pulling Jack close to him. "She's mute," he said, "not deaf."

Jack sprouted an embarrassed grin.

"Can I buy you a Diet Coke?" Henry said, pointing the way to the bar.

"You remembered my brand," Jack said, feeling relieved that Henry had changed the subject.

Henry and Jack moved through the crowd, shaking hands and slapping backs until they arrived at the bar. Glasses were clinking and a blender was whining in an effort to fill the overflow of orders being shouted at the wait staff. Henry reached behind the counter and rescued two diet sodas out of an ice-filled container. A large man with a bad toupee wedged his body up against the bar next to Jack and shouted out an order for a margarita. The bartender, looking annoyed by the man's demanding tone, took his time acknowledging the request but then stepped over to the blender and began to prepare the drink.

Jack's eyes tracked the movement of the bartender's hand as he wrapped his fingers around the ice scoop that was sitting on the counter. It disappeared below Jack's line of sight and then reappeared, having gathered a load of the small cubes of ice. The hand lifted the load to the edge of the blender and then dumped the frozen ingredients into the bottom, covering the blades that would shred them and make them one with the liquid ingredients that were to follow. The sound of the ice hitting the bottom of the glass body of the blender caused a faint twitch in Jack's neck muscles. He knew the process—

every step. Next, the hand grabbed the bottle of tequila and tipped it over just above the edge of the blender. As the liquid emerged from the spout, its flow was interrupted by a jigger thrust into its path. The jigger tipped twice without any change in the flow from the bottle. The tequila was a golden brown and glistened as it flowed. Jack's brain filled in the sensory gaps by recalling the smell and the faint bitter taste of the raw liquid. The hand grabbed the bottle containing the greenish-yellow mixer to complete the tart concoction, and then punched a button on the face of the machine to send the blades screaming into action. Jack's hand trembled as he grabbed his diet soda and lifted it to his lips. It didn't taste right.

Henry put his hand on his shoulder. "Must be good to be home," he said, "remembering old times."

Jack stared at the can of diet soda. "Yes," he said. "Remembering old times."

His senses were jerked away from the bar by a gust of air that had a distinct odor of stale cigars. At the far end of the bar, next to a double door opened to a courtyard, Jack spotted the source of the pollution. A group of large and small men with large and even larger cigars were huddled in a cloud of whitish-blue smoke, laughing, puffing, and exchanging stories. There were two women among the group as well, one smoking a cigar and the other appearing to enjoy the attention. Bruno was one of the characters. Stewart Ramsey was another. There was a group of classmates including Frank, Joshua, and Jessie just outside the door, listening to the storytelling but avoiding the carcinogenic atmosphere.

Jack left Henry at the less polluted end of the bar, chatting with classmates, and weaved his way toward the fog bank that was oozing out the open doors. Stewart Ramsey was the shortest and loudest man in the group. He held a very long cigar between his thumb and the rest of the fingers on his left hand. He waved it in the air as he spoke, creating swirls of new smoke in the mist of cloud surrounding the group. It was his rapier, to thrust at a particular point he was driving home to his audience. He had gained a little weight in twenty years, Jack thought, but the face was surprisingly youthful. A handsome face almost void of middle age wrinkles, with light-brown hair combed straight back and neatly trimmed around the ears. An expensive suit, too.

Bruno saw Jack moving toward the group and raised his hand in invitation to join them. The cigar in his hand sent the same message in swirling smoke signals.

"McCall, you son of a bitch," Stewart said, grabbing Jack by the elbow. "You've been in town since yesterday and you haven't come out to the house to say hello." The short man reached his short right arm up over Jack's high-altitude shoulder, causing his right heel to lift off the floor.

Jack was mystified by this show of camaraderie from a man who had been a casual friend at best in high school. "I've been a little reluctant," Jack said, following a big gulp of Diet Coke. "Afraid you might decide to charge me for the use of that black Mustang your son delivered to the airport."

Stewart let out a laugh that was twice his size and audible throughout the room. Fresh cigar smoke spewed out of his mouth to track the sound of his laughter. "Great boy, isn't he?" he said. "Takes after his mom, luckily for him. How about joining us for a round of golf this afternoon at the country club, Jack? My treat."

"Who's going to play?" Jack said.

"Bruno, you, Sterling, and me," Stewart said. "Tee off at three. What do you say?"

Jack hadn't started playing golf until after he graduated from college. When he had watched and listened to the country club kids swimming and driving their golf carts around, he had wanted to join them. It looked like fun. He used to find some reason to pass by the pool, so he could watch Betty Hendricks swim and play tennis on the nearby courts. Great legs, huge boobs, terrible tennis. Legend had it that Betty was equally ungifted on the golf course. Seems her caddy spent a lot of time replacing divots and looking for her golf ball—but the caddies didn't seem to mind. Jack used to see her, Stewart, and Sterling playing golf in the mornings when he rode his bicycle down

Sweetwater Circle, the street that ran alongside the first fairway. The chain-link fence along the fairway kept undesirables out. Bruno hadn't played golf then either, Jack recalled.

"Love to join you, Ramsey," Jack said.

"Bring your checkbook with you, McCall," Stewart said, blowing out another plume of smoke and dabbing the cigar ashes in the general direction of an ashtray. "We play serious golf at the Caldwell Country Club."

Bruno looked down at the cigar ash that missed the ashtray and landed on his carpet. He motioned for one of the attendants working the room to clean up the mess. "You ruin my carpet," he said, leaning down towards Stewart's face, "and I'll come down to your car lot and piss on your desk."

Stewart blurted out another laugh and grabbed one of the women in the group, dragging her toward the bar. "See you at three, Jack," he said over his shoulder. "And don't forget to bring your checkbook."

"The kid does take after his mother," Jack said to the rest of the group. He patted Bruno on the arm, then made his way back through the crowd to find Mollie. She was seated at a patio table, drinking some sort of tropical concoction with Jennifer Coleman. They seemed to be content, so Jack headed back up to the room to change clothes for his upcoming golf match.

Jack entered the room and gave the door a push to close it behind him. The balcony doors were open, and a hint of a breeze pushed the folds in the linen curtains in a subtle slow motion. He walked into the bathroom and turned on the shower, intending to clean up before going over to the country club. He walked back out into the room and stopped in front of the chest of drawers. His left hand grabbed the wrought-iron drawer pull, and as the drawer opened his right hand reached inside for a pair of shorts.

He heard a rattle, and a long gray object flashed from inside the drawer and struck at the underwear in his hand. He leaped and fell backward onto the floor. His feet alternated between slip and grip on the carpet as he scrambled to move away from the chest. A three-foot-long rattlesnake draped itself across the edge of the drawer at the extension of its striking motion, then dropped to the floor, coiled, rattled, and struck at him again. His heart rate quadrupled in an instant, and all he could hear was the rattler, his own gasping for air, and the thumping of his shoes against the floor as his legs flailed to propel him away from the snake. He backed up against the overstuffed chair near the fireplace. The snake paused, coiled, and continued to rattle its warning. Jack scrambled up onto the chair. "Damn," he said. He stared at the snake.

Someone knocked on the door. "Housekeeping," the voice said. "Everything okay in there?"

"No!" Jack yelled.

A key clicked into the lock and the door opened. A rather large woman in a housekeeping uniform took one look at the snake in the middle of the room, let out a scream, and took off down the hall to get help. Jack stood with one foot on each arm of the overstuffed chair and his ankles shaking as he watched the snake uncoil and slither back toward the dresser.

"What the hell are you doing, McCall?" a voice said from behind him.

Jack half-turned to see who was talking, while struggling to keep his balance on the arms of the chair. Frank Kirby, Joshua Pitts, and several people who looked familiar were standing in the doorway, staring at him standing atop the chair. Several members of the crowd, including Frank, were chuckling just loud enough to cause Jack to forget about his fear of snakes and realize the embarrassment of the moment. Frank grabbed a sponge mop off the housekeeping cart, walked over to the rattler, and pinned its head to the floor. He grabbed the snake behind the head and picked it up. "You can come down now, McCall," he said. "It's safe."

Jack wanted to crawl into the drawer where the snake had been hiding. More people gathered outside the door to his room, laughing at him and applauding Frank as he dropped the snake into a large cloth laundry bag on the housekeeping cart and tied the top closed.

"You shouldn't keep your pets in your room, McCall," Frank said. "They might get out and hurt someone."

"Damn near got me," Jack said, stepping down from the arms of the chair and trying to act nonchalant. "Since you're the town detective, tell me: how'd a rattlesnake get in that closed dresser drawer anyway?"

"You mean it was in a closed drawer?" Pitts said, nudging his way past Frank and several other people standing just inside the door. "Sounds suspicious to me, like someone wanted to hurt you bad."

"Or scare the piss out of you," Frank said. "Sounds more like a practical joke to me."

Jack walked over to the fireplace and grabbed the poker off the tool stand. "I'm going to check the rest of these drawers, just in case," he said. He stood at maximum distance from the chest of drawers and slipped the poker hook through the iron pull of the top drawer.

"Careful, Jack, there might be a bunny rabbit in that one," said an anonymous voice from the crowd. The comment provoked another round of laughter. Jack flashed an annoyed glance toward the door and pulled the drawer open. No snakes.

Similar inspection of the remaining drawers failed to turn up any more reptiles, so the crowd dispersed while Frank grabbed the bagged rattler and headed down the hall.

"Aren't you going to check to see how that thing got in here?" Jack said, sticking his head out the door.

"McCall, you're a pussy," Frank said, not looking back. "You've always been a pussy." He disappeared through the stairwell door.

Jack was both embarrassed and disgusted. He slammed the door closed and threw the fireplace poker in the general direction of the fireplace, taking out a chunk of rock, which ricocheted onto the floor behind the overstuffed chair. The balcony doors were still open, so he brushed aside the curtains and stepped out into the sunlight. *Maybe someone got into the room by way of the balcony and put the snake in the drawer to scare me. Or kill me.*

Most of his classmates knew he was afraid of snakes, and now half the people at the inn knew it too. Someone wanted to shake him up and picked the best possible way to do it. Henry used to tease him about being afraid of snakes when they were growing up. Bruno—hell, the whole football team—knew he was afraid of snakes. "Damn," he mumbled.

Drops of sweat seeped from his pores and dropped to the concrete balcony, where the heat of the day made them vanish in an instant. Jack looked over to the balcony next door. There she was, Blondie—sunbathing. Not a stitch of clothes on. "Damn," he mumbled again. She started to stir, so Jack ducked back into the room before she had the opportunity to strike up a conversation again. Passing the mirror, he also realized that the front of his pants was wet. "Damn."

Jack went into the bathroom, giving extra scrutiny to everything in his path. The water had been running continually since he first entered the room, so he stripped, took a quick steamy shower, and put on clean clothes. He was ready for the day to start going his way. A good round of golf, and relieving Ramsey of some of his money in the process, would make him feel better. Jack was very good at golf.

The door to the room opened and Mollie came in. "You decent, Jack?" she said. "Bruno is here. We heard about the snake and came up to check on you."

"In fact," Bruno added, as he stepped into the room, "everyone in the lobby heard about the snake. Frank paraded through the lobby with that bagged snake like it was the Lombardi Trophy."

"Damn."

Bruno inspected the room and then picked up the room phone. "I'll have all your stuff moved to a room two doors down the hall and then have this room thoroughly searched," he said.

Jack didn't say so, but changing rooms would be the only way he would be able to sleep that night. Good thing Bruno suggested it. It saved Jack the further embarrassment of asking.

"I'll supervise the move and then probably take a nap," Mollie said. "Where you headed?" she asked Jack.

"Bruno is taking me to the country club to play golf," Jack said.

"Oooooh, the country club," Mollie said. She turned and walked into the bathroom, closing the door behind her. As soon as Bruno finished instructing his staff, he and Jack headed down through the lobby and out to the parking lot, where the Mustang was parked at the curb waiting for them. Jack's golf clubs were in the back seat.

Jack climbed into the car and unfastened the latches that secured the convertible top to the windshield frame.

"Better leave the top up," Bruno said, sliding into the passenger seat. "Crown Construction is remodeling the west wing of the clubhouse, and they're having a labor dispute. Things have gotten nasty on a couple of occasions."

Jack refastened the latches. "Are you going to be my bodyguard?" he said to his large companion.

"You shouldn't need one," Bruno said, "but I might need one."

"A lovable guy like you?" Jack said, as he put the car in gear and headed down the driveway.

"I'm the chairman of the facilities committee at the club," Bruno said. "The laborers' union is trying to put pressure on the committee to influence Crown."

"Say no more," Jack said. "I get the picture."

Sterling Whitehurst turned into the entrance to the country club just ahead of Jack and Bruno in the Mustang. A group of picketers crowded the driveway, impeding the movement of both cars as they entered. One of the picketers pounded on the trunk of the Mustang as it passed through the entrance.

"That was mild," Bruno said, looking back at the group. "You should see what they do to *my* car when they see it."

"Have they threatened you personally?" Jack said.

"No," Bruno said. "I've had a few phone threats saying they'll trash my hotel, but nothing has happened yet."

Bruno directed Jack to the bag drop area and motioned for assistance from one of the attendants. The kid took Jack's clubs to a nearby golf cart, then hopped in the Mustang and took the long way past the pool to find an empty parking space. Jack chuckled as he watched the mating ritual of the boy slowly cruising past the pool and the girls pretending not to notice him. *Some things never change, it seems.* An image of Betty Hendricks entering the water to finish a springboard dive flashed through his mind. The girls around the pool on this day were the same age as his image of Betty, which reminded him that Betty was as old as he was now. But seeing the young girls lounging by the pool made him feel younger, or at least brought back the memory of how he had felt back then.

The swimming pool was to the left of the entrance to the single-story clubhouse. The clubhouse building was framed with brick columns on each side and had ivy covering just enough of the brick to give the whole thing a luxurious look. Spreading out in both directions from the entrance was a brick wall that devolved into a chain-link fence, which encircled most of the grounds, keeping out the unwanted.

Jack climbed into the passenger side of Bruno's golf cart, and the two friends headed down the path to the first tee. Stewart Ramsey was sitting in a golf cart, with Sterling standing at the rear of the vehicle supervising a young attendant who was cleaning his clubs. Cigar smoke drifted downwind from the oversized ashtray built into the dashboard of Ramsey's golf vehicle. The mock license plate read "KARZ." Bruno and Jack gave a wave to the opposing team as they passed by Ramsey's cart and then stopped in front of the steps leading to the tee box.

The fairway on the first hole was a long par five. Ramsey stepped up to hit first, proclaiming that the match was his idea so he should have the honors. No one argued, so he dropped his stogie on the ground and hit a modest drive down the right side of the fairway. Sterling stepped up to hit second. He was dressed appropriately for the country club set—very stylish. Jack watched him go through his routine, set the club head down, then—SWISH—miss the ball completely. Jack managed to suppress his desire to laugh, but Bruno chuckled audibly and Stewart almost swallowed his cigar he was laughing so hard. Sterling shot a death-ray stare at Stewart, then ripped a long drive about a hundred yards past Stewart's. Bruno and Jack both hit their drives down the middle, hopped in their cart, and headed down the cart path.

Stewart hit his second shot, then both carts headed up the fairway to wait for Jack and Bruno. Bruno parked the golf cart about twenty feet behind Jack's ball, then Jack got out and hit his second shot. The ball headed right, hit a tree limb, and bounced backward into a brushy area to his right.

"Damn."

"I'll help you look for it," Bruno said, climbing out of the cart. "I know that patch of brush pretty well."

"We'll go up ahead so Sterling can hit," Stewart said. "We'll come back behind Hackett's ball after Jack gets out of the woods—if he ever does." Their cart roared off, cigar smoke leaving a telltale trail, like a high-altitude jet.

"Let's walk over in this direction, Jack," Bruno said, pointing toward a large oak tree in the stand of timber. "I saw where it bounced."

Bruno and Jack walked over to the edge of the brush, then spread out to search the area.

BOOM. A shock wave hit Jack from behind, sending him flying face first into a shrub, his arms and legs flailing like a rag doll. It felt like someone had hit him from behind with a piece of plywood. His face and chest were impaled with tiny twigs from the bush. He rolled over onto his left side and off the bush, ending up on his back in the dirt, looking up at the oak tree. His ears were ringing, and his vision was a little blurred. He tried to push himself to a sitting position but couldn't. He rolled onto his side, then propped himself up by his elbow. His ears were still ringing. He heard a muffled noise that sounded like shouting, but it seemed very distant. He looked around and saw Bruno making an effort to get himself up off the ground.

He looked back toward the fairway. The cart that he and Bruno had been riding in was in a thousand pieces of varying size, and there was a huge hole in the ground where it had been parked.

"You okay, Hackett?" Jack said. His lips moved, but the sound of his voice barely registered in his brain.

"Yeah, I think so," Bruno said, elevating himself to a wobbly standing position and rubbing his head. "What the hell was that?"

"Look at the cart," Jack said, pointing to the hole in the ground.

"Holy shit," Bruno said.

Jack stood up, and the two men walked out onto the fairway, scratching their heads in dismay. Jack felt something running down his right cheek. He swiped at it with his hand, and his hand turned red. His face began to sting. Bruno stopped him by putting his hands on Jack's head, then surveyed the wound.

"Looks nasty, but not fatal," Bruno said. "Looks like part of that bush is still embedded in your face." He took out his handkerchief and dabbed at the wound to clear away the blood and branches. "You'll live," he said. "You just won't be as pretty."

Jack chuckled. It hurt when he did it. The two men walked toward what was left of Bruno's golf cart. Stewart and Sterling had their cart at full throttle coming back down the fairway. Their mouths were open, and they looked a little pale as they reached Bruno and Jack. People were rushing toward the scene from all directions. Somewhere in the distance, there was a siren moving closer. Jack wobbled and shuffled closer to the hole to survey the damage.

"What the hell caused that?" he said, looking up at Bruno.

Bruno just shook his head in disbelief, then fainted and fell face first into the hole.

CHAPTER 5

JACK DIDN'T LIKE HOSPITAL ROOMS, they were sterile and people died there. But he felt guilty about Bruno's condition, so he stepped into Bruno's room, joining the gathering of friends and investigators.

"He looks okay, doesn't he?" Joshua Pitts said, leaning over the hospital bed and gawking at the abrasions on Bruno's face. He pointed toward a large gash. "There's still blood oozing out of that cut."

Frank Kirby grabbed Joshua by the elbow and tried to coax him away from the bed. "Let the man breathe, Pitts," he said.

Joshua resisted Frank's tugs and continued to hover over Bruno's head.

"You part vampire, Pitts?" Frank said. "You seem to be fascinated by blood."

Pitts appeared to ignore the remark.

"You got here awfully fast, Pitts," Frank said. "How'd you hear about this, anyway?"

"Heard the blast from inside my car ten blocks away, Frank," Joshua said. "Sounded like a sonic boom."

Frank wedged himself in between Joshua and the stainless steel bed rail. "Let the man rest," he said, eyeball-to-eyeball with Joshua.

Joshua backed away and joined Stewart and Sterling, who were on the other side of the nightstand.

Jack stood at the doorway, rubbing the back of his neck to ward off the onset of stiffness and pain the doctor had predicted. "Still think the rattlesnake in my dresser was a prank, Frank?" he said.

Frank turned to Jack. "What makes you think that blast was meant for you?" he said. "It was Bruno's cart, and he was standing right beside you when the bomb went off. It makes more sense to conclude that it had something to do with the labor dispute at the clubhouse than someone trying to scare or kill you."

Frank walked over to the door and motioned for everyone to leave the room. "Everyone, into the hall so we can talk."

Jack, Joshua, and Stewart immediately stepped out into the hallway. Sterling hesitated, so Frank took him by the arm and escorted him out of the room. A nurse walked through the group in the hallway and into Bruno's room. She closed the door behind her.

"Let's start with you, Ramsey," Frank said, nodding toward Stewart. "Did you see anything or anyone unusual around that cart, prior to heading out to the first tee?"

"Nope," Stewart said. "Andy, the boy who shuttles the carts to the bag drop, brought Bruno's cart up to the front of the pro shop with Jack's and Bruno's club bags strapped to the back like everyone else's."

"You see anything unusual, Whitehurst?" Frank said, turning to Sterling.

"No, nothing at all," he said.

"How 'bout you, Pitts?" Frank said. "You see anybody unusual around the area?"

"Couldn't have, Frank," Joshua said. "I was ten blocks away. Remember?"

"Oh, yeah," Frank said. "Guess I forgot. Any of you guys see anyone around holding something the size of a garage-door opener?"

"You'd have to be pretty close to the bomb to trigger it with a mechanism that small," Jack said.

"Very good, McCall," Frank said. "You really do have some experience in this kind of stuff, don't you?"

Frank walked over to the drinking fountain on the other side of the hallway, took a quick taste of water, and walked back to the group. "Andy Robinson, our explosives guy, told me that the device was triggered close in. Probably with a remote radio signal from a device about the size of an opener."

"That was a fast diagnosis," Jack said.

"Andy's retired FBI," Frank said. "Knows his stuff. Seen a lot. Doesn't miss much. He figures that whoever it was had to be watching you when he set it off."

Sterling shifted his weight and leaned back against the wall. "That means he probably knew that the two of them were out of the cart, and that they weren't going to be seriously hurt by the blast," he said.

"Probably," Jack agreed.

"Sounds like a waste of a good bomb to me," Joshua said. "A lot of work just to scare someone."

Stewart pulled a big cigar out of the chest pocket of his shirt and lit it. "Maybe he just didn't like golf carts," he said.

Jack fanned the cigar smoke and moved to the opposite side of the group. "With a triggering device that small," he said, "the 'perp' could have been standing right next to someone and they wouldn't have known he'd set it off." He looked at Frank. "I'd like to talk with Andy to find out more about the trigger device. Maybe I can use some of my contacts to—"

"You guys keep saying he," Sterling interrupted. "How do you know it was a he?"

"I don't," Frank said. He turned and gave the evil eye to Jack. "And no, you can't talk to Andy, McCall. You're going to stay out of this."

The nurse came out of Bruno's room and stopped in front of Stewart. She took the cigar out of his mouth, walked to the water fountain, extinguished the tip by soaking it thoroughly, brought it back to Stewart, placed it in his shirt pocket with a love pat, and then headed down the hall. Stewart gave a glance down at his pocket and started to walk off.

"Where are you going, *Mister* Ramsey?" Frank said.

"I'll be available anytime you want to talk to me, Frank," Stewart said. "Except now." He kept on walking and then disappeared around a corner.

Frank waved his hand in the air in disgust. "The rest of you can go, too," he said. "But my people will call you tomorrow to arrange for a formal statement."

"Even me?" asked Joshua. "I wasn't anywhere near this or the other incident."

"Can you prove that?" Frank said.

Joshua looked puzzled for a moment, shifting his weight from one foot to the other. "I'll be available tomorrow," he said.

The group started to disperse. "Not you, McCall," Frank said. "We need to talk some more."

Jack stopped in his tracks. "You ignored my complaint this morning when someone tried to kill me with that snake," he said. "And now I'm starting to get a terrible headache. Can't we talk later?"

"No," Frank said.

Jack walked across the corridor to a seating area and plopped himself down in one of the institutional chairs. "If I can't go, I'm going to sit," he said.

"I think this incident is connected to the labor conflict," Frank said, from across the corridor. "But I can't ignore the possibility that it was directed at you."

"Very good, Kirby," Jack said, mocking Frank's earlier insult. "You really do have some experience in this kind of stuff, don't you?"

Frank was not amused.

"Come over here so you don't have to shout," Jack said. "Remember, I have a headache."

Frank walked over and stood in front of Jack.

"Sit down," Jack said, looking up at Frank. "My neck hurts, too."

"You're enjoying this, aren't you?" Frank said, taking an adjoining seat. "You think you have my attention now, don't you? Well, personally, I could give a shit if this guy blows you to kingdom come. I just want him to do it somewhere else."

"That's it, Frankie boy," Jack said, rubbing his neck with his eyes closed. "Vent that anger."

Frank grunted out a disgusted version of a laugh.

"Actually, it's a good sign that you're angry," Jack said, continuing his patronizing psychoanalysis. "It takes a certain amount of feeling to be angry. We just have to focus on the source of your anger."

"Now you're a damn shrink?" Frank said.

The two men sat in silence for a few moments, each seeming to wait for the other to speak. The hospital intercom periodically called out doctors' names, directing them to a phone number or a room. Jack continued to rub his neck. He was glad to have Frank's attention, even if his entire body was beginning to hurt.

Jack opened his eyes and leaned forward in his chair. "Look, Frank," he said. "I don't know how many people could want to kill me. I've been a federal prosecutor for ten years. I've crossed paths with and pissed off a lot of bad people. But how would one of them know I was here? And why would they want to come after me here? It wouldn't make sense."

Frank didn't say anything. He just shifted his weight from one cheek to the other in his chair.

"What does make sense," Jack continued, "is that someone got very nervous when I started speculating about how Annie died."

"Ah, not that shit again," Frank said, rising abruptly out of his chair. "You're never going to let go of it, are you?" He turned toward Jack and bent over, pointing a finger as if scolding a child. "You just have to find someone to blame, don't you? Once someone else gets accused and is in jail or on death row, you think you won't feel guilty anymore."

"Like you?" Jack said, without looking up at his accuser.

"What the hell do you mean by that?"

"I know you were in love with her too," Jack said, raising his head to a position where Frank's accusatory finger was pointing right between his eyes. "Maybe it was you in the car with her that night." Jack rose to his feet and towered over Frank. "Maybe you're the one who wants people to stop asking questions."

Frank drew back his left arm and landed a swift punch to Jack's unsuspecting abdomen, sending all the air rushing out of his lungs and dropping the big man back into his chair. "Now your gut hurts too, McCall. It'll go well with your sore head and your sore neck."

Frank started walking down the hospital corridor. "I'm going to find out who planted that bomb in Bruno's golf cart," he said. "Then, if it was meant for you, I'll give him a few pointers, help him do the job right next time."

Jack steadied himself on the arm of the chair and slowly rose to his feet while struggling to get his lungs working again. The sounds of the staff moving and working in the hallway were hurting his head. He shuffled over to the elevator and made his way out of the building, just as Mollie rolled the Mustang to a stop in front of the hospital's main entrance. Jack stood by the door with one hand on his stomach and the other on his head while Mollie got out of the car and walked over to him.

"The people at the country club asked if you were okay, honey," she said, lifting Jack's hand off his head to see if there was a hole or something being covered up. "You don't look so good, though. You should go back in and have a doctor take another look at you."

"I'll be fine," Jack said. "Let's go back to the hotel. I just need to lie down for a while. My whole body hurts."

"That generally happens when you get knocked on your ass by a bomb," Nurse Mollie pointed out while loading her patient into the car.

Jack adjusted his position in the passenger seat to minimize his discomfort. "I'll bet that Frank's retired FBI guy used some resources in the Bureau to identify that detonator so quickly. Maybe I need to make a few inquiries myself. It's a cinch Frank's not going to give me any info."

"You're not going to be able to do much but sleep for the rest of the day," Mollie said. "Maybe you should let me do your legwork for you."

"Doesn't involve legs," Jack said. "Although you certainly have a nice pair of legs for the job." He winced in pain as he held back a chuckle.

"What do you want me to do?" she said.

"E-mail Malcolm Hayes, back in Hartford," he said. "Ask him to check with his contacts in the Bureau, and find out if they helped good ol' Andy identify the detonator for that bomb. And get them to send me a copy of the report, if they have one."

Jack closed his eyes and leaned his head back against the headrest. The acceleration of the Mustang convertible, under the command of Mollie's heavy foot, forced his neck sideways, generating a twinge of pain. As soon as the pace of the car stabilized, the wind rushing against his face soothed his nerves and helped him relax as they drove back to the Caldwell Inn.

Mollie helped Jack out of the car and served as a crutch on his journey from the parking lot through the crowded lobby of the inn toward the elevator. Jack was a little self-conscious as he walked through the lobby. His glance at an expansive mirror on the lobby wall revealed that he still had several pieces of shrubbery stuck to his shirt. He wanted to act somewhat dignified in front of the reunion crowd, but his body just wasn't moving the way he wanted it to.

Just as he reached the safety of the elevator, a small group of classmates came out of an adjacent meeting room. Joshua Pitts led the way, followed by Stewart Ramsey, Joe, Jessie, Sterling, and Victoria. Joshua stopped right in front of Jack and Mollie, bringing the entire herd to a standstill.

"Jack, you don't look so good," Joshua said.

Stewart stepped around Joshua and grabbed Jack's other arm to become a second crutch. "Let me help you upstairs, Jack," he said. "This elevator is kind of shaky."

Jack managed a polite smile and lifted his forearm off Stewart's shoulder. "Thanks, Stewart," he said. "Mollie's a pro at this. We'll manage."

"Anything we can do for you, Jack?" Sterling said from the back of the group. Jack shook his head and punched the button to summon the elevator. The car arrived and the pair got in, along with several of the hallway crowd.

As the door began to close, Joe poked his head out from behind his dad. "Does this mean we won't be able to go flying tomorrow, Mr. McCall?" he said.

Mollie put her finger on the "door open" button and leaned forward from the elevator car. "We'll go, Joe. If Mr. McCall doesn't feel like flying, I'll take you and your friends." She winked at the young man. "I'm a better pilot, anyway. See you at the airport at nine a.m. sharp. I'll stop in the restaurant and get a thermos of coffee, some sodas, and maybe a sandwich or two for a light snack while we're sightseeing." She leaned back, and the young man's smiling face disappeared behind the closing doors.

At the fourth-floor landing, Mollie assisted Jack as he exited the elevator, walked down the hall, and entered their room. He slumped onto the bed and moved only when required to cooperate with Mollie's efforts to undress him and maneuver him under the covers. It was only late afternoon, but he was exhausted and sore, and he had a terrible headache. Mollie got some aspirin out of her travel bag in the bathroom and brought it to him.

"Thanks, hon," he mumbled, as he downed the medicine and chased it with the tap water she provided. "Don't forget to contact Malcolm. I need him to check on that bomb stuff right away."

"I'll set up my laptop right now," she said. "Close your eyes and sleep for a while. I'll e-mail Malcolm, and with a little luck I'll have some answers for you when you wake up."

Jack rolled over onto his back and wedged a pillow under his neck to straighten out his spine. The technique helped a tension headache go away, so he figured it might help with an "explosion headache." Anything to allow him to get comfortable and to make the pain in his head disappear.

He heard Mollie get her computer out of its carrying case and plug in all the wires. The noise was irritating, but he knew she was trying to be quiet. It was her way. She would deliberately agitate him when he was feeling good, but when he was down she was his number-one pal, as he was hers.

Gradually, the aspirin and the neck pillow began to have their desired effect. The noise became distant and his body went into sleep mode.

Mollie set up her laptop computer and connected to the building's Wi-Fi. This was her specialty. She took great delight in gathering information when Jack was at an impasse. He relied on her. She was his go-to person.

A few quick clicks of the mouse and she was in cyberspace, heading toward Jack's office computer. It wasn't exactly legal, but she had access to everything. Everything. She logged into Jack's office e-mail system and routed a message to Malcolm, inquiring about the bomb information Andy Robinson might have obtained from the FBI.

Mollie looked over to the bed to check on Jack. He was asleep and emitting some telltale snoring, which was common when he slept on his back. It usually bothered her, but right now it sounded reassuring. She walked over to the bed and pulled the covers over his shoulders.

Her immediate assignment completed, Mollie decided to do a little investigating on her own. Her main tool, the Internet, might yield some insight that the people involved wanted to keep hidden. She did a Web search on Wainwright Industries to check out Sterling's in-laws and his professional ties to them. This is interesting, she thought, as she scanned through the Web information. Good ol' Sterling was listed number two on the corporate menu. Pretty prominent fellow. Did he have something to hide back here in Caldwell that might prevent him from ascending to the throne? He seemed very nervous about Jack's asking questions about Annie. Might be something there. She saved all the downloadable pages available through the Wainwright Industries website to a thumb drive.

Nothing was available on Jessie Dalton, unless she used the alias Matilda Dalton, an eccentric painter from Sydney, Australia, specializing in nude self-portraits. Likewise, nothing was available on Frank. She'd have to do some legwork to investigate him as well.

Joshua Pitts, on the other hand, had a website. Pitts Photography, the family business name, was now his. The website didn't reveal much other than very expensive prices for his services, an address, telephone, fax, and e-mail. His advertisement read "Historic Events Photography." She thought it an odd specialty. No weddings, babies, portraits, that kind of thing. Just "historic." She wondered how his clients decided what would qualify as historic. For that matter, how did he decide what would qualify as historic? Might be an interesting dinner conversation. Stewart Ramsey also had a website for his car dealership. Nothing unusual there.

Mollie got up from the desk and walked over to check on Jack again. She watched him for a moment. His snoring serenade had ended, and she wanted to make sure he was breathing. After reassuring herself that he was okay, she grabbed the coffee thermos from her flight bag and headed down to the restaurant. She had promised the younger Mr. Ramsey that she would take him flying, complete with luncheon service. She always kept her promises.

Mollie opened the door and stepped into the hallway. She was heading toward the elevator, a route that took her past the open door next to their old room. A slender, well-dressed blonde woman stepped out into the hall, closing the door behind her.

"How's your hubby?" the woman asked.

"He's fine, thank you," Mollie said. "You look too young to be one of his classmates. How do you know him?"

"Oh, we shared fashion tips early this morning, out on our adjoining balconies," the woman said with a smile. She made an abrupt turn and disappeared through the stairway exit door.

Mollie made a mental note to ask Jack about the sexy neighbor and exactly what she meant by "fashion tips." She summoned the elevator to the fourth floor and headed down. When the elevator stopped at the second floor, the door opened to reveal Jessie Dalton, waiting to get on.

"Mollie," Jessie said, with a startled look and a slight shudder. She took a hesitant first step into the elevator and caught the heel of her shoe on the metal strips separating the elevator car from the landing. Mollie reached out and kept her from falling face first into the elevator.

"Careful there, Ms. Dalton," Mollie said. "You're falling for the wrong member of the McCall household."

Jessie straightened up, then brushed the wrinkles from her pale-yellow silk dress in an attempt to regain her dignity and composure. "Thank you for catching me," she said. "I'm just as glad it was you and not Jack."

"How's your hand?" Mollie said, as she pushed the lobby button.

"Oh, it's fine," Jessie said, raising the wounded appendage and rotating it in the air. "You must think I'm an awful klutz."

"No, you just seem very nervous. Like something is really bothering you, you know."

"Well, I guess I am. This trip was very hard for me to make. My counselor practically forced me to come, though."

"I'm headed for the restaurant to order some coffee and food for tomorrow," Mollie said, as the elevator door opened to the lobby. "We could sit and talk awhile."

Jessie hesitated. "Well, I don't know. I heard about Jack's troubles today. You probably want to be with him, not me."

"The doctor said he'll be fine, and he's upstairs sleeping like a baby. Let's go have a cup of coffee. I'm a great listener."

Mollie didn't allow Jessie to answer. She grabbed her by the arm and coaxed her toward the restaurant. She wanted to find out as much as she could about Annie, Jessie, Frank, and all the rest. She figured getting Jessie to open up and confide in her was the quickest way. The two women finished off the evening with food, conversation, and half the coffee supply in the building before retiring for the night.

******

Jack awoke as he had the day before, somewhat disoriented and in pain. But this time, the pain wasn't from growing old. It was from his close encounter with high explosives. His mind was a little cloudy. He could remember being in the car on the way back from the hospital but couldn't remember much after that. A sliver of sunlight sliced its way through the curtains, crossed his face, and continued down his right arm, which hung out over the side of the bed. The light was hot and cutting. With Mollie's dormant body on the other side of him, the only escape from the discomfort was to get out of bed.

Reunion activities officially commenced at breakfast, so he needed to get up. The football team was having a special gathering that included the rally squad. Jack figured that the state championship game would be relived over and over and over again before breakfast was finished. It wasn't that great of a game the first time, and he wasn't looking forward to its resurrection. But the opportunity to visit with his teammates appealed to him. Besides, maybe during the latest telling of the tale they would win the game.

His legs felt rubbery, and he wobbled back and forth as he rose out of bed. His mind was telling his legs to move, but they were not fully cooperating with his commands. He hobbled to the bathroom and turned on the shower. A nice hot shower always loosened up his stiff muscles, so he gave the hot-water valve an extra twist and stepped in. It was usually akin to magic. The warm water sucked all the stiffness out of his muscles and the tension flowed from his body, disappearing down the drain. At least that's how his mind pictured it.

As he stood in the shower with the water running over his head, he thought about Coach Grady. Two images flashed through his mind: the coach standing on the sidelines in the pouring rain, signaling a play for Jack to run; and the coach lying in the nursing home bed and looking off into space, with no sign of life except the rhythmic beep of the heart monitor. *Why did I wait so long to come home?*

The team would be at breakfast, but he doubted that the coach would be there. The team wanted to honor him, but with no way for Grady to communicate with the world, Jack felt that to wheel him into the room and have him just sit there in front of everyone like a vegetable would be cruel. He lifted his face into the shower with the hope that the water would wash away the vision from his mind.

He stepped out of the shower and toweled off. His body felt better and his mind was a little clearer, but the image of the coach lingered, making him feel depressed. He got dressed without turning on lights or closing any doors in the room, so Mollie could sleep. He knew the team breakfast wasn't high on her list of priorities.

He got on the elevator and went down to the lobby, where his teammates, a few wives, and a few vintage cheerleaders were milling around, waiting for breakfast to begin. A plume of cigar smoke was rising from the middle of the pack. Stewart Ramsey was somewhere in the crowd, he guessed. Jack shook hands and said hello to several people he recognized (and a few he didn't recognize) as he made his way through the group and toward Henry, who was standing near the entrance to the banquet room along with Jessie, Sterling, and Victoria.

"You're looking a little better today," Henry said, leaning forward to shake Jack's hand. "How do you feel?"

"Better, I guess," Jack said. "Bit of a headache, but I can walk without getting dizzy. Did I see you yesterday?"

"Yes," Henry said. "I was in the group by the elevator when you got back to the inn."

"Did we talk?" Jack said.

"No, you looked a little out of it."

Sterling Whitehurst leaned forward, nudging Henry sideways. "Mollie's not joining us for breakfast?" he said. "Victoria was looking forward to having some female companionship during this gathering."

"No," Jack said. "She's sleeping in. She's going to take Mr. Ramsey the Younger and his friends flying sometime this morning. She'll probably a have a light breakfast when she gets up."

"Are you going flying with them?" Jessie said.

"Yes," Jack said. "She's a great pilot, but I always feel better if there are two pilots onboard."

"Excellent," Sterling said. "Always good to be safe."

A puff of smoke drifted across Jack's face.

"Have you figured out who blew up Bruno's golf cart, Mr. Prosecutor?" the elder Ramsey's familiar voice asked from the back of the crowd.

The group turned toward the source of the air pollution and collectively glared down at Stewart. "Would you mind putting out that cigar, Stewart?" Sterling said. "Victoria's sinuses don't tolerate smoke very well." Victoria was fanning the air and sneezing at this point.

"Well, excuse me, Mrs. Whitehurst," Stewart said. "I wasn't aware of your condition." He stepped over to a large tray inside the banquet room and scraped the ash and fire off the burning end of the cigar into one of the half-full coffee cups. He stuck the remainder of the cigar in his shirt pocket and then walked back to the group. "Now, as I was saying," he continued, "who's trying to scare you into leaving, McCall?"

Victoria took a prolonged drink of her modified morning tomato juice. "Probably someone bumped off ol' Annie twenty years ago and doesn't want y'all asking questions," she said.

"Now, Victoria," Sterling said, taking her arm and leaning down to her ear. "We talked about that and decided that was highly unlikely. Remember?"

"Yes," Jessie added. "No one could have wanted to hurt her, let alone kill her. The whole idea is ridiculous."

"Sounds like an intriguing puzzle to me," Joshua Pitts said, stepping into the group and the conversation. "Why else would someone want to destroy Bruno's golf cart and hide a rattlesnake in Jack's underwear drawer?"

Jack stepped toward the banquet room door. "Someone doesn't want me asking questions," he said. "I think when we get back from taking Joe and his pals sightseeing, I'm going to find some answers."

Henry followed Jack into the banquet room and put his hand on Jack's shoulder. "Why don't you and Mollie come out to the farm after you get back from your excursion?" he said. "We'll talk."

"Okay," Jack said. "It'll be good to see the old place again."

The two men wandered among the tables, looking for a place to sit that would allow them a good vantage point for the proceedings, and a good escape route if they wanted to leave early. Taking seats near a side door, they listened to the welcoming speeches, which included Stewart Ramsey broadcasting his intention to run for state senator. Then came the droning noises that made up the introductions, which required everyone to stand and be recognized by the group. In some cases, recognition was difficult. More weight and less hair was the general rule for the team; and more weight and different-colored hair was the general rule for the rally squad.

"When did Ramsey get pumped up on politics?" Jack asked Henry.

"Oh, he's been playing at it for a while now," Henry said. "He's been dabbling in city politics for years, but he couldn't get anyone to listen to him until he got elected to the city council. Then they had to listen. He liked the results so well he decided to find a bigger soapbox to stand on."

"So the state senate would be the bigger soapbox?" Jack said.

"Yup, biggest soapbox around here."

"Does he do any good, or is he just up there to hear himself talk?" Jack said.

"He's had a few good ideas, and he hasn't gotten in the way of the good ideas from other councilors. I guess that makes him a little better than your average politician."

Before Henry could comment, their attention was drawn to a commotion by the entrance to the room. Coach Grady was at the doorway, sitting in a wheelchair and escorted by a nurse. Jack got up and walked back to where the nurse was standing. He recognized her as the nurse who had taken him into the coach's room the day before. "You're not going to bring him in here to be gawked at, are you?"

"Yes," she said. "We are bringing him in here, thanks to you."

"I don't understand," Jack said, as he put his hand on the arm of the wheelchair.

"We'd never been certain whether he was aware of what was going on around him until your visit yesterday," the nurse said. "I went into his room right after you left and saw something I had not seen since he had his stroke." She moved closer to Jack and put her hand on his arm. "Tears."

Jack looked down at the coach, who was staring straight ahead, motionless.

The nurse leaned forward so she could look Jack in the eye. "Your being with him yesterday sparked an emotional response in him," she said. "He knows you are here with him now."

Jack squatted down beside the chair and put his hand on the coach's hand. "Are you sure?" he said.

"Ask your friend over there," she said, pointing toward Henry. She moved into position behind the chair and took hold of the grips. "The doctors think being here with this group will be good for him," she said, as she started moving him forward at a snail's pace into the room.

Jack stood and watched the coach being wheeled into the room. Everyone stood and applauded as the coach moved past them.

Jack joined Henry at the table near the back of the room. "The nurse said the doctors are pretty certain the coach is aware of what's going on around him, even though he can't communicate," he said, as he sat down next to his friend. "I asked her if she was sure, and she said to ask *you*."

Henry grinned and shrugged his shoulders. "She knows I'm a farmer," he said. "Guess she thinks farmers have a connection with the universe or something."

Jack crumpled his face to signal that Henry's explanation was suspect.

"You were asking about Ramsey's political aspirations," Henry said, in an obvious attempt to change the subject. "He seems intent on winning the upcoming election."

"Takes quite a bit of money to run for state senator," Jack said.

"He's got that covered," Henry said.

"The car business must be pretty good if he's using his own money," Jack said.

"He's not using his own. US Senator Bob Mason, from Illinois, is flying in to do a fundraiser for him," Henry said. "They're having a big family barbecue lunch on Sunday."

"Bob Mason—risky," Jack said. "Couldn't he get anyone other than Mason to endorse him?"

Henry turned his head upward as if looking for divine wisdom to guide his answer to Jack's question.

"Mason isn't exactly a stand-up guy," Jack continued. "He's a take-no-prisoners politician who isn't very popular with his colleagues."

"Doesn't seem to matter these days," Henry replied.

"Why would he come here to do a fundraiser for Ramsey?" Jack said. "And why would Ramsey want someone as scandalous as Mason to campaign for him?"

"Speculation is that Mason's going to run for president, and Stewart convinced him that State Senator Stewart Ramsey would be a quality ally and an effective fundraiser in this state."

"Still the used-car salesman, isn't he?" Jack said.

Henry chuckled at the remark. "He was aided by the fact that Mason has pissed off both Pritchard and Wilson, his senatorial colleagues from the State of Oregon. He has to find support on a state level, and the old guard in the capitol building are aligned pretty close to Pritchard and Wilson. Mason's probably willing to help Stewart—or anyone else—get elected in this state, if they promise to help him in a presidential campaign."

"When'd you get so deep into politics?" Jack asked his friend.

"Oh, you know us farmers," Henry said with a straight face. "We just keep an ear to the ground and pick up a little bit here and a little bit there."

"Right."

"Jack," a muffled voice said from behind him.

Jack turned to see Mollie standing at the doorway, motioning for him to join her. "I'll get the car and meet you out front," she said.

He turned back around and leaned over toward Henry. "Gotta run," he said. "If I get any awards, accept them for me with great pride and humility, just as I would."

"If you get any awards, I'll accept them with great surprise and arrogance—just as you would."

"Whatever," Jack said, starting to rise from his chair.

Henry grabbed his arm and pulled him back down. "Don't forget to come out to the farm when you get finished with your tour," he said. "We need to talk about Annie and all this stuff that's been happening."

Jack gave him a thumbs-up and said, "I'll call you when we land."

CHAPTER 6

MOLLIE MANEUVERED THE MUSTANG around the traffic circle in front of the inn, stopping just long enough for Jack to get in before heading down the drive toward the street. "You sure you want to come with me and miss all the hoopla?" she asked Jack. "I'm going to be flying anyway. No sense in missing your party if you want to stay."

Jack thought a second. "No," he said. "I got to see the coach and talk with Henry for a few minutes. That's enough."

"The coach was there?" Mollie said. "I thought you said he was totally out of touch with the world."

"I spoke with the nurse who brought him over," Jack said. "She said that my visit yesterday triggered a response in him that the doctors hadn't seen before. They now think that he's totally aware of what's going on around him."

"Wonderful," Mollie said. "I'll bet that made your day."

"Yes," Jack said.

"Well," Mollie said, "I found out some things last night that you might find equally interesting."

Jack tipped his head back against the headrest and let out a moan. "What did I do? Did I do something weird last night?"

"No, it has nothing to do with you," Mollie said. She stopped the car at the main entrance to the inn and then pulled out onto the street, heading toward the airport.

"Mollie," Jack said with a scowl, "what have you been up to?"

"I had a long conversation with your pal Jessie Dalton last night," she responded. "You know, woman to woman."

"Oh?" Jack said, lifting his head off the headrest and directing his attention toward his wife.

"Turns out that she and Annie had a relationship going."

Jack leaned his head back against the headrest. "Sure they did," he said. "Everyone knew that they were close."

"No, Jack," Mollie said. "They had a *relationship*—as in intimate relationship."

Jack stared straight ahead, putting all the pieces together in his mind. "Annie and Jessie, and Annie and me," he said, from his statue-like position. "That's why . . ."

"Why what?" the driver asked.

Jack didn't answer. He leaned forward, massaging his closed eyelids with the palms of his hands.

"Jack," Mollie said, taking her right hand off the steering wheel and rubbing his shoulder. "Talk to me, Jack."

Jack shook his head. "She said no."

Mollie waited for a few moments for him to say more. "No to what?" she asked, when her patience expired.

"The night before we graduated," Jack said, "I asked her to move to Hartford so we could be together."

"So, was that like a proposal or something?" Mollie said.

Jack shrugged his shoulders. "I guess—kind of," he said. "As close to one as an eighteen-year-old boy could get."

"And she said no?" Mollie said.

"She said no," he continued, "and that she wanted to go to college too, but she'd just figured out how to pay for it, so she hadn't made plans yet."

"So you got pissed off and broke up with her."

"Yes."

A quizzical look emerged on Mollie's face. "Do you think she was going away with Jessie?" she said.

"You tell me," Jack said. "You were the one playing parish priest last night."

Mollie flipped on the right turn signal and slowed the car to turn into the airport entrance. "Well," she said, "I do know that she's been in therapy for a couple decades trying to deal with her past and her present. She confessed that she tried to kill herself once."

"Oh, man," Jack said. "I didn't need to know that."

"What do you mean?" Mollie responded. "I thought she was a friend."

Jack took a deep breath and leaned his head back as far as it would go, staring at the tree limbs overhanging the road. "Yes, she was—is," he said. He straightened his posture, then turned sideways to face Mollie. "But it makes me wonder if the past she's dealing with is having her lover die, and the present she's dealing with involves blowing up a golf cart because Annie died going up the mountain to see me."

Mollie steered the Mustang through the main entrance to the aircraft parking area. "So you think Jessie might be secretly angry at you, and she's trying to kill you because Annie felt guilty about dumping you and died driving up to the park to make sure you were okay?" she said.

Jack shrugged his shoulders again. "I've sent people to prison for stranger reasons than that."

"She doesn't strike me as the high-explosives type, Mr. Prosecutor."

"You'd be surprised," Jack said. "I've heard of cases where little old ladies—you know, Granny types—buy hand grenades and blow up little old men who piss 'em off."

Mollie brought the Mustang to a halt in the vehicle parking lot adjacent to where the Aero Commander was parked. "Speaking of women getting pissed off at men," she said, getting out of the car and closing the door with a thud, "you want to explain the blonde I met in the hallway last night who said she'd been sharing fashion tips with you?" She put her hands on the door of the convertible and leaned forward. "She expressed great concern about your welfare, too, by the way."

Jack's mind went blank. *Blonde? Fashion?* His brain kicked into hyper-drive to come up with an answer—a good answer. An answer that wouldn't get him into trouble. But first he had to figure out what she was talking about. *Blonde? Fashion? Oh, yes.*

"Did she have on sunglasses, by any chance?" he said.

"In the hallway, outside our room?" Mollie said. "I don't think so."

"That must be the gal in the room next to ours," he said. "She was out on her balcony yesterday morning. I'd forgotten about that."

Mollie took off her sunglasses, giving her husband one of those "sure, you forgot" looks of disbelief, complete with raised eyebrows and penetrating stare. "She didn't appear to be the type of girl you would—just forget," she said. "What was the 'fashion' comment about?"

"Oh, it was just a joke about the towels and linen here at the hotel." *Change the subject, McCall.* "Let me get those box lunches out of the back seat. Those look good. Did you get them at the hotel?"

Mollie wasn't that easily distracted. "Yes. Right after meeting your friend in the hallway outside our room. So, did you have a long conversation about the linen?"

"Let me get that coffee thermos too." *I can't believe I didn't tell her about the blonde. Idiot.*

As they walked toward the Commander, Mollie stared at him, waiting for an answer to her question.

"Just a few words," Jack said, turning away from her glaring eyes. "Like I said, I had forgotten all about it. Did you get some Coke for the kids and some Diet Coke for me?"

"Yes," she said. "They're in the trunk, in a small Styrofoam cooler that the cook gave me."

"I'll load the plane while you file our flight plan," Jack said.

"Okay," she said, as she turned and headed toward the flight service office. "But I want to know more about your fashion tips before we close this topic of conversation." She crossed the parking apron and went into the office to file a flight plan for their trip, leaving Jack to prepare the airplane for the excursion.

He climbed into the airplane and strapped the coffee thermos in place on the side of the main console, then made several trips back and forth to the car to stow all the gear. He was walking back to the airplane with his last load when Joe Ramsey arrived at the vehicle parking area.

"Where are your friends?" Jack shouted, as the young man and his date got out of their car.

"Their parents wouldn't let them come," Joe said. "They didn't want them flying with someone they didn't know."

"Their loss," Jack said, shrugging his shoulders and gesturing for the young couple to come out to the airplane. "We'll just have to eat all the food ourselves."

The trio walked to the door of the airplane while Joe introduced his girlfriend, Carrie, to Jack, and then the youngsters climbed into the middle row of seats. Mollie walked back across the parking apron and climbed into the pilot seat, while Jack began his preflight walk-around of the aircraft.

He checked the oil level in both engines, removed the wheel chalks, and did a visual inspection, looking for any problems. He opened the cargo and removed a small stepladder.

"Did you get the fuel receipt?" he shouted at Mollie, who was doing her cockpit preflight.

She answered by holding up a wad of papers.

Jack checked the fuel levels in the tank on each side of the airplane, then stowed the ladder and climbed into the cabin. Turning forward, he gave Mollie a thumbs-up. Joe and Carrie were in the seats just behind the cockpit. Jack moved forward and motioned for Joe to get up. "You sit in front with Mollie, Mr. Ramsey," he said. "Carrie and I will sit behind you and guard the sandwiches."

"Cool," the boy said, and in a flash he was out of his seat and into the copilot seat.

Jack sat down across the aisle from Carrie, who by this time had her iPhone blaring music into her earbuds and was tapping her fingernails on the seat belt's metal buckle while staring out the window. Mollie finished the preflight checklist, then started the engines, all the while explaining the process to her attentive student copilot.

When she finished the checklist, she keyed the radio mic. "Caldwell Ground Control, Commander Six-two-seven-eight-Bravo, taxi for takeoff on runway three-five, over," she said.

"Seven-eight-Bravo, Caldwell Ground Control, current altimeter two-eight-seven-three, wind calm, taxi and hold to runway three-five, over."

"Roger, Ground Control, altimeter two-eight-seven-three, wind calm, taxi and hold, runway three-five."

She nudged the throttles, coaxing the big plane forward, and headed down the taxiway. The plane bounced and swayed all the way to the entrance of the runway.

"Caldwell Tower, Six-two-seven-eight-Bravo for takeoff runway three-five, over," she said into the microphone of her headset.

"Six-two-seven-eight-Bravo, Caldwell Tower," a voice said, "wind one-seven-zero at five, you are cleared for takeoff runway three-five. Be advised, Seven-eight-Bravo, there is a mill fire one-five miles to the east of the airport. The smoke is pretty bad in that direction, and those crazy news helicopters are all over the place. You may want to avoid the area."

"Roger, Caldwell Tower," Mollie said. "Wind one-seven-zero at five, cleared for takeoff runway three-five. We're heading north for a few miles, then west to the coast. Thanks for the advisory." Mollie eased the throttles forward, sending the airplane onto the runway. A little more throttle as she started her turn to the centerline, then full throttle sent the Commander racing down the runway. The day was warm, and the hot air rising off the concrete surface distorted their view of the end of the runway. The plane pitched left and then right, movements countered by Mollie's manipulation on the rudder foot pedals. It rolled ever faster until it eased upward into the air. Free at last.

Jack slumped back into his seat. He didn't like sitting in back. He was just doing it so the kid could sit up front with Mollie. Carrie was still staring out the window, apparently lost in her own thoughts and her music, so Jack watched the ground fall away under the plane as it rose higher into the air. He could see Mollie and Joe exchanging questions and answers, but his headset was tucked in the pouch on the back of the pilot seat in front of him. He left it there, to escape the conversation for a while. The vibrations and sounds of the engines, and the air rushing across the skin of the aircraft, carried his mind off to the past. A melody entered his mind. It was a song his mother had sung to him when they traveled cross-country in his father's airplane. She would put him in the back seat, wrapped in a blanket, with a big pillow, and sing to him until he fell asleep. The memory of the melody was hypnotic.

Joe seemed totally engrossed in this new experience. His hands rested on the yoke, which guided the aircraft's elevator surfaces and ailerons. Mollie's hands were firm on the controls as well. She kept the Commander about a thousand feet off the ground and heading north up the valley to allow her young student to get a sense of speed and a feel for the movements of the controls. The plane bounced a little from the heat rising off the fields below. Mollie pulled back on the yoke to guide the plane to a higher and safer altitude. Joe's tense limbs resisted her movements, so she reached over and put her right hand on his left as it rested on the controls. "Relax," she said. The boy responded, and the plane eased upward.

"How high will she go?" Joe said.

"Service ceiling for this aircraft is nineteen thousand feet," Mollie said.

"I've been up to thirty-five thousand feet in an airliner," Joe said, scanning the horizon, "but it never felt like this. This is so cool."

Mollie, remembering her own first flight in something other than a passenger jet, grinned in response to the boy's expression of joy. She pulled back on the controls, increasing the rate of climb. "When we get a little higher, you'll be able to see the ocean," she said, pointing to the west.

The boy's head turned to follow the direction of her gesture.

"We'll turn west now and head toward Mount Dixon," Mollie continued. "We'll fly around the mountain and then head toward the coast."

Mollie banked the aircraft to the west and continued the climb.

"You want to take the controls for a minute while I pour some coffee for myself?" she said.

The young boy didn't hesitate. "Sure," he said. He tightened his grip on the controls and nodded.

Mollie eased her hands off the yoke but kept her feet on the foot pedals, just in case. The airplane rose abruptly and pitched to the left, causing her hand to fly back to the yoke. "Easy there, my friend," she said to her apprentice pilot. "Relax and loosen your grip a little. You have to be able to feel the airplane."

Mollie could see his fingers change color from white to pink as his body relaxed, so she let go of the controls again. The airplane wiggled up, down, then sideways, but not enough to cause concern on her part. "That's it," she coached. "Nice and easy. Don't overcorrect."

Keeping one eye on the kid and one eye on the lookout for air traffic, she reached down to retrieve her thermos bottle from its cradle and set it in her lap. Without conscious effort, the chrome-plated lid was off and the stopper threaded out, and coffee magically appeared in the cup. The distinct aroma drifted upward with the steam in front of her face, then spread out to the rest of the cabin. The plane jostled a bit to demand attention. Mollie glanced at Joe, who seemed to handle the movements of the aircraft. She raised the cup to her mouth and let a small amount of the brew slide past her lips. The coffee was strong and hot. The aroma blasted up into her nostrils, and the steam warmed her face and fogged up her sunglasses.

"Smells pretty good," Joe said, looking over at his instructor. "Can I have some?"

"Keep your eyes on the road," she pretended to scold. A turned-up corner of her mouth revealed a camouflaged smile. "When you're learning, you fly the plane or you dine. One or the other."

"Yes, ma'am," Joe said.

"You want me to take the controls for a few minutes while you have something to drink or eat?" Mollie said. "You can fly the plane again when you're finished."

"I am a little hungry," the boy said.

Mollie put her left hand back on the controls. "Okay," she said. "I've got it."

Joe let go of the controls and grabbed the thermos bottle. His hands, still charged with adrenaline, shook a little as he poured the coffee into a Styrofoam cup. "That really does smell good," he said. He sat for a minute just looking out the window and holding the cup in his hands. Finally, both hands brought the cup to his mouth, and he sipped a small amount of the steamy drink. "Tastes good, too," he said. "You want something to eat, Mrs. McCall?"

Mollie shook her head. The kid turned his upper body back toward the lunch sack and rummaged around for a sandwich. In a matter of seconds, the wrapper was off his selection and the first bite was through his mouth and halfway down to his stomach. "Sandwiches are really good, too. Sure you don't want one?"

"In a minute," Mollie said. "See if Carrie and Mr. McCall have eaten."

Joe twisted backward again to check on his fellow passengers. Neither showed signs of life. Jack was staring out his window, deep in his own thoughts, and Carrie was staring out her window, deep in her own personal sound system. "Don't think they're interested right now," he reported back to Mollie.

"Okay, then hand me a sandwich," she said. To prepare for lunch she reached down to set the autopilot. The back of her hand hit the control switch when her fingers failed to spread apart to manipulate the device. She stared at her hand for a moment and then, focusing her thought on moving her fingers, gripped the control knob and activated the guidance system. She raised her hand and shook it. The nerve must have been pinched somehow, she thought.

"She's on autopilot," she said to her apprentice. "I can eat and drink while it flies itself. We're headed directly for Mount Dixon. The autopilot will keep us on a direct course and at a constant altitude."

Joe thought for a minute while chewing his sandwich. "Will it automatically pull up if we get too close to the mountain?" he said.

"No," Mollie said, shaking her hand again to restore sensation. "It'll fly us right into the dumpster at the picnic ground if we let it." She cracked a grin and glanced at the boy to observe his reaction.

"Cool," he responded, without a change in body language.

Mollie turned her attention back toward the front of the plane and raised a sandwich to her mouth. The sandwich fell into her lap.

A rustling noise caught the boy's attention. He turned to observe his girlfriend's left hand sunk deep into the sandwich sack, searching for just the right flavor combination. Joe smiled and turned back to finish his meal and watch the scenery. "Mrs. McCall, my lips feel numb."

Carrie continued to check out the sandwich selection until she found one that appealed to her. She, too, unwrapped the sandwich in short order, eager to satisfy the empty feeling in her stomach.

Sandwich in hand, Carrie turned her attention back to the scenery below. The ground seemed to be getting closer as the airplane headed toward the mountain rising straight ahead.

As the level flight path of the plane brought it closer and closer to the landscape, she began to see the park features in more detail. She wanted to see if Joe was enjoying the sights as much as she was, so she loosened her seat belt, eased herself forward, and stuck her head into the center of the cockpit area to get his attention. She could see straight ahead now. The plane was getting closer to the trees below, and the parking area for the picnic grounds was dead ahead. The airplane was approaching the terrain at 210 miles per hour.

Carrie reached up and touched Joe's shoulder, giving him just a little shake to get his attention. The boy's upper body fell to the left and slumped across the instrument console between the two front seats. Carrie let out a scream.

Jack banged his head against the window as every muscle jumped to attention. He put his hand on his injured head and leaned into the aisle to see what was going on. Carrie was still screaming and flapping her upper arms up and down like she was trying to fly. Jack looked to the front of the plane and saw Joe draped over the console. His seat belt was off in a flash. His feet stumbled on the sandwich sack as he rose out of his seat, and he went crashing into Carrie's seat, pinning her against the window. She screamed even louder. He pushed off the window to get back on his feet and landed on his butt in the aisle instead. "Mollie," he yelled as loud as he could. No response. He rocked forward onto his knees, grabbing Mollie's arm. Her head flopped forward but her body was restrained by her shoulder harness. He looked out the front windshield. The plane was heading straight for the parking lot. The roar of the engines was starting to echo off the ground. Jack grabbed Joe and tried pulling him up out of his seat. The boy was strapped in, and his body flopped back into his seat.

Carrie started to shout, "We're going to crash—we're going to crash." She was crying and screaming and shouting all at the same time.

Jack unbuckled Joe's seat belt and jerked the boy out of his seat and into the empty seat in the back. He looked ahead. Ten seconds and they would crash. *No time to get to the controls. The plane is on autopilot.* He reached down to the console in front of him and moved the altitude selector on the autopilot backward, causing the nose of the airplane to rise. The centrifugal force drove him back down to his knees and caused Mollie's head to flop backward in the seat. He looked out the windshield and was staring at the top of a picnic shelter. The plane was rising. He swallowed hard and stared straight ahead.

The plane's engines made a deafening roar as it cleared the shelter by just a few feet. Jack lifted Mollie and leaned her upper body against the pilot's side window. He looked forward again to make sure the airplane was not headed for anything else. He grabbed Mollie's wrist and checked her pulse. It was faint but definitely present. He checked Joe. Same result. He strapped Joe into the back seat, then turned to check on Carrie. She was silent now, tears running down her face and body shaking like a leaf. "We're okay," he reassured her. "Joe's alive, and so is Mollie. I'm going to get in the front seat now. I need you to keep an eye on Joe. Check his pulse every two minutes. Can you do that?"

Carrie answered with a nod. Jack took Joe's limp wrist and put it in her trembling hand. He turned the boy's hand over and found his artery. He guided the girl's fingers down the boy's wrist. "Can you feel his pulse?" he said. The girl nodded. He took off his wristwatch and put it in her lap. "Count the beats for fifteen seconds, multiply by four, then tell me the result," he said. "Do that every two minutes." The girl looked down at the watch and nodded. Knowing his pulse wouldn't help the boy, but Jack figured the girl needed something to do. He also figured that whatever was affecting the boy was also affecting Mollie. If he was still alive, then she was still alive. He straightened up as much as possible and braced himself as he slid into the copilot seat. He checked Mollie's pulse again, then put his feet and hands on the controls and switched off the autopilot. He got his bearings and put on his headset, then banked the airplane back toward the east.

"Caldwell Tower, this is Six-two-seven-eight-Bravo declaring an emergency, over," Jack shouted into the mic. No answer. "Caldwell Tower, Caldwell Tower, this is Six-two-seven-eight-Bravo declaring an emergency, over."

"Six-two-seven-eight-Bravo, this is Caldwell Tower, what is the nature of your emergency, over," the reply finally came.

"Caldwell Tower, I have two, I say again two unconscious passengers. Both have a weak pulse but I don't know what caused them to lose consciousness. I am four-zero miles west of the airport at Mount Dixon at eight thousand feet. I'll be on the ground in one-five minutes. I need an ambulance standing by, over."

"Seven-eight-Bravo, this is Caldwell Tower, wilco on the ambulance. Understand estimated ETA one-five minutes. How many souls on board?"

"Four souls on board, Caldwell Tower."

"Roger, Seven-eight-Bravo, understand four souls on board. How much fuel do you have, and do you have any mechanical problems?"

Jack took a few deep breaths before he answered. "Negative on the mechanical, Tower," he said. He checked the fuel gauges. "One-zero-seven pounds of fuel."

He pushed forward on the yoke, sending the nose of the airplane downward, and pushed the throttles forward. "Hang on, Mollie," he said, as if she could hear him. "I'm not going to let you die." He reached over and checked Mollie's pulse again and then turned back to check on Joe. "How's he doing?" he asked Carrie.

The girl had Joe's hand in her lap, with her fingers against his wrist. "No change, Mr. McCall," she said.

"Good girl," Jack said. "An ambulance is going to meet us when we land in just a few minutes. They should be just fine in no time." *I hope.*

"Six-two-seven-eight-Bravo, this is Caldwell Tower, over," the voice said into Jack's headset.

"Seven-eight-Bravo, go ahead," Jack responded.

"We've got a problem, Seven-eight-Bravo. All the ambulances are deployed at the mill fire. We can't get one to the airport for another hour."

"Shit," Jack said.

"What's wrong, Mr. McCall?" Carrie said.

"Nothing, honey," Jack reassured her. "Just keep checking on Joe. Things are going to be just fine," he lied.

Jack's mind was going 800 miles per hour. No ambulance. A doctor at the airport without an ambulance might not do any good. What to do? How can I get them to the hospital? I have to get them to the hospital now. Now.

Jack keyed the mic. "Caldwell Tower, this is Seven-eight-Bravo. Call the Caldwell police department and tell Frank Kirby that I'm going to land on Macadam Boulevard right in front of the hospital. I want the street blocked off in ten minutes."

"Say again, Seven-eight-Bravo," the tower controller said.

"You heard me," Jack yelled into the mic. "I'm going to land right in front of the hospital. I'm not going to wait an hour for an ambulance. These people need to be in that hospital five minutes ago. They can't wait. They may die if they have to wait." Jack put the Commander in a steep left-banking turn and headed for downtown Caldwell.

Carrie pushed on the back of Jack's seat. "Are they going to die?" she said.

Jack grimaced when he realized he had shouted out his fears in front of the girl. "No, Carrie," he said. "I just said that to get everyone on the ground moving so Joe and Mollie get the best possible care when we land."

"Okay," she said. "Good."

Jack pushed the throttles full forward, sending the engine noise to a higher pitch and creating a pronounced vibration throughout the cabin. The streets in the town were becoming more visible by the minute. He didn't see any flashing red lights in the vicinity of the hospital, though.

"Caldwell Tower, this is Seven-eight-Bravo. I don't see any action in town yet. What did the police say?"

"Seven-eight-Bravo, Caldwell Tower, they said it's impossible to clear the street in ten minutes."

"Listen, dammit," Jack screamed. "You tell those clowns I've got two people on this plane who are dying. One of them is my wife. The other is Stewart Ramsey's boy. Now I want that street cleared in five minutes or I'm landing without their help. You got that?"

"Roger, Seven-eight-Bravo, we'll pass along your message," the tower controller said.

Jack's eyes were glued on the north end of town, looking for signs of compliance with his demands. The plane descended lower, with the engines still racing at full power. He turned back to check on Joe and Carrie, then checked Mollie's pulse. He held his breath until he found a faint trace on her wrist, then banked the plane to line up for an approach to Macadam Boulevard. He pushed the nose of the plane to a steeper angle of descent and pulled back on the throttles to slow the airspeed.

Police cars with flashing lights began to appear on the street near the hospital. "You'd better clear it out," he said to no one. He turned back to check on Carrie. "Make sure his seat belt is tight, Carrie, then bend him over so his head is down by his knees." The girl did as instructed, then looked up at Jack. Her lip was quivering, and a tear trickled down her cheek. "They'll be fine," Jack assured her. "Now snug your seat belt and put your head in your lap just like his, okay?" The girl nodded and bent forward with her head down.

Jack lined up the nose of the Commander with the street in front of the hospital. The straight section of the street was only eight blocks long, but it was the longest section of street that was wide enough to land the Commander. He didn't have another option. The police had both ends of the boulevard blocked. Houses sat at one end and the shopping mall at the other. Power lines flanked both sides of the street, but the street was four lanes wide with a turn lane in the middle, so he figured he had just enough width to land safely. If nothing went wrong, he had just enough length too.

The Commander dropped lower as Jack pulled the throttles back to slow the airspeed. He lowered the flaps and the landing gear. The Commander shook and rumbled. Jack checked the landing gear lights, and three green dots appeared on the console. So far, so good. He put the flaps on full and pushed forward on the throttle to keep the plane from stalling and dropping out of the sky. The Commander floated just over the houses and trees. He cut the throttles and let the Commander drop toward the street, just missing the power lines and the police cars. The airplane hit the concrete street hard. Mollie's upper body bounced back and forth between the seat and her shoulder harness. Jack worked the controls and rode the brakes. The plane shifted left, then right, as his feet and hands corrected for the plane's unwanted movements.

Jack brought the Commander to a stop in the middle of the cross street at the end of his makeshift runway. He immediately pushed the right throttle forward and pushed hard on the left wheel brake, causing the Commander to spin around 180 degrees. He released the brake, brought both engines to full power, and headed back down the street toward the entrance to the hospital. Red lights were flashing everywhere, but his eyes strained to find someone in a white coat with a stretcher for his wife and the boy.

Jack rolled the Commander to a stop right in front of the hospital and cut the engines. A multitude of white coats descended upon the plane even before the propellers stopped turning. Someone opened the door and was inside the cabin before Jack could catch his breath. "What are the symptoms, Jack?" a voice said from behind.

"They just aren't able to move," Jack said, without looking back.

"Don't move," the voice instructed. "We'll get these three out, and then you can get out." Jack complied and didn't move as several white-clad bodies unbuckled Mollie's seat belt and eased her upward and sideways out of the airplane. When Jack finally got out of his seat and made his way to the door at the back of the cabin, Mollie and Joe were already on gurneys, headed into the emergency entrance of the building. Jack tumbled to the ground. His body shut down.

CHAPTER 7

JACK WAS SITTING ON THE FLOOR in the hallway across from the emergency room. His head hurt and he felt groggy. "You'll have to move your airplane, mister," a voice said. He lifted his head off his knees and looked up. A very large, very round man wearing a red hardhat was looking down at him. "It can't stay there," the big man insisted, tapping on Jack's shoulder.

A nurse grabbed the big man by his colorful, striped traffic safety vest. "Burt, can't you see he's in no condition to walk, let alone move an airplane?" the woman said, as she attempted to pull him away from Jack. "You'll have to excuse Burt," the nurse said. "He's been with the street department for fifteen years, and he thinks he's in charge of everything."

Jack just looked up at the pair. "Where's Mollie?" he mumbled to the nurse, who had returned to his side. "She's in the Intensive Care Unit," she said. "If you can stand up, I'll take you to see her."

"Yeah," Jack said, trying to push himself up. His effort failed, and he plopped back down on the floor with a thud.

"Don't just stand there, Burt," the nurse said to the man wearing the hardhat. "Help the man up."

Jack rose off the floor like a rag doll into Burt's arms. "Sorry to bother you about your plane, mister," he said, supporting Jack with a huge arm around the rib cage. "Can I help you down the hall?"

Jack just nodded, and the odd couple shuffled down the hall, led by the watchful nurse. They passed several doors, went down an elevator for a few floors, and then headed down another hallway. The movement of his legs, aided by Burt, his rotund crutch, revived Jack's senses and got his limbs working reasonably well by the time the group reached the ICU.

"She's in here," the nurse said.

Jack looked in the door, then back at the nurse. "Where's the kid?" he said.

"He's in the next room," she said.

Jack nodded and walked at a cautious pace to a chair positioned by Mollie's bed. A doctor stood on the other side of her bed, reading something on a clipboard. "What's wrong with her?" Jack said.

"We don't know yet, Mr. McCall," the doctor said, looking up momentarily and then back down at the paper on the clipboard.

Jack looked over at his wife, lying in the bed. Her face was peaceful and her eyes were wide open, but there was no expression on her face. An IV drip hung from a stand next to her bed. The other end of the narrow tube snaking out of the hanging plastic bag disappeared into a patch of tape on Mollie's forearm. Jack reached out and touched her arm. He was surprised that her skin felt very warm. His brain had expected a corpse-like cold and clammy feeling.

Frank Kirby came into the room and walked to the end of Mollie's bed. "How are she and the boy doing, Doc?" he said, avoiding eye contact with Jack.

"They don't know yet," Jack said.

"Do you know what it is?" Frank asked the doctor.

"Since it happened to both of them," the doctor said, "we think it is some sort of drug-induced paralysis, but I've never seen anything like it before. We're checking with every medical database we can think of to see if we can get a match on the symptoms. We hope to have an answer within a couple of hours."

"So what's the plan until then, Doc?" Frank said.

"Their vital signs are stable, and they don't show any signs of being in immediate danger," the doctor said, walking toward the door. "So we'll just keep a close eye on them and see what happens between now and when we hear back from our sources. I'll let you know as soon as we hear something."

"Convinced now?" Jack said, looking up at Frank.

"Yes," Frank said in an indignant tone and emitting a muffled snort to punctuate the point. He walked over to Mollie's bedside. "You started this, McCall, and I'm going to finish it."

"Maybe you and I can figure this thing out together," Jack said.

Frank scowled at Jack. "To start with," he said, ignoring Jack's overture to collaborate, "I'm going to have your airplane moved to the parking lot, and I'll have the state forensics team go over it with the proverbial fine-toothed comb. If there's something there, we'll find it. But you are going to stay out of this. I don't want you getting anyone killed."

Jack stood up and walked to the end of Mollie's bed. He took the patient's clipboard off the hook and stared at it.

"Are you a doctor too?" asked the policeman.

Jack sneered at Frank, put the clipboard back on the hook, and walked to Mollie's side. He put his hand on her face and then took her hand in his. "Test the coffee."

"Already on it," Frank said. "The container, the lid, and the Styrofoam cup the kid drank out of are all on their way to the lab. I take it you and the girl didn't drink any coffee."

"Correct."

"I'll have the lab phone the results to the hospital as soon as they get it," Frank said.

"Let me know what you find too, please," Jack said.

"Not a chance, hot shot," Frank said, on his way out the door.

Jack walked to the window and twisted the rod that controlled the blinds, letting sunlight enter the room. He spread the thin horizontal aluminum slats apart and peered outside. The city public-works crew, with yellow lights flashing on top of their trucks, finessed the Aero Commander into the parking lot. He watched for a minute to make sure the plane wasn't damaged. The two most important things in his life were in the care and keeping of other people. The doctors had Mollie, and Burt, the rotund city worker, had his airplane. But he had to do something, and since he seemed to be the catalyst for everything that had happened, he figured he would have to be the one to find out who was doing all this and put a stop to it.

******

Jack guided the Mustang down the long driveway that led to Henry's farmhouse. The driveway was lined with Douglas fir trees, which shaded the car as it made its way to the large house that sat on a ridge overlooking the Willamette River. The house had been built by Henry's dad. Every stick and stone was personally crafted by him. Jack recalled watching the process, which had lasted the entire time he and Henry were in junior high school. He and Henry had helped tear down the old house when the new one was finished.

The driveway looped around some landscaping at the side of the house, then ended at a parking area next to a large deck overlooking the river. Henry was sitting in a patio chair and motioned for Jack to come up the stairs leading from the parking area to the deck.

"It's changed some," Jack said, arriving at the top of the stairs.

"Yup," Henry said. "I just heard what happened. How's Mollie doing?"

"The doc says she's stable and doesn't appear to be in immediate danger," Jack said. "I felt like I needed to do something, but I didn't know what. So I came out here."

"You hungry?" Henry said. "Got some ham in the fridge, and I can have Jennifer fix you a sandwich."

Jack shook his head. "Got any Diet Coke?" he said.

Henry broke into a big grin and reached down into a cooler next to his deck chair, rattled the ice around, and produced a can of the requested beverage, which glistened in the sunlight as it was offered to the guest.

"Guess we still have some things in common, don't we?" Jack said. He lifted the metal tab of the can and settled into a lounge chair that faced the river. The sun was warm on his face, and his eyelids closed halfway to block the glare from the water below.

"Mollie's in very good hands," Henry said. "That hospital may be small, but the people and the technology are world-class."

Henry rose from his chair and patted Jack on the head as he walked by, heading toward the house. "I'll be inside for a few minutes," he said. "You just rest your eyes. You look like shit."

Jack shook his head. "Can't rest yet," he said. "Mollie's in the hospital, and the Commander is in a parking lot downtown."

Henry took out his cell phone and punched in a number.

"Who are you calling?" Jack said.

"Mike," Henry said. "He runs the flight service at the airport. I'll have him tow your airplane back to the airport after the forensics team is through with it."

"Tow?" Jack said.

"Trust me," Henry said. He turned and headed into the house, talking with Mike as he walked.

Jack leaned his head back against the cushioned chair, took a long drink of cola, and closed his eyes. The rush of the rapids upstream from the house became a hypnotic time machine that transported him back to his youth. The smell, the sound, the warm sun were all as much a part of his existence back then as breathing in and out. He relaxed in the security of the place. He fell asleep.

******

Jack felt a jostle on his arm. "Hey, wake up." It was Henry.

"How long have I been asleep?" Jack said.

"About an hour," Henry said. "Someone is here to see you."

Jack looked up to see a squatty middle-aged man, with thick glasses and thin hair above a round face with a hint of a smile on it.

"Hello, McCall," the man said. "Frank asked me to do some research to find out what kind of drug was given to your wife and the Ramsey boy." The man sat down next to Jack, leaned forward, and stared directly at Jack's still-blurred eyes. "Chief Kirby also instructed me specifically to not give you the results."

Jack gave a halfhearted smile and nodded as he straightened his posture and took a drink of the cola. The now hot liquid no sooner hit his tongue than it was propelled out of his mouth. Henry grabbed a cold one out of the cooler, without being asked, and handed it to his guest.

"You don't remember me, do you?" said the researcher.

Jack shook his head. The little man let out a squeaky, high-pitched laugh that sounded like a pig being murdered. A smile popped onto Jack's face.

"Porky," he said, leaning over to give the man a hug.

"No one's called me that in decades," the man responded. "Most of the time nowadays it's Doctor Timothy Jones, or Professor Jones, or sometimes Doc Jones."

Jennifer came out of the house with a variety of chips and dips and scooted a footstool into the middle of the huddle. She set the food down, winked at her husband, and walked back into the house.

"Thank you," they all said in unison.

"Well, what did you find out, Tim?" Henry said, grabbing a big corn chip and scooping up a glob of guacamole.

The professor jiggled with excitement as he began his report. "Turns out the serum is from Brazil. A native tribe, in a region known as Mato Grosso, brews a particularly nasty potion that paralyzes movement but leaves the person totally conscious and aware of what's going on."

"You mean Mollie has been awake the whole time?" Jack said.

"That's my very educated guess," Dr. Tim said.

"How long does the paralysis last?" Henry said.

"According to what I've been able to find out, although the effect is not permanent, the duration varies based on the potency of the serum, the dilution factor of the host liquid, and the size and weight of the victim," Tim said. "I told Chief Kirby to expedite the coffee analysis, since that's the likely delivery mechanism. Once we know the dilution factor, I can make some calls to Brazil and find out how long their paralysis should last."

"Someone's trying to kill me," Jack said. "At first they were just trying to scare me off, but now they are definitely trying to kill me."

"I think everyone's figured that out by now, Jack," Henry said. "What can we do to help?"

"You've already done enough," Jack said. "I started this twenty years ago when I broke up with Annie and picked that lock on the gate. Now Mollie and Joe are in the hospital, and I don't want anyone else becoming collateral damage. I need to go make a pact with the devil and put an end to this, one way or another."

Henry stood up. "What happened twenty years ago was an accident," he said.

"Was it?" Jack said. "Was it, Henry—just an accident? Nobody's fault? That would be the easy solution." He rose out of the lounge chair and shook Tim's hand. He gave Henry a handshake and a hug and headed for the car, leaving his companions with puzzled looks on their faces. He hopped in the Mustang and roared down the long driveway, heading toward the police station.

Traffic was light so Jack arrived at the station in short order. He wasn't looking forward to declaring a truce with Frank. Pride and habit were tough meat to digest, but he knew it was the only way he would have a chance of getting to the bottom of this without getting someone else hurt or killed.

Frank was walking out of the men's room when Jack walked into the lobby. "We need to talk," Jack said, confronting The Devil, who was zipping his pants as he walked.

"Why don't you just leave town, McCall?" Frank responded. "That way no one else gets hurt, I can investigate this and close the books, and everybody's happy."

"You amaze me," Jack said, shaking his head in disbelief. "If you really cared about justice and the truth, you would be leading the charge to find out what really happened."

Frank turned and grabbed Jack by the shirt, then pushed his elbows up into Jack's stomach, pinning him against the wall with his feet barely touching the ground. "Don't question my commitment to my job, McCall," he said.

Jack tipped his head downward to look Frank in the eye. "Put me down or—badge or no badge—I'll kick your ass," he whispered. "And you know I can do it."

Frank tightened his grip and pushed Jack sideways toward the door.

"Get out of here, and don't come back unless I send for you," Frank instructed.

Jack straightened his shirt and stood his ground. "I'm not going anywhere," he said. "You're going to listen to me, and then we're going to figure this thing out. Once that's done, we can see who's going to kick the shit out of who."

The two men had a stare-down that lasted about ten seconds before Frank turned and headed for his office. "Follow me," he said. The two men walked in silence to Frank's office. Jack closed the door behind him.

"Who knew you were going for a high-altitude joy ride with the kids?" Frank said.

Jack was silent for a moment as he reran in his mind images of the events leading up to the flight. "Mollie called the kitchen directly to order the coffee, so the person who took the order knew, and the person who made the coffee might have known."

Frank pushed the intercom button on his phone. "Shirley, see who was working in the kitchen over at the Inn this morning."

"Sure, chief," came the reply.

"Sterling and his wife, Ramsey, Henry, and Pitts," Jack continued.

Frank sat down at his desk and wrote the names on a pad of paper by the phone. "What about the girl?" he said.

"What girl?" Jack said.

"The one in the plane," Frank said. "Her parents probably knew."

"Carrie?" Jack said. "Yes, she and her parents would have known, but their kid was on the plane. They wouldn't be suspects."

"No," Frank said, "but they might have mentioned the flight to someone, and that person might have a motive."

The reasoning was sound, but Jack didn't want to score a point for Frank, so he ignored the comment, walked to the window, and looked out toward the city park across the street. His mind flashed back to a childhood moment. He was pushing Jessie in the swing that still stood next to a large Douglas fir tree near the center of the park.

"And Jessie," he said.

"What?" Frank said.

"Jessie was there this morning. She knew we were going flying," Jack explained.

"But what about the coffee?" Frank said. "How would someone be assured that you would both drink the coffee?"

Jack grimaced, straining his brain's memory cells. *How would someone know? Why would someone assume both of us would drink the coffee?* He turned, walked to the chair across from Frank's desk, and plopped down, placing his head in his hands. His head still hurt a little.

Seconds, then minutes passed. Frank scribbled notes on the pad on his desk.

"Day before yesterday," Jack said, raising his head, then rising to his feet. "You were there, remember? You, Jessie, Sterling, Vicky, Ramsey, Pitts. And Rosemary Poole, she was there too. Mollie was teasing me about how much I *loved* coffee."

"Yeah," Frank said. "Anyone who heard that conversation would have assumed that you would both drink the coffee. So why didn't you drink any?"

"Can't stand the stuff," Jack said.

"But the other day you and your wife made such a big deal out of how much you loved coffee," Frank said.

"You've never heard of sarcasm?" Jack said.

Frank shook his head and pushed the intercom button again. "Have Officer Davis and Officer Schmidt report to my office," he instructed.

Within a minute, two uniformed police officers knocked once and entered the room.

"I want you guys to escort Mr. McCall here wherever he goes," Frank told the officers.

"Come on, Frank," Jack said. "That's overdoing it a little, isn't it?"

"It's not for your protection, hotshot," Frank said. "It's for the protection of anyone who happens to be unlucky enough to be standing near you when someone tries to kill you again."

Jack was tired and didn't want to argue anymore, so he just nodded and headed for the front door. "Come on, Beavis," he mumbled under his breath. "And bring Butthead with you."

The late afternoon sun flooded Jack's eyes as he exited the building with his escorts, so he put on his sunglasses as he headed for his car. Officer Schmidt split off from the procession and disappeared around a tall hedge at the side of the building.

"Where's he going?" Jack asked the remaining attendant.

"Officer Butthead is getting a patrol car from the motor pool, Mr. McCall," Officer Davis said with a glare, as he looked Jack directly in the eye. "In these situations we pick the oldest car in the fleet, in case we have to sacrifice the car to save the lives of our fellow citizens."

"That's comforting," Jack said, as he continued toward his car.

"I wasn't referring to you," the deadpan policeman continued. "You're not a citizen. Wait at your car until Officer Butthead pulls the car around."

Jack grimaced and tipped his head downward from embarrassment, not fatigue. He had vented some of his frustration and anger by mocking the officers.

"Look," he said, "I'm sorry about the Beavis and Butthead thing. The chief and I have a history, and I took it out on you guys. That was disrespectful, and I apologize."

Officer Davis acknowledged the apology with a subtle nod.

Jack leaned back against the Mustang and waited for the patrol car to arrive. When the unmarked car pulled up, the second officer got in and motioned for Jack to move out. He got in the Mustang and pulled out of the parking lot, heading back to the hospital. He needed to rest again, but he hadn't heard from the doctors who were taking care of Mollie and Joe, so his first priority was to check on their condition. The car found its way to the hospital while Jack's mind replayed as many of the past events as possible. There had to be a common thread in all this. The other person in Annie's car the night she crashed, the attempts on his life—what was it? His brain was fuzzy and he couldn't concentrate. *Better go check on Mollie.*

When Jack arrived at Mollie's hospital room, a doctor and two nurses were hovering around her bed. "I was just going to call you," the doctor said. "She moved her arm a few minutes ago. I think the drug is starting to wear off."

"How 'bout the kid?" Jack asked, taking Mollie's hand.

"Nothing yet, but he's a little smaller than she is, so it may take a little longer," the doctor said. "I'll go check on him now." The doctor handed Mollie's chart to one of the nurses and left the room.

Jack looked at Mollie's face. Her expression had not changed from when he had seen her that morning, except now her eyes were closed. "Did she close her eyes?" he asked the nurse.

"No, Mr. McCall," the nurse said. "I closed them."

Jack clenched his fists. "Doc Jones says she is probably wide awake," he said in a raised voice.

"Yes," said the nurse, putting her hand on Jack's upper arm. "I know, but she needs to sleep, and it will be easier for her if her eyelids are shut. She'll open them when she regains her ability to move. It will be okay."

Jack stood motionless for a moment, thinking about what the nurse had said, then relaxed his hands and nodded to acknowledge the logic. He decided that he needed sleep too.

CHAPTER 8

JACK ARRIVED AT THE HOSPITAL early the next morning, with his police escort in tow. There wa s a different nurse on duty, and she displayed a tense smile as the trio walked by the desk. Mollie's eyes were open when Jack entered the room.

"Thank you for saving my life," she said in a faint voice.

Jack took her hand in his and kissed it. A tear rolled down his face, then disappeared with a quick swipe of his sleeve.

"You scared the hell out of me, Mrs. McCall," he said. "For a while there, I thought I might lose you."

"And let you take all the money from my life insurance and go play with that blonde fashion expert you met the other day?" she said. "Not on your life."

Mollie tried to laugh, but her body jerked as the laugh turned into a cough.

"Take it easy, girl," Jack said. "You'll have plenty of time in the future to give me grief about being so irresistible to women."

Mollie closed her eyes. "I'd better rest for a while," she said. "I'm starting to hallucinate. I thought I just heard you claim to be irresistible to women." She patted him on the hand and let her head roll sideways to rest against her pillow.

The doctor came into the room and checked the monitors and Mollie's chart.

"How's the kid, Doc?" Jack said.

"He's coming out of it slower than your wife, but I think they'll both recover," the doctor said. "We'll see how they are doing in twenty-four hours, then decide if they can be released."

"Thanks, Doc," Jack said. "I owe you one."

Jack rose and walked out into the hall. His two guardian angels were seated, but they stood when he came out of the room.

"How's she doing, Mr. McCall?" Officer Davis said.

"Getting better," Jack said. "Thank you for asking."

"Where to now?" Officer Schmidt asked.

"To visit an old friend," Jack said. "I'd tell you that you don't need to watch over me, but somehow I don't think it'd do any good."

The two men nodded in unison and fell in step behind Jack as he headed down the hall toward the elevator.

As he left the parking lot in the Mustang, the patrol car followed. He wanted to put the convertible top down, but the summer sun was too intense, so he just rolled down the windows and cranked up the music to clear his mind. His normal process when he wanted to organize and make sense of case details was to talk the whole thing through with someone. Mollie served as his sounding board when he wasn't at his office, but she was still recuperating from the effects of the Mato Grosso cocktail she'd consumed. He needed to find Henry. Henry had been his friend and co-conspirator since childhood. It was time to go back to the one person he trusted as much as he did Mollie.

Jack glanced in the rearview mirror to check on the position of his guardians, then guided the Mustang out of town on Highway 99. As he headed south, Jack eased the car into a faster pace, until a flashing red light in his rearview mirror caught his attention. He could see Officer Davis wagging an index finger back and forth, reminding him that this was Oregon, not Montana, where you can go really fast because there's nothing to run into. He backed off the throttle, and the patrol car dropped back into a "follow," as opposed to "pursue," position. With the wind channeling through the car and blowing against the back of his head, Jack's brain flashed back to the first time he had driven a car down this highway. The sense of freedom he had felt back then was intense. The recollection of it was stimulating too. Heading into farmland, it struck him that zoning had probably prevented the stark changes to this region that the rest of the town had experienced. The familiarity of the road, the trees, and the land helped his brain relax a little.

The Mustang found its way to Henry's farm without conscious effort on the part of its pilot. Jack needed a grounding point from which to organize his thoughts and create a plan.

Henry's farm was about as grounded as a place could get. There weren't many childhood memories in Jack's mind that didn't include this place. It had almost been his home until he and Henry got into high school. Then they had drifted apart. *What a loss.* His life might have been much different if he had stayed connected with his childhood friend. As he drove down the private lane toward Henry's place, the sights, sounds, and smells brought floods of memories.

With Mollie in the hospital, he felt alone and vulnerable, although his ego did a quick delete on the thought of being vulnerable. He readily admitted to himself, though, that he could sure use an ally, and Frank wasn't volunteering for the role.

The only change Jack noticed on the journey from the highway to the farmhouse was that the road was paved. He hadn't noticed that when he came out to the farm the day before. In fact, he didn't remember traveling to the farmhouse at all. Probably because of fatigue. He scanned the house and the surrounding grounds as he arrived. He could see the big oak tree where he and Henry had built tree forts and battled imaginary invaders. The forts were gone, just a memory now. Jack parked the Mustang in the circular drive in front of the house and made his way up the steps to the covered front porch that spanned the width of the house. Henry's mother's rocking chair was still in its place on the porch, just beyond the living room's picture window. Jack rang the doorbell and stepped back a little.

The front door opened, and a smiling Jennifer Coleman motioned for Jack to come in. She welcomed him with a hug, then walked to a computer station on a bar-height table in the entryway. She typed him a message that displayed on the monitor:

> Henry is in the field, but I'll text him and let him know you're here. Would you like some lemonade? I just made some fresh.

"Yes, please," Jack said.

The hostess picked up her cell phone and typed a quick message to her husband as she led her guest through the kitchen and onto the back deck. She made him sit in the shade beneath a tree on one side of the deck, then went inside to pour the drinks. Jack sank into the deck chair and surveyed the landscape that had been so familiar to him as a boy. He could see a prominent cloud of dust rising above the trees to the south. He recognized the unmistakable sign of harvesters at work, extracting seed from the rows of cut grass stalks that lay on the ground. As he continued his scan of the area, he saw something he hadn't expected. Just above the roofline of a long two-story outbuilding to the north, he saw a windsock. The bright orange fabric cone, tethered to a vertical pole and hoop, was used by pilots to show wind direction. Its presence told him that there was an airstrip nearby. He recalled that Henry's father never flew. He'd had an intense dislike for airplanes. To the east of the house was the river. Jack could see that the riverbank on the opposite shore had been washed away over the years. The pilings, which had once provided an anchor point for the bridge that the senior Coleman used to access his land across the river, were now just gathering points for debris that floated down the river.

Jack's attention was drawn back to the present by the squeak of the kitchen screen door being coaxed open by Jennifer's backside. She exited the house carrying a tray with a pitcher of lemonade and two tall glasses already filled with ice and the pulpy, sour drink. She set the tray on the table next to Jack's chair, then handed him a note saying that Henry would be back at the house in a few minutes. Jack mouthed the words "thank you," triggering a broad smile from the hostess. She moved in front of him to ensure his undivided attention, then pointed one index finger at her eye. "I?" Jack said. She nodded yes, then pointed to her ear. "You can hear," he said, rolling his eyes. "My apology, Jennifer," he said. "You can hear, but I can't think." Jennifer let out a laugh that was mostly muffled bursts of air accompanied by some muted sounds, and patted his hand to comfort him. "How long have you been married?" Jack said.

Jennifer held up both hands, with all her fingers extended. "Ten years," he acknowledged. She nodded.

Their attention was drawn to the sound of a vehicle approaching from the south. Jack instantly recognized the old Jeep that was rumbling up the graveled road alongside the tree-lined field. He had ridden in that Jeep with Henry when they were both still in junior high school. Farm kids learn to drive at an early age. The old Jeep rattled and clunked its way up to the parking area by the equipment shed on the far side of the drive, and stopped in the shade. Henry slid out of the seat and walked to the shed, where he grabbed an air hose that was coiled on a bracket attached to the side of the structure. He took off his hat and used the compressed air to blow away all the dust on his clothes and body. He emerged from a small cloud and put his hat back on as he walked toward the house.

Jennifer rose from her chair and walked to the edge of the deck, greeting her husband with a hug and a kiss on the cheek. The couple walked over and sat down in the shade, where their guest was sipping his glass of lemonade. "How're Mollie and the boy?" Henry said.

"They're both recovering, and the doctor thinks they'll be okay after the stuff wears off," Jack said.

Henry raised his glass to his lips and downed about half his glass of lemonade. "How are you doing?" he said.

"I feel okay," Jack said, "but I need your help."

Henry smiled and finished off his drink. "From the looks of the patrol car parked out front, I'd say you already have some help," he said.

"That's the first thing I need help with," Jack said. "I need you to call Frank and convince him to call off the protection detail. It's like having a big banner flying overhead announcing where I am."

"I think Frank doesn't want to see you get hurt," Henry said, "but I'll call him right now and be your advocate." He extracted his cell phone from his pocket, tapped on the face a couple of times, and held the instrument to his ear. "Frank? Henry," he said. "I have a request." He paused for a moment, listening to the response. "I need to have you call off the guard detail on Jack," he said. Another moment of silence, then he nodded. "I would consider it a personal favor." He listened to Frank's answer. "Thanks."

Henry tapped the face of the phone again and looked at Jack. "Done," he said.

"Thanks," Jack said, as he grabbed the pitcher and poured another round of drinks. "I think he's more worried about collateral damage than damage to me. He'd just as soon I got blown up if no one else got hurt in the process, and if it didn't happen on a city street that would have to be repaired."

Henry chuckled and shook his head in disagreement. "I think he wants to keep you alive," he said. "I also think he has a subconscious need to compete against you, as you do with him."

"When did you become a psychologist?" Jack said.

Henry and Jennifer both laughed at the question. "Come on in the house for a minute," Henry said, rising from his chair and kicking off his work boots.

The two men walked into the house, and Jack followed Henry through the hall to a room that Jack recognized as "the office." It was Henry's father's hideaway—the only place in the house the two boys had never been allowed to play. Henry walked to a picture and document grouping on one of the walls and lifted one of the documents off its hook. "You weren't the only one to go off to college," Henry said, handing the document to his friend.

Jack looked at the diploma, then up at Henry. "You *are* a psychologist," he said.

"Yup," Henry responded, as he took the document out of Jack's hands and placed it back on the wall.

"Wow," Jack said. "Why are you working the farm?"

"Plants don't commit suicide," Henry said.

Jack was caught off-guard and didn't know what to say. He stood silent, waiting for Henry to say more. Henry said nothing.

"So you're a psychologist," Jack said, after an awkward amount of time. "Got any more surprises for me?"

"Just one," Henry said. He turned and headed down the hallway toward the kitchen door leading to the back deck. He motioned for Jack to follow him. "I want to show you something," he said.

Jack followed his host out the back door, across the deck, and along a tree-lined path that led to an area with several buildings. He recognized some of the buildings as equipment sheds and workshops, where Henry's father had repaired and stored tools and farm equipment. Henry headed toward the large two-story building with the windsock mounted on the far side.

"I had a small practice in Portland," Henry said as they walked. "Then Dad died, and I came home to settle the estate. I planned on going back to Portland to resume my practice, but by the time I settled the estate and had to sign the papers to sell this place, I couldn't do it."

"Where did suicide enter into the decision?" Jack said.

Henry kept walking and didn't answer. The two men arrived at the entrance to the large building. Henry grasped the doorknob and went inside. Jack followed, tethered to his host by curiosity. Henry flipped a light switch just inside the door.

When Jack entered the building, he stopped dead in his tracks. His mouth opened slightly, and his eyes became twice their normal diameter. There in front of him was an airplane: a Piper Tri-Pacer in perfect condition. He read the tail numbers. "Seven-one-two-five-Sierra," he said. He looked at Henry, then back at the airplane, his mouth opened even wider to attest his amazement. "Is that really my dad's airplane?" he said.

Henry smiled as he walked over and opened the front door on the copilot side of the aircraft. "I've owned it for about ten years," he said.

Jack inched his way toward the airplane as if he feared it was just a mirage; he wanted the moment to last as long as possible before it disappeared. He reached out his hand and touched the taut fabric skin that covered the airframe. It felt smooth as a drum, and the polished, brilliant white paint was immaculate. Tan-and-dark-brown stripes decorated the side of the aircraft. It looked just as he remembered it. "Where did you find it?"

"It was at an airport in Idaho," Henry said, as he walked to the hangar doors and began to open them. "It was in pretty bad shape, so I had it disassembled and sent back to the factory to be completely rebuilt. Grab the tow bar and pull her out."

Jack went to the front of the airplane, lifted the handle of the tow bar that was attached to the nose wheel, leaned back, and began to coax the flying machine out of its hideaway. Images of his father flashed through his mind as the airplane rolled slowly out of the building.

Henry took his cell phone out of his pocket. "I'm letting Jen know that we'll be gone for a while," he said, as he typed the text message.

Jack brought the airplane to a stop and disconnected the tow bar. He walked to the cargo door, put the bar inside, and then walked to the front access door. He leaned inside the cockpit. The smell of the brown leather seats surprised him. They looked and smelled just like the seats in his Aero Commander. His friend had made a substantial investment in restoring this machine and had even upgraded some of the creature comforts.

"Do you remember how to do a preflight inspection on this machine?" Henry said, walking by Jack on his way to the front of the plane.

"We'd both better do it," Jack said. "No sense in letting ego ruin the day."

The two men walked around the airplane, following the preflight routine to ensure they didn't fall out of the sky, and then Henry climbed into the pilot seat. Jack climbed up and slid into the copilot seat. He closed and locked the door. Henry brought the engine to life, and the airplane slowly made its way to a mowed strip of grass next to the river that served as a runway. After a short run-up of the engine and final checks, the Tri-Pacer rolled down the grass strip and lifted into the air. Jack could see the patrol car that had followed him to the farm turn onto the main highway, signaling the end of his guard detail.

Henry contacted the flight center and gave a brief description of their intended flight itinerary while Jack peered out the window, recalling childhood memories of sitting in this very seat, looking down at the farms and the valley landscape below. The plane headed west from the farm and climbed to 1,500 feet, allowing the occupants to see most of the surrounding countryside. The engine sound was muffled slightly by the headphones the two men wore while on their journey westward.

"Where are we headed?" Jack said.

"Up to Dixon Park Road, and then south," Henry said.

The reference to the park brought Jack out of his semi-trance and re-engaged his anxiety about the death of Annie and the attempts on his life. "Which reminds me why I came to see you," he said. "I need to put some pieces together, and the only way that works for me is to talk to someone. Will you help me?"

Henry nodded and banked the airplane to the south. "We'll follow the foothills south to Veneta, then come back up the valley," he said.

"There are several possibilities, when you consider opportunity and suspicious behaviors," Jack said. "Sterling Whitehurst is very anxious to have me drop the whole subject of Annie's death. He went so far as to try to persuade Mollie to get me to let it be."

"But what would motivate him to the point of trying to kill you?" Henry said.

"That's one item for my task list," Jack said. "Do you have something I can write on?"

"In the pouch behind my seat," the pilot responded. "Jen keeps a notepad there, and a pen."

Jack reached into the pouch and extracted the tools to continue his process. "So what do you know about the Whitehursts?"

"No skeletons in their closet that I know of," Henry said. "Gloria runs the remaining businesses, and his sister Grace lives in Denver. I think she married a dentist."

"How did he end up in Louisiana, tied to the Wainwrights?" Jack said.

"He met Victoria at Arizona State, and she led him back to Louisiana by the zipper," Henry said. "Between good old Uncle J.J. and her daddy, poor Sterling didn't have a chance. He got sucked into that culture—and pretty much drowned in the mint juleps. His father told my dad several times that he wanted Sterling to come back and run the business. But the only time he came back to Oregon was when the old man died. He left town a few days after the funeral, and I hadn't seen him again until yesterday."

"He never came back to Caldwell?" Jack said.

"Not that I know of," Henry said.

"I wonder why he came back for the reunion," Jack said.

"He said it was because his sister Gloria was having cancer surgery," Henry said.

"Is she?" Jack said.

"Yes," Henry said. "The whole town probably knows by now."

"Have you ever heard him mention Annie before this visit?" Jack said.

"Never."

Jack jotted down a few more notes, then gazed out the window to clear his mind. "What about Frank?" he said, turning back toward his companion to resume his analysis. "You must have had lots of conversations with him over the years. Could he have been the one in the car with Annie that night?"

Henry made a slight course correction to avert a pending conflict with a local hilltop, then shook his head. "Can't tell you anything about past conversations with Frank, Jack," he said.

"Doctor-patient stuff?" Jack said.

"Yes," Henry said. "But I can tell you that he wasn't the one in the car with Annie. I personally saw him in town that night, about the time the crash happened."

"How about Pitts?" Jack said. "His behavior has been borderline bizarre."

Henry let out a chuckle and nodded. "I'd love to get him on the couch for a session. That would be an interesting conversation. His whole family was weird. They pretty much disappeared not long after Josh graduated. We've seen an occasional photo credit by Pitts Photography in a newspaper or magazine, but that's it. Like you, this is the first we've actually seen of him in twenty years."

"And how about his fascination with blood?" Jack said. "Talk about bizarre."

"Like I said," Henry responded, "a very interesting session on the couch."

The sun traversed the cabin as Henry banked the aircraft to the left and headed toward a reservoir to the east of their location. He pushed forward on the yoke, causing the Tri-Pacer to descend lower for a better view of the lake. It was Friday, and the weekend boaters were already launching their vessels and icing down their beer. The small airplane made a long, gradual turn around the south end of the lake and headed north toward the dam and valley beyond.

"Then there's Jessie," Jack said. "She was in love with Annie too." He glanced at the pilot, who showed no signs of surprise or any other reaction to the statement. "That doesn't seem to surprise you."

"It doesn't," Henry said, without further explanation.

Jack waited for a moment to see if an awkward silence might extract a response from Dr. Coleman. It didn't. "Well, maybe she hates me because Annie died on her way up to the park to find me," Jack said. "And her 'aw, shucks' shyness is just a smokescreen."

"Could be," Henry said. "But then again, I'm not really qualified to be a criminal profiler."

"You'll do for now," Jack said. "She may know something, though, that she doesn't want anyone else to know. Can you talk to her and see what you can find out?"

"Yes," Henry said.

"Then there's Stewart Ramsey," Jack continued. "He stated specifically that he doesn't think we should drag up the past. I wonder if the past might be a roadblock to his future. If he was involved in Annie's death in some way, that would be a real downer for his political aspirations," Jack said, writing on the notepad.

"You're getting ahead of yourself there, Sherlock," Henry said. "The word 'involved' implies that she was murdered. The only thing that might lead you to that conclusion is the fact that someone is trying to kill you. What if the two aren't related?"

Jack pondered the question for a minute, then made another notation on the pad.

"Seems to me," Henry continued, "you need to go back to the original incident and determine if there was anything overlooked in that investigation. If there's a possibility that she was murdered, then you can tie that to the present situation."

Jack nodded in agreement. The good doctor was right. He needed to review all of the documents and evidence from Annie's crash. But to do that, he was going to need the cooperation of the one guy who was most antagonistic toward him, Frank Kirby. *Damn. That's going to be the hardest part.*

Henry grabbed the microphone, changed the radio frequency, and keyed the mic. "Caldwell Tower, this is Piper Seven-one-two-five-Sierra, over."

"Two-five-Sierra, Caldwell Tower, go ahead," came the response.

"Caldwell Tower, Two-five-Sierra will be passing through your airspace two miles to the east at one thousand feet, requesting traffic advisory, over," Henry said.

Jack put his hand on Henry's shoulder. "Let me shoot a touch-and-go," he said.

Henry looked at his copilot.

"Two-five-Sierra, Caldwell Tower. Traffic is light today, Henry. Just a King Air on final to runway one-seven."

Henry keyed the mic. "Tower, Two-five-Sierra requesting a touch-and-go for runway two-seven."

Jack felt his stomach muscles tighten.

"Two-five-Sierra, Caldwell Tower. Altimeter two-niner-niner-three, wind calm, cleared for approach to runway two-seven for touch-and-go. Report on final."

"Roger, Two-five-Sierra, cleared for approach to two-seven. Report final," the pilot said.

"Thank you, my friend," Jack said.

"She's all yours," Henry said.

Jack slipped his feet onto the control pedals and grasped the yoke. The knot in his stomach doubled in size, and his mind went blank for a moment. The last time he had held the controls of this aircraft, his dad was in the left seat, and the results were disastrous. He felt Henry's hand on his shoulder, bringing him back to the present. He pushed forward on the yoke to begin his descent to the runway and made a slight course correction to a heading parallel with the highway below. The sun was on his left as he descended on the base leg of his approach.

"Caldwell Tower, Two-five-Sierra turning final for runway two-seven," Henry said.

Jack banked the Tri-Pacer to the left and pulled the sun visor down from overhead to aid his vision, as the aircraft turned directly into the late afternoon sun.

"Two-five-Sierra, Caldwell Tower. Wind calm, cleared for touch-and-go, runway two-seven."

"I'll get the flaps," Henry said. He reached up to a handle on the overhead and started turning it to lower the flaps on the wing, increasing the lift characteristics and allowing the aircraft to stay in the air at slower speed.

Jack pushed on the throttle to speed up the engine so the plane wouldn't stall. The airplane passed over a railroad track and then the highway, as it settled closer and closer to the runway. Once he was past the power lines next to the highway, Jack pulled back on the throttle and let the Tri-Pacer ease down to the runway. Just before the wheels touched he cut the throttle, and the aircraft settled smoothly onto the runway.

I did it, Dad.

A smiling Jack McCall pushed forward on the throttle and worked the foot pedals to keep the aircraft headed straight down the runway. As the Tri-Pacer picked up speed, it lifted off the runway and began to climb to the west. The sun was directly in the face of both men.

Henry keyed the microphone. "Caldwell Tower, Two-five-Sierra requesting right turn for departure to the north."

Jack grasped the control handle for the flaps and cranked them back into the wing.

"Two-five-Sierra, Caldwell Tower. Clear to depart the control zone to the north," came the reply. "Remain at or below 1,000 feet. We have commercial traffic on approach to Eugene from the north."

"Roger, Caldwell Tower, Two-five-Sierra, out," Henry said.

Jack banked the airplane to the right as it continued the climb out of the traffic pattern. "She's all yours, Captain," he said.

"I've got it," Henry responded.

Jack took his hands off the control yoke and held them up in front of his face. They were shaking, and he couldn't seem to make them stop. He shook them, as if trying to eject the adrenaline out of his fingertips, then grabbed the notebook to give them something to do.

As the small aircraft rose upward and headed to the north, both men surveyed the landscape below in silence. Teams of grass seed harvesters traversed the fields below, leaving clouds of dust and rows of chaff. To the east were the river, the valley, and the Cascade Mountains. The Tri-Pacer leveled off at 500 feet and continued north toward Caldwell. The landscape of fields and farms gave way to houses and some light industrial buildings on the outskirts of town. The lone eyesore, from the air at least, was the LCT auto-wrecking yard that had collected the area's destroyed and derelict vehicles for fifty years. It had quadrupled in size since Jack was a boy. It was the only wrecking yard in town at that time, and Jack's grandfather, an auto mechanic who owned his own shop, sent many a car there that had been damaged beyond repair. A quick scan from the air revealed several competitors, but none were as expansive as LCT. Henry banked the Tri-Pacer to the right and headed east toward the river and the landing strip at his farm. As they passed over the wrecking yard, Jack surveyed the rows of tattered cars.

"Do you suppose Annie's car is still there?" he said.

Henry looked down to survey the yard. "At LCT?" he said. "I doubt it. It was a '56 Chevy. A classic car even then. It's probably been parted out and the carcass shredded by now."

"I wonder," Jack said, making a notation on his writing pad. "It would be interesting to see if it's there."

"It's on your way back into town," the pilot responded, as he pushed forward on the control yoke to begin the descent to the landing strip.

The Tri-Pacer banked to the right and turned south, as it dropped below the tree line and floated onto the grass landing strip. Henry taxied the plane to the hangar and shut off the engines. The two men exited the plane, grabbed the tow bar from the luggage compartment, and dragged the airplane into the hangar.

"I have to get the fuel trailer and top off the tanks," Henry said to his guest. "Why don't you head on up to the house and grab a Diet Coke while I finish up here? I'll be up in a few minutes."

Jack thought for a second. "I think I'll take a rain check on the Diet Coke and head over to the wrecking yard to snoop around a little," he said. "Give my thanks to Jennifer for her hospitality."

"Okay," Henry said.

Jack headed off at a fast pace toward the front of the house, where the Mustang was parked. He hopped in the car and headed toward the wrecking yard. Maybe he would get lucky and find the remnants of Annie's Chevy. It was a long shot, but he had a little time before he had to be at the reunion's happy hour.

As he pulled into the parking lot, he was greeted by a large "LCT Wrecking" sign. The building had undergone a facelift since his high school days, but once inside the door he recognized the smell. Oil and grime covered the same counter over which his grandfather had retrieved parts to be transplanted into comatose automobiles, bringing them back to life. The faces were new, but the look and the smell of the place were unaffected by time.

Jack looked around to see if he recognized anyone, but he had to settle for a tall, redheaded counterman who was finishing a transaction with a customer in Ramsey Motors coveralls. He stood in line behind the mechanic and waited.

"That'll be fifty-five dollars," the redheaded kid said. "I suppose your boss is going to charge a hundred fifty-five after you install that thing."

"Isn't capitalism great?" said the mechanic, as he signed the invoice and headed out the door.

"Can I help you, sir?" the counterman said, looking at Jack.

Jack glanced at the name badge on the kid's blue-striped work shirt. "Sure, Steve," he said. "How good are your records for the cars that have been brought here?" He figured Steve probably hadn't heard that question before, so the puzzled look on the kid's face wasn't a surprise.

"We have records, sir, but I'm not sure how far back they go," Steve said. "The manager isn't here right now, and I don't think he would want me to go digging through the file cabinet."

Jack decided to grease the wheels a little. He pulled out his Department of Justice business card and handed it to the kid. "Official business, Steve," he said, flashing his badge too. "We're doing some background work on the auto-wrecking business, in preparation for congressional hearings on trafficking in stolen cars," he lied. "Your cooperation would be most helpful."

Steve was duly intimidated, and he motioned for Jack to follow him as he headed toward a door directly behind the counter. Behind the door was a very wide hallway with several computer workstations. The keyboards were covered with flexible plastic sheets that were heavily spotted with grease. The chairs were protected with covers that bore the same logo as the floor mats guarding the doorways, to what Jack guessed were offices. The kid sat down at one of the terminals, typed some characters, and waited for the magic to happen.

"Just type in the make and model you are looking for, Mr. McCall," Steve said. "You'll get a list of every car we've processed back to 1960."

Steve got up, pulled the protective covers off the keyboard and the chair, and motioned for Jack to sit.

"Thank you, Steve," he said, taking his place at the keyboard. He typed in "1956 Chevrolet," hit "enter," and waited for the machine to respond—and for Steve to go back through the door to the customer counter area. The machine moved faster than Steve. Once Steve closed the door behind him, Jack scanned the list that the machine produced. It looked like Annie's car was one of four on the list. He concluded it was hers based on the date it was brought into inventory. There were some numbers indicating the location of the car in the yard. Jack rose from the chair and navigated his way to the counter area to find Steve, who was working at a computer terminal. He stopped at the doorway.

"Steve," Jack said. "I need your help."

A startled Steve snapped his neck around and lurched toward the door where Jack was waiting. "Yes, sir," he said, falling in step behind Jack, who turned and headed back to the work-station displaying the list.

"I have to do a random review of cars, to validate the sample for the investigation," Jack told the kid. "I want to use at least one really old car for that purpose. How do I find this one?" he said, pointing at the line that identified Annie's car.

Steve leaned over and wrote down the location numbers. "That's a really old section of the yard," he said. "You might find this one, because this car is considered a classic and we don't send them to the shredder until there are absolutely no salvageable parts left." Steve stood and headed out the back door of the building, and Jack followed.

"The rows are alphabetical left to right, and the spaces are numerical front to back," Steve said. He started to head toward the space indicated on Jack's list.

"That's okay," Jack said. "I can find the sample car. You can go back and help your customers. I just need to verify the vehicle identification number for the records."

Steve nodded and headed back into the building, leaving Jack to work his way through the rows of "junkers," as his grandfather used to call them. A row of tall cottonwood trees to the west of the yard provided some shade and relief from the afternoon sun as Jack made his way to the location written on the sticky note. What he found didn't look like a '56 Chevy. But it was her car all right. The color was right, and the left rear quarter panel hadn't been damaged very much and was consistent with a '56 Chevy. Jack looked inside the passenger compartment, which had been long ago been stripped bare. The only things that remained were some glass and a damaged section of the dashboard. The rear drive train was gone, so he inspected the front brakes. They had been beaten up pretty badly in the wreck, but the hydraulic lines were intact. The hood for the engine compartment was sitting on top of the car and was crumpled like an accordion, which made it worthless for parts. Jack looked in the engine compartment, which was missing the engine and most of the other components normally found there. There were some wires and hoses, but little else. The steering column was bent but intact. The police report had stated that there was nothing wrong with the brakes or the steering at the time of the accident.

Jack wrapped his hand around the top of the steering column and slid it down the shaft. Halfway down, his fingers felt something on the underside of the shaft. He moved his hand slowly across the area again and felt the same sensation. It felt like a groove. He wrapped his hand tighter around the shaft and attempted to rotate it so that the groove would face upward and he could examine it. The shaft wouldn't rotate. Maybe, he thought, he could use the steering wheel to rotate the shaft. The driver's door was missing, which allowed him easy access to the steering wheel, so he reached in and grabbed the top of it and pulled. Still no luck. He braced his left knee against what was left of the dashboard and leaned backward, pulling with all his weight and muscle. The steering wheel rotated a quarter of a revolution, so he took a fresh grip on the top of the wheel and gave it one more pull. The wheel rotated again. He moved forward to the engine compartment and examined the steering shaft.

The shaft was rusty, but there were distinct grooves around the portion of the shaft that was now facing upward. They only ran partway around the shaft, so they hadn't been visible before Jack rotated the steering wheel. *Curious. What would cause that kind of groove in the shaft?* He examined the area of the metal car body adjacent to the groove. The only thing he found was two holes about a quarter inch in diameter. He took out his cell phone and snapped some pictures of the shaft and the sheet metal. He would find some pictures of a stock engine compartment and compare them to these pictures.

Jack headed back toward the office area. He walked over one row to stay in the shade of the cottonwoods. The gravel roadbed, now in shade, still radiated the solar heat stored from its earlier exposure to the summer sun, making his journey still a little uncomfortable. He walked at a casual pace, letting his mind mull over the facts at hand: The police had ruled the crash an accident; Rosemary had seen someone else in Annie's car that night; there was a strong possibility that the car had been tampered with; he, Jack, had openly questioned the conclusion that her death was accidental, and, subsequently, several people were quite insistent that he drop the subject of Annie Ridgeway altogether; and someone had tried to kill him several times. He also knew that there were only a handful of people who had known he would be taking coffee on the sightseeing flight with Mollie, Joe, and Carrie. The only logical conclusion was that someone had killed Annie and was now trying to kill him because he was stirring the pot.

Steve was still at the front counter, helping another customer, as Jack passed the lobby, so he raised his hand in recognition, mouthed a "thank you," and kept on moving out the front door. Steve looked momentarily confused but went back to his duties. Satisfied that he had not aroused suspicion about his true motives for snooping around the wrecking yard, Jack exited the building and started toward the car. As he opened the door of the Mustang, he caught a glimpse of something that grabbed his attention. He stopped and stared at a large red-white-and-blue building that shared parking and street access with the wrecking yard. Atop a two-story steel pole on the front of the property was perched a red-white-and-blue sign that read "Cramer Towing & Repair." Jack closed the car door and stood looking at the sign. He recalled that Lamont Cramer had retrieved Annie's car the night she was killed and had towed it back to town. Maybe Cramer could tell him something about the car. He walked over to the building and went inside.

"Can I help you, sir?" a young, dark-haired girl said from behind a short counter in what appeared to serve as a lobby and office area.

"Is Lamont Cramer around?" Jack said.

"He's in his office," the girl said. "Your name, sir?"

"Jack McCall."

The girl picked up the phone and punched two numbers. "Grandpa," she said, "there's a Jack McCall in the lobby. He wants to talk with you." After listening to Grandpa's reply, she hung up the phone. "His office is at the end of the hallway to your right," she said, pointing toward a passageway. "You can go ahead and go in."

"Thank you," Jack said.

The hallway was unlit and had an odor like the degreasing solvent Jack's grandfather had used in his auto repair shop. His foot caught on a crumpled section of carpet as he walked toward the end of the hall, where a partially-open door revealed light coming from inside the room. Upon arriving at the doorway, he gave a light tap on the door to announce his presence.

"Come in, McCall," a voice said.

Jack entered the room.

"Forgive me if I don't get up," said the old man, from behind a cluttered oak desk. "By the time I got up, shook your hand, and sat back down, we'd have to send out for dinner." The old man smiled, seemingly entertained by his own wit.

"Your grandfather was a good friend of mine," he continued. "I knew your dad too. Good men, both of them. What can I do for you?"

Jack sat down in an oak chair in front of the old man's desk. "I appreciate your taking time to see me, Mr. Cramer," he said. "I am trying to find some information about the accident that killed Annie Ridgeway the night of my high school graduation party."

The old man's head moved up and down in slow motion. "I remember that wreck," he said, grabbing a pack of cigarettes off his desk and lighting one up. He leaned back and flipped a switch on the wall behind him, starting both an electric fan to the right of his desk and an exhaust fan in the exterior wall to the left of his desk. "Earl fixed this up for me so I could smoke in here and not drive out my guests," he said. The smoke from his cigarette followed the airflow out of the room. "Pretty clever, huh?"

"Yes, sir," Jack said. "About that wreck, would it have been possible for someone to tamper with the car after you brought it back to the city?"

"Tamper with it?" Cramer said. "Hell, they could have done a complete overhaul. It sat over in the wrecking yard for two days before the state boys arrived to check it out. We didn't have anyone local at the time who could do an adequate job of analyzing the thing for mechanical failures."

"Two days?" Jack said.

"Yup," Cramer confirmed. The old man used his arms to raise himself out of his seat a few inches, then shifted his weight to the left. "Damned leg gives me fits. Sometimes I think I should just cut if off."

Jack pulled out his smartphone. He poked and swiped the face until the first picture he'd taken of Annie's car was displayed on the screen. "What might cause a groove like this on a steering shaft?" he said, setting the phone on the desk and sliding it in front of the old man.

Cramer picked up some eyeglasses sitting on his desk and examined the picture. "Looks like something scraped against it," he said, looking back up at Jack. "This from the dead girl's car?"

"Yes," said Jack. "Could that groove have been created over a long period of time?"

The old man looked at the picture again. "Not likely," he said. "If it'd been cut over a long period of time, the edges would be more rounded. The edges of this groove are square, like it was cut all at once."

Jack took out the notes he'd started in Henry's airplane, picked up a pencil from the old man's desk, and scribbled an entry. He put the pencil down and brushed his finger over the screen on the phone, changing pictures.

"Could there have been a part or an accessory mounted on the engine compartment wall that would explain these holes?" he said.

The old man stared at the picture for a few moments, rubbing his chin with his hand. "Maybe," he said, "but I can't think of one, off the top of my head."

Jack rose, picked up his phone, and leaned forward to shake the old man's hand. "Thank you for your help, Mr. Cramer. I hope your leg gets better."

The old man just mumbled and shook Jack's hand.

Jack exited the building, hopped in the Mustang, and headed back to the inn.

CHAPTER 9

SUMMER IN CALDWELL had been a great adventure for young Jack McCall, but even the memories of those happy times weren't enough to take away the present-day anxiety that forced his fingers tight to the steering wheel of the Mustang as he cruised toward town. He had more facts and evidence after visiting with Henry and then snooping around at the wrecking yard, but there were still too many variables and unanswered questions to give him a starting point for a plan of action. He felt a strong urge to start doing something to solve the mystery. He was trapped between being Jack McCall, prosecutor, and Jack McCall, small-town boy.

The boy just wanted to enjoy the moment and ignore the mounting evidence that led in too many directions, and the prosecutor wanted to see someone pay for Annie's death. And then there was Jack McCall the man, who had to deal with the guilt of possibly being at least partially responsible for Annie's death. He had pushed it back into the recesses of his mind since leaving Caldwell, but now speculation about the past, and the events of the present, were impossible to ignore. The prosecutor headed for the hospital.

Mollie was sitting up in her bed, with a spoonful of hospital cuisine at her lips, when Jack entered her room. "Be careful, gorgeous," he said. "That stuff can kill you."

She finished the food delivery and labored to swallow. "Just hanging out with you will probably kill me first," she said, when her throat was clear. "Have you found out who tried to kill us?"

"Not yet," Jack said. "But I'm working on it. I see they've removed your IV."

"Yes," Mollie said. "I told them if it was still in my arm at five p.m., I wanted the bag filled with margaritas—blended, no salt."

"Salt's bad for your health," Jack said. "It can kill you, you know."

She smiled and pushed away the cantilevered tray holding her half-eaten plate of food. "So fill me in on the facts, Mr. Prosecutor," she said.

"I think that someone messed with the steering mechanism on Annie's car," Jack said, as he helped her wedge another pillow behind her back. "I found the car in the wrecking yard, and there was a rusted groove on the steering column that look like something might have been clamped around it, preventing the shaft from turning. There were also some holes in the sheet metal next to the shaft that looked out of place."

"Was that ever mentioned in the newspaper reports back then?" Mollie said.

"No," Jack said. "All the headlines at the time focused on too much speed, swerving to avoid a deer, or suicide."

"So they ruled out mechanical failure?" Mollie said.

Jack nodded. "But if I had been investigating a car going over a cliff," he continued, "and there weren't any overt signs of mechanical malfunction to the brakes, it would've been easy to arrive at the conclusion stated in the newspaper. And I don't know that I would do any close inspection of the steering column."

"So," Mollie said, "does this new information clarify logical suspects?"

Jack let out a sigh and sat down in the chair next to Mollie's bed. "Well, if you assume that Annie's death was not an accident, and that the attempts to discourage me from investigating her death—and then to kill me when I wouldn't stop—were committed by the same person, then the suspect would logically be someone who knew we were going flying yesterday."

"Who *did* know?" Mollie said.

"Do you remember the conversation we had with that group as we were getting on the elevator the day the golf cart exploded?" Jack said.

Mollie closed her eyes and sighed. "Vaguely."

"You mentioned in that conversation that you were going to take coffee from the inn on the flight," Jack continued. "It's logical to conclude that one of the people in that group was responsible for trying to kill us by poisoning the coffee. That group included Frank Kirby, Stewart Ramsey, Sterling and Victoria Whitehurst, Joshua Pitts, and Jessie Dalton."

Mollie opened her eyes and adjusted her hospital bed to a more upright position. "Doesn't make sense that Ramsey would do it, since Joe was on the plane."

"Agreed," Jack said. "And the only thing Victoria would put in a container of coffee is Kahlua. That leaves Frank, Sterling, Joshua, and Jessie as possible suspects."

"Jessie?" Mollie said. "Really? I still don't think she's the killer type."

"Agreed," Jack said. "But I've seen too many killers that 'didn't seem the type.' I can't rule her out at this point."

"Well, it's obvious that someone is trying to kill you," Mollie said, "but why did he or she kill Annie?"

"Yes, why?" Jack said. "If I knew why, it'd be easier to figure out who."

Mollie nodded and closed her eyes. "I'm tired of this place. Can we go home now?"

"Do you mean back to the inn, or home?" Jack said, knowing full well that the answer was home, to Hartford.

She answered his question with a subtle smile.

"I want you to go back to Hartford to rest," Jack said. "I can resolve this thing, and then I'll come home."

"Not a chance, McCall," his wife said. "If the plane goes down, we'll both be in it."

"Well, that's heroic," he responded. "Stupid—but heroic. I'd go if the situation were reversed."

"Would you go if I didn't have life insurance?" she said, seeming to mock his self-sacrifice.

He knew he couldn't win this contest, so he gave up with a smile and changed the subject. "I'm going to go check on Joe," he said. "I'll be back in a few minutes."

Jack rose from his chair and left the room. He checked at the nurses' station and was told that the boy was in Room 212, in the next corridor. While navigating the hallways, he spotted Mollie's doctor. "When will Mollie be released?" he said. The doctor, caught off-guard, said he needed to check on her progress and would leave instructions with the nurse, so Jack kept moving toward Room 212.

When he arrived at the room, Stewart Ramsey was seated outside the door, chewing on an unlit cigar. "A waste of good tobacco," he said, as Jack approached. "Fine tobacco is meant to be inhaled, not digested."

"It wasn't 'meant' for either," Jack said. "How's your son doing?"

Stewart rose from the chair and turned toward the boy's room. "Come on in and see for yourself."

Jack followed Ramsey into the room. A woman was seated by Joe's bed. The boy's eyes were closed, and a set of earbuds seemed to induce twitching, in rhythm with music only he could hear.

The woman looked at Jack. "I'm not sure whether to thank you for saving my son's life, McCall, or kill you myself for putting his life in danger."

Jack wasn't expecting the "mama bear" hostility, and he hesitated before answering. Her voice sounded familiar, but he didn't recognize her face. "Have we met before, Mrs. Ramsey?" he said, to divert her attention from the subject of her son's condition.

A faint grin peeked out from behind Mrs. Ramsey's anger-tightened lips. A heavy coat of lipstick accented the subtle change in facial expression that would have brought a rush of pride to the heart of any self-respecting mime. She lifted the walking cane that rested against her leg and pointed it at Jack. "You never could remember anything," she said. "I almost gave up teaching because of you. I was fresh out of college when I had the great misfortune of being tasked with teaching you history." She laughed, then her face retreated into anger.

Jack face contorted as he strained to remember. A name flashed into his brain. "Miss Danielson?"

"Shirley and I got married after I graduated from college," Stewart said.

"Shut up, Stewart," his wife barked. "It's none of his business."

Stewart walked back out into the hall. Shirley took a cell phone out of her purse, punched in some numbers, and put the phone to her ear. "Kirby, I want this situation with McCall cleared up immediately," she ordered. She waited for a moment as Constable Kirby replied. "Good. See to it."

"You lucked out, McCall," she said, turning her attention back to Jack. "If your wife hadn't been in the same predicament as Joe, I would have concluded that you were just being reckless."

"I'm sorry that Joe got dragged into this," Jack said. "I would never intentionally put the boy in harm's way."

Stewart stepped back into the doorway. "We know that. We just want to get this resolved so everyone is safe. And it's a huge distraction from the upcoming campaign."

Shirley nodded and rose to adjust the covers on Joe's bed. "Just fix it, McCall," she said.

Jack nodded and left the room while there was a lull in the antagonism. He was pleased that he had a new, and seemingly influential, ally. He grabbed his cell phone and called Henry's number, which was now stored in his phone for permanent use.

"Henry, it's Jack," he said. "What's the story with Ramsey and Miss Danielson?" An orderly walking by turned his head as Henry's laughter escaped from the listening end of Jack's cell phone. "Just give me the *Cliff's Notes* version." He held the phone to his ear as he navigated the corridors back to Mollie's room. Upon arrival, he gave a quick "thank you" to Henry and put the phone back in his pocket.

"What was that about?" Mollie said.

"Just some background stuff on the Ramsey clan. Interesting, but not relevant to the task at hand."

"Come on, McCall," his wife prompted, "don't keep the interesting stuff all to yourself. It's getting a little boring sitting here in this bed."

Jack headed for the door again and begged her indulgence while he checked in at the nurses' station. Upon arriving back at the room, he said, "Grab your stuff, Rocco, I'm bustin' you out of this joint."

She gave him one of her "huh?" expressions.

"Come on, the doc said you could leave."

"You could have just said that," Mollie barked, pivoting her legs to the side of the bed and easing her way to the floor. "Sometimes your attempt to be humorous is so far off the wall that it's in the next township."

Jack accepted her discontent and wrote it off as her just not being in the mood for his clever wit. He helped her gather her things, then exited into the hallway to stand guard while she got dressed. An orderly showed up with a wheelchair, and after a brief visit from the discharge nurse, they headed out of the building and into the sunlight.

"God, that feels good," she said. "I want to walk."

The orderly looked a little confused, but Mollie stopped the wheelchair and flipped up the footrests to facilitate her escape. The wheelchair driver shrugged and headed back into the hospital.

Jack walked beside Mollie, letting her set the pace as they headed toward the parking lot. He usually was out in front, coaxing her to speed up. But at this moment he was just glad she was alive, so he was content to help her shuffle her way toward the Mustang. He helped her into the car and stowed her overnight bag in the back seat. The convertible top was down, so he flipped a switch to raise the fabric roof.

"Leave it down," Mollie said, leaning her head back so her face was covered in sunlight.

Jack did as he was told, then guided the car out onto the street and headed toward the inn. His mind refocused on the reunion events and the mystery they had spawned.

"Once you are safely back at the hotel, I have to attend a happy hour sponsored by the reunion committee," Jack said. "Henry is meeting me there, and we are going to see if we can ferret out some answers."

Mollie rolled her head toward her husband and rubbed the back of his neck for a moment, then returned to her sun-worshiper position.

When they arrived at the inn, Henry and Jennifer were waiting for them. Henry opened Mollie's door. A young valet opened Jack's door and took the keys to park the car.

"I thought Mollie might need someone to stay with her while we attend this function," Henry said. "Jen volunteered."

Mollie put her arms around Jennifer and thanked her with a hug. The foursome walked slowly into the building, where the two women disappeared into the elevator.

"I found an interesting piece to the puzzle," Jack said, as he and Henry headed for the ballroom, where drinks and finger food awaited. He looked around as they walked, to make sure no one was in earshot. "I found Annie's car in the wrecking yard, and there were some suspicious marks on the steering column."

"What do you mean, 'suspicious'?" Henry said.

"There was a groove in the shaft, as though something had been pressed against it, but in a place on the shaft that wouldn't logically have anything attached," Jack said.

"Interesting," Henry observed.

"But I'm not sure," Jack continued, "that it would mean anything if you were examining the wreckage as part of an accident investigation. If the brakes looked okay and no one saw the car go off the road, the logical conclusion would have been speed, or else dodging a deer. Besides, the groove was on the bottom side of the steering column as it sat in the yard. It's possible no one saw it."

Jack grabbed Henry's arm and moved to the side of the hallway. He stopped and leaned closer to his friend so their conversation would remain private. "And another thing. I found two rusted-out holes on the inside of the fender wall that aligned with the grooves on the shaft. They were about a quarter inch in diameter."

Henry looked away, and Jack's head followed to see what had captured his attention. It was Frank Kirby, walking past them with a benign expression that suggested his hostility toward Jack might have begun to fade.

Henry looked back at Jack. "You should tell him what you found."

Jack squirmed a little and ran his fingers through his hair. "He's just going to tell me I'm nuts and go on a rant about how her death was my fault."

Henry put his hand on Jack's shoulder, as if to stabilize the squirm and reassure him. "Give him a chance," he said. "I think you will be surprised."

Henry nudged Jack back into the flow of bodies that were migrating toward the ballroom and the open bar. "Frank's at that table in the back," he said, steering Jack in that direction. As they walked toward the table, two alumni moved over to where Frank was sitting. They were well into their "good ol' days" conversation when Henry and Jack arrived at the table.

"Can we have a word with you in private, Chief?" Henry said.

Frank stared at Jack for a moment, then asked his two guests to excuse him. He rose and followed Henry and Jack to a private corner of the room, next to a tall window. "What do you need?" he asked Henry.

"Jack has some very interesting information to share with you."

Frank turned toward Jack. "Okay, whatcha got?" he said.

Jack hesitated, expecting Frank's body language to broadcast anger. But Frank's blank stare, his arms at his side, seemed almost inviting. Maybe Frank was ready to work with him. So Jack went over the day's events and findings, emphasizing what he had found on Annie's car.

"I didn't know that car was still around," Frank remarked. "So your conclusion, at this point, is that someone killed Annie twenty years ago, and now that same person is here for the reunion and is messing with you because you're trying to find out what happened back then."

"Yes," Jack said.

Henry leaned toward Frank and said, "That sounds very plausible to me, Frank."

Frank slowly nodded. "Sounds plausible to me too," he said. "I'll have her car transported to the station, and we'll get the State's forensics team to look it over."

Jack took his smartphone out of his pocket. "I have pictures of the steering column and fender wall, if that would help."

"Be at my office at seven tomorrow morning," Frank said, as he turned and started walking toward the door. "You can download them onto my computer."

"I didn't expect that," Jack said, as he dragged Henry toward the bar. "You were right about his being more willing to listen, but I have to admit that he was on my list of suspects, and I'm not sure I'm ready to take him off the list."

"You really don't think he killed Annie," Henry said. "Do you?"

"No, but that doesn't mean he's not trying to kill me," Jack said. "I know it's a stretch."

"You just don't like him," Henry said. "And he doesn't like you, so he probably changed his mind as a favor to me."

"Or in fear of *Mrs.* Ramsey," Jack said.

"And speaking of favors," Jack added, as they weaved their way through the crowd, "have I ever thanked you for saving my butt from the Jimmerson brothers?"

"Yes," Henry said. "You used your sources to get me my first pint of vodka, when we were in high school."

Jack smiled at the dim recollection. "You sure you want to count that?"

"We'll just let it retain the value it had back then," Henry said. "If we tried to revalue past events, we'd be here forever."

Jack nodded and turned to the bartender. "Diet Coke for me," he said, and turned back to Henry. "What'll you have, Doc? I'm buying."

"Don't start with that Doc business," Henry said. "That's ancient history too. I'll have a root beer."

Jack retrieved the drinks issued by the bartender, and the two friends found an empty table. As they sat and watched the crowd mill about, Jack spotted Sterling Whitehurst. He was walking away from the bar with a drink in his hand, so Jack hollered at him and invited him to join them. Sterling stopped, and Jack could see his eyes squint and his mouth curl into a forced smile, as if he were trying to think of a reason why he couldn't join them. Before he could invent a reason to keep going, Victoria appeared and grabbed him by the arm.

"Come on, sugar lips," she said. "I need another drink."

Sterling looked at Jack with a "sorry, what can I do?" expression and followed his leader back toward the bar.

"Something tells me he didn't want to talk with us," Jack said to Henry. "I wonder what he's hiding."

"Well, we can start to put all the pieces together tomorrow when we meet with Frank," Henry said.

"Hold on, partner," Jack said, jerking his head back toward Henry. "I don't want you becoming a target too. I appreciate your willingness to help, but I created this mess. You need to stay out of it. Or at least stay in the background."

"I can help," Henry said.

"You can help by keeping an ear to the ground and letting Frank and me know anything you hear," Jack insisted.

"Okay," Henry said. "If that's the way you want to work it."

"*Yes*" was Jack's emphatic reply.

The two men rose and walked toward the door, shaking a few hands and exchanging greetings on the way out. Jack went up to his room to relieve Jennifer of her nursing duties. When he opened the door to the room, Jennifer held her index finger to her lips to signal that Mollie was asleep, then went downstairs to join her husband. Jack walked over to the bed and did a visual survey of his wife. She seemed to be okay, so he took a shower, set his alarm clock for six a.m., and went to bed. He wanted to be rested and on time for his meeting with Frank.

******

The next morning, the alarm clock rousted Jack out of bed. Mollie was already awake but still in bed.

"How are you feeling?" Jack said.

"Pretty good, considering," she said.

"I have a meeting at the police station at seven," Jack said. "Do you want me to get someone to stay with you this morning while I'm away?"

"No," Mollie said. "Jennifer invited me to have breakfast with her, and then she is going to show me around town."

"Great," Jack said. "I'll meet you back here for lunch." He hopped out of bed, took a quick shower, got dressed, and gave Mollie a kiss on the cheek as he headed out the door.

"Don't worry about me," she shouted after him. "I'll be fine, now that I'm not dying."

Jack stopped and walked back to the door. He gave his wife a long kiss. "I'll fill you in on everything at lunch," he said. "Call me if you need me, and I'll drop whatever I'm doing. Promise?"

"Okay," she said.

Jack decided to skip breakfast and head straight to the police station. He didn't want to be late. When he arrived, the lobby area was vacant except for Trina at the front desk.

"I have a seven o'clock meeting with the chief," Jack said.

"You'll have to wait for a few minutes, Mr. McCall," Trina said. "He's got two people in his office right now."

Jack sat in the reception area and fidgeted with some magazines on the end table beside him. Impatience oozed out of his fingers and toes until Trina finally told him the chief was ready to see him. He rose and opened the door to Frank's office. He expected the two people with Frank to be gone, but they weren't. The man and woman were still seated in front of

Frank's desk, and they didn't acknowledge his entrance into the room.

"Have a seat, Jack," Frank said, directing him to a chair at the side of his desk. "I'd like you to meet Agents Wilder and Simpson, from the FBI."

"Peter?" Jack said, extending a hand in greeting. "Peter Wilder."

Peter, dressed in a wrinkled suit that suggested he'd been wearing it for at least three or four days, rose from his chair and greeted Jack. "How are you doing, Jack? Been a while."

"Yes, it has," Jack said. "What brings you to this little burg in Oregon?"

"You," Peter said.

Jack's face muscles tightened, signaling that his brain was straining to understand Peter's response. "Me?"

"Jack, I'd like you to meet my partner, Agent Kate Simpson," Peter said.

"Nice to meet you, Mr. McCall," Agent Kate said, shaking Jack's hand. "Peter has told me a lot of stories about your years together at Trinity."

Jack's face muscles again tightened, and he again directed his attention to Peter. "You didn't tell her everything, did you?" he said.

"Only the fun stuff," Peter said.

"Chief," Peter said, turning toward Frank, "Kate and I haven't eaten breakfast yet. Is there somewhere close where the four of us can grab a bite to eat while we fill Jack in on the reason for our visit?"

"Sure," Frank said, then rose from his chair and headed toward his office door. Kate, Peter, and Jack followed. "Trina, we're going to breakfast. Back in an hour." The foursome went out the front of the building and headed down the street.

Peter and Kate may have been partners, but as they followed Frank down the sidewalk, Jack observed that they were about as different as two people could get. Peter was short and rumpled-looking, while Kate was a good half foot taller and perfectly coiffed, not a hair out of place. And if she and

Peter had been traveling together for the same amount of time under the same conditions, Jack concluded that her suit must be 200 percent polyester, because neither the skirt nor the coat had a wrinkle on it. Peter looked disheveled. Kate looked precise. An odd couple, if ever there was one.

Their short journey ended as they entered Wagner's Café, a few blocks away from the station.

"Someplace private, Susie," the police chief said to the hostess. Susie headed toward a table near the rear of the dining area with the group in tow, except for Peter, who peeled off the formation and headed toward the men's room.

Jack's curiosity was at a level that would have killed off all nine lives of every cat within ten blocks. Instead of sitting down when they arrived at the table, he excused himself and headed to the restroom.

Peter was returning to the table when Jack stopped him in the hallway, out of sight and sound of Frank. "What the hell's going on, Peter?" he said.

Just as Peter began to answer, a female customer walked out of the bathroom toward the two men. "It's okay, buddy," Peter said. "We can talk in front of the chief."

"No, we can't," Jack said. "In case you haven't read his body language, he and I are not exactly bosom buddies."

"It'll be okay," Peter said, taking Jack by the arm and nudging him toward the dining room. "I've got your back."

Peter kept walking, and as they arrived back at the table Frank gave Jack a confused look. "That was a short trip to the john," he said.

Jack put on a fake smile and mumbled something about Mother Nature changing her mind, then sat back down next to Kate. "So what's going on?" he said to the group.

Peter looked at his partner. "Kate, please bring Mr. McCall up to speed on our case."

Kate picked up an attaché case from the floor next to her chair. She removed a file folder and returned the case to the floor. "The Bureau has been tracking a hired killer, code name 'Magellan.'"

"Magellan?" Jack interrupted. "Weird code name for a hired assassin."

Kate looked at Peter, crumpled her lips, and nodded.

"He travels all over the world to kill people," Peter responded. He looked at Jack, then Kate, then Frank. "All the good code names were taken."

Kate shook her head.

"Well, I thought it was good," Peter said, waving his hand in the air to prompt Kate to continue with the briefing.

"We believe he is responsible for an assassination in Florida a month ago," Kate said. "A charge on a stolen credit card that we suspect he's currently using was traced to a convenience store in Salem, but the trail ended there. The store's video records were destroyed in a fire, after the time/date record from the card company shows that the charge was made."

"How does that tie in with me?" Jack said.

"I'm getting to that part," Agent Simpson said. "We have been monitoring law enforcement chatter in the region, looking for something that might indicate where he went."

"That's where you come in, Jack," Peter said. "The effects of the poison used on your wife and the kid matched the evidence in the Florida case."

"When the hospital made the inquiry to identify the drug, it was flagged and directed to us," Kate continued. "Then Chief Kirby sent a request for information on you, and that was flagged as well."

"When I saw your name, Jack," Peter interjected, "I decided to personally do the legwork on this lead."

Frank coughed and let his spoon drop to the table, drawing the group's attention. "Couldn't believe he would be worth the effort for someone to kill him, huh?" he said.

Peter laughed and patted Jack on the shoulder. "I don't want anything to happen to him," he said. "He still owes me money."

"Thought maybe you'd forgotten about that," Jack said, lowering his head in mock shame. "So let's go over this file. What do you know about this guy?"

"Wait a minute, hotshot," Frank interrupted, leaning forward with a scowl. "I allowed you to join us as a courtesy to Agent Wilder. This is my case, not yours. You are going back to the inn and confining your activities to scheduled reunion events so we can keep an eye on you. If you can't do that, you are leaving town, permanently."

"I'm afraid I have to include him in some parts of this investigation, Chief," Peter said, shaking his head. "The assistant director thinks that Jack's case experience, on top of his personal involvement in this situation, will be an asset to the Bureau's investigation."

Frank rolled his eyes with an exaggeration that dragged his entire head into the process. "Jesus. You guys are going to get me killed."

Jack resisted the temptation to gloat and brought the conversation back to the file. "What can you tell us about Magellan, Kate?"

Kate looked at Peter, who nodded his authorization to proceed. "We're not sure at this point whether Magellan is a he or a she," she said. "I've referred to Magellan as 'he' for the purpose of this discussion because men have a greater tendency to be psycho killers." The men at the table each faked a smile. "We think he has been active for quite a few years," she continued. "Maybe decades. Most of the hits in which we have begun to suspect his involvement were political or business-related. No domestic dispute stuff or the like. No direct ties to organized crime, either. He's a freelancer. We have intel that leads us to believe he is very selective about his contracts. High-profile stuff. Big risk, big reward."

"Any idea why he's in this area?" Frank said. "Other than to kill McCall here."

"Well," Peter said, leaning forward and lowering his voice, "we understand that there's a US senator coming here to do some campaigning for one of your local guys."

"Yeah," Jack said. "Henry told me about that. He's coming to campaign for Stewart Ramsey. He's coming in tomorrow so

Ramsey can make his big announcement on Sunday afternoon at a big family barbecue whing-ding at the football stadium."

"Also," Kate added, "one of your classmate's wives has an uncle who is a US senator. The former Victoria Wainwright, now Victoria Whitehurst."

Jack looked at Frank, who apparently had already been briefed on the details, since he was surveying the menu in search of an appetizing breakfast entrée. "Anyone else around who might be a target, Chief?" Jack said.

Frank glanced up from the menu and stared at Jack. "What?"

"Is there anyone else, besides the senator just mentioned, who might be a target for this assassin?" Jack repeated.

"No," Frank said. "I already went over that with Agents Wilder and Simpson. We even went through the list of attendees for the reunion activities. Only one classmate was on the list developed by the Bureau."

"What list?" Jack said, turning his attention to Peter.

"We compiled a list of possible targets, based on what we deduced from our profiler about Magellan," Peter said. "Mostly business and political people who are engaged in controversial policies or transactions that involve a lot of money, or people who have potential to influence actions where a lot of money can be gained or lost. Your classmate, actor Dakota Douglas, was on our list, but only because he's well known. He doesn't really fit the profile of Magellan's past targets."

"And no one who lives here is on the list or even comes close to that profile," Frank added.

"Well, I certainly don't fit the profile of one of his victims," Jack said, shaking his head. "So the only thing linking me to Magellan is the stuff he used on Mollie, right?"

"Yes," Kate said. "And the target that brought this guy here is most likely someone traveling here from out of the area, someone with a high-profile schedule that would allow Magellan to plan way ahead."

"But why try to kill me?" Jack said.

"Maybe he's just bored or needs the practice," Frank said, with a healthy dose of sarcasm.

"Maybe . . . ," Peter said, pausing to complete his thought before continuing. "Maybe you know something that you don't know you know, that would reveal his identity."

"Maybe," Jack said. "It has . . ."

"What'll it be, folks?" the waiter asked. The middle-aged man was dressed in black slacks and a white shirt, with the name "Bob" on the badge clipped to his shirt pocket.

Frank handed the waiter his menu. "I'll have the usual."

"Don't know why you even bother looking at a menu, Chief," Waiter Bob said.

Bob wrote down each order and headed off to the kitchen.

"You were saying?" Kate said, prompting Jack to continue his thought.

Jack looked at Frank. "What if the connection has something to do with Annie's accident, which may not have been an accident?"

Frank let out a contemptuous, guttural noise that had no literal translation but spoke volumes about his feelings. He squirmed a little, while holding up his coffee cup to signal Waiter Bob for a refill.

"Well, Chief?" Peter said.

"Okay," Frank responded, "just suppose that Annie's death wasn't an accident and that Magellan was somehow involved. That might lead us to conclude that he was either a member of our class or someone who lived around here at the time she was killed."

Jack nodded and continued the line of logic. "If he is trying to discourage us from investigating Annie's death, then there must be a link between that event and the reunion that would lead us to his identity."

"Or her identity," Kate added.

"Right," Jack acknowledged.

"Or maybe he's just playing with you to feed the thrill factor," Peter said. "You know, kind of a 'catch me if you can' thing."

Waiter Bob arrived with a pot of coffee, causing a lull in the group's discussion as he poured a second round. "Your food will be right up, folks," he said, before disappearing into the kitchen.

"It could be a thrill factor," Jack said, "but why me? Logically it would need to be someone who knows me and was part of the conversation the other day about flying."

"Or was told about the sightseeing tour you were going to take," Frank added.

Waiter Bob appeared once again with a tray of food and distributed the institutional cuisine for consumption. As he was doing so, several office workers, wearing building access badges, laid claim to the booth next to the law enforcement team, stifling the group's confidential conversation. Jack and Peter switched the conversation to college memories, and their two dining partners ate and listened in silence.

Once the meal was completed, the group exited the café. The confidential conversation resumed in the chief's office, and Jack wasted no time injecting himself into Peter's investigation.

"You think he's here on another contract, don't you?" Jack said, sliding to the front edge of his chair. "I can be as valuable to your investigation as you can be to mine."

"What the hell do you mean, 'your investigation'?" Frank said, slamming his hand down on his desk and leaning across it toward Jack. "I agreed to let you help with this as a favor to Henry and to Shirley Ramsey, so sit your ass back in that chair and keep your mouth shut."

Jack was surprised by the apparent renewed hostility on Frank's part. "Relax," he said, sliding back in his chair. "Just a slip of the tongue. It's a phrase I use a lot in my line of work."

Frank straightened his posture and waved his hand in the air as if erasing something. "Yeah," he said. "Slip of the tongue." He turned to Peter and Kate. "I get a little touchy when it comes to crime in my town."

Peter, in an apparent attempt to ease tensions, started to chuckle and shake his head. "I can see you haven't lost your ability to bring out the best in your teammates, have you, Jack?"

"I think we can all benefit from sharing information and resources," Kate said.

Frank took a deep breath and walked toward a door to his left. "Yes, we can," he agreed. "If you will follow me, we'll get started."

The three guests followed the chief through the doorway and into a conference room. In the room were three large, portable whiteboards, with photos of each attempt to either kill or scare Jack since his return to Caldwell. Each board also contained names of what he assumed were witnesses and possible suspects, since some of the names were people who weren't present when the incident occurred. Jack turned his attention to the conference table. It was covered with similar documents and materials relating to Annie's death twenty years earlier.

"Impressive," Jack said. "We can cross-reference the FBI material on Magellan with your material, Frank, and that should start to bring some things into focus."

Frank didn't look at Jack, nor acknowledge the compliment. He just moved the two outer whiteboards away from the center one, then picked up the telephone handset from the unit located on the conference table. "Beth, bring two more portable whiteboards to the conference room," he said, then paused a moment, listening to Beth's reply. "Well, get some from the squad room. We need them up here ASAP." He hung up the phone.

Peter moved in for a close inspection of the center display. "Kate," he said, "please contact DC and have them make sure all the latest material is on the task force server."

Frank picked up the phone again. "You can set up your laptop in the office on the other side of mine, Agent Simpson," he said, then punched zero on the keypad and instructed Trina to make arrangements to facilitate their use of the office.

"Thank you," Kate said. "This all looks promising. Maybe we can find this guy—or gal. Whichever."

Jack started for the door. "I have a few things to do," he said. "Frank has my cell number if you need me. I'll check back with you this afternoon."

"Do not start your own investigation, McCall," Frank hollered, as Jack left the room.

"Of course not," Jack said, to the ceiling of the lobby. "Wouldn't think of it."

CHAPTER 10

THE BLONDE WOMAN that Jack had met on the balcony was in the lobby when he arrived back at the inn. She was seated in a conquistador's version of a loveseat in the middle of the room, wearing dark glasses and dressed in a pure white swimsuit cover that displayed an abundance of leg. The sight caused one businessman to trip over the carpet as he walked past her. Jack, not immune to such distractions, walked at a fast pace, hoping she wouldn't notice him pass by on his way to the front counter.

"I have some fresh towels in my room," she said, when he was close enough to hear. "I'd be happy to show them to you—since you have such a keen interest in towels."

Jack just smiled and kept walking. His reaction appeared to please her; he saw the hint of a smile flicker onto her face. Bruno was exiting his office when Jack reached the front desk. He motioned for Bruno to move to the end of the counter so they could speak in confidence.

"Who is the hottie in the sunglasses and the virgin's uniform in the middle of the lobby?" Jack whispered.

Bruno peered around his guest to get a good look at the body in question. "I have no idea," he said, "but if she's a virgin, she won't remain so for long wearing that outfit."

"She's in the room next to the first room you put us in," Jack said. "Look up her name."

"You know I can't divulge guest information," the proprietor said. "But she doesn't look old enough to be here for the reunion, as far as I can tell."

Jack leaned against the counter and gradually turned his head and torso, as if inspecting the room. He guessed she was spying on him from behind the dark glasses, based on the slight grin that appeared on her face when his gaze turned in her general direction. He turned back toward his host. "Just look up her name in the register and tell me if you recognize it," he requested.

Bruno exhaled his frustration, then walked over to a nearby computer terminal and poked at the keyboard. After about thirty seconds, he came back. "The name doesn't look familiar," he said.

"I think she wants me," Jack said, glancing back in her direction.

"I've heard you say that about every female you've ever known," Bruno said, leaning sideways to take another look at the topic of discussion. "Besides, I think she wants *everybody*." He patted Jack on the back, then resumed his journey to the customer service section of the front counter, where there was a short line of guests waiting for assistance.

Jack headed for the elevator, following a route that avoided the hottie and the mental complications she presented. "See you at the luncheon," he said to Bruno, as he passed the line of guests. Bruno just raised and lowered his head to acknowledge the comment in a manner that wouldn't require him to take his fingers off the computer keyboard.

Jack removed his cell phone from his pocket and called Mollie. "How are you doing?" he said.

"I'm a little tired," Mollie said. "Jennifer's not going to the class lunch, so she invited me for lunch at her house. I think I'll stay with her for the day. You go ahead without me."

Jack camouflaged his disappointment with an artificial "okay." His mood degenerated further when he got to the ballroom, where the official luncheon was being set up. He had looked forward to introducing Mollie to the rest of his classmates, and now he wouldn't have her company as refuge from the awkward moments he knew would be forthcoming.

Jack entered the room where the reunion committee was busy setting up table decorations. The tables were evenly spaced, with a long table and podium in front of the "CHS Class of 1997" banner that was secured high on the wall. Sterling Whitehurst, atop a small step stool, and Victoria, who was holding a rope in one hand and a drink in the other, were among a group setting up decorations to welcome the participants. Jack's mind immediately went into prosecutor mode, and he headed directly toward Sterling.

"Can I talk with you for a minute, Sterling?" Jack said.

"I'm rather busy, Jack," Sterling said. "Can it wait?"

"No," Jack said.

Sterling crumpled his face and let out a sigh of inconvenience, as he climbed off the stool. "What do you want, McCall?"

Jack started walking toward a private area by the window and motioned for Sterling to follow him.

"You know your problem, McCall?" the irritated Mr. Whitehurst said, as the two men walked toward the window. "You can't just let things be. You're like Victoria's poodle—you grab onto someone's pants leg and growl and yap until someone finally has to swat you with a newspaper."

Jack stopped short of the window area and got into Sterling's face. "I'm not a poodle, Whitehurst," he said. "I'm a pit bull."

Sterling backed up.

"And this dog wants to know why you tried to convince my wife that I should stop asking questions about Annie."

Sterling pursed his lips and returned Jack's intimidation stare.

"And my second question," Jack said, "is to what lengths would you go to make sure I don't investigate her death?" Jack moved closer to his adversary, causing Sterling to start inching his way backward. "Would you try to scare me by putting a snake in my room, or blow up a golf cart?" He matched the movements of Sterling's slow retreat, step for step. "And if I didn't stop, would you try to kill me by putting poison in my coffee?"

Sterling backed away again. "You don't have any authority here, McCall," he said. "I don't have to answer your questions." He turned and walked out of the room.

Jack's mouth gave a hint of a smile as he congratulated himself on provoking a reaction from the suspect. Usually he could just flash his Department of Justice credentials and get people to talk. But Sterling was right. Here he had no authority, and the authorities here, in the form of Chief Kirby, didn't want him asking questions. But, having rattled Sterling's nerves, he wanted to see what the transplanted southern gentleman did next. Jack couldn't call Frank, who would just as soon throw him in jail for interfering with the investigation, so he called Peter.

"Peter," Jack said, moving to a remote part of the room for privacy. "Jack here. I need your help."

"What do you need?" Peter said.

"I just lit a fire under Sterling Whitehurst, and I need you to put someone on him to see how he reacts," Jack said.

"I already have agents watching all the people who were present during your coffee conversation the other day," Peter said.

"Oh," Jack said. "Well—good. I was going to suggest that anyway."

"Sure you were," Peter said with a chuckle.

Jack disconnected the call and slid his cell phone into his pocket just as Joshua Pitts walked into the room, carrying his camera.

"Smile, everyone," Pitts said. "You are about to become famous. A Joshua Pitts portrait is prized by the rich and famous all around the world." With that declaration, he started taking pictures of all present.

"Smile, Jack," he said, as he walked up to Jack, who wasn't smiling. "I know you've had a rough two days, but these pictures will be on the class website, so try to smile, at least a little."

Jack continued to frown at the annoying photographer.

"You and Sterling both seem to be in a mood today," Joshua said. "He just stormed through the hall like someone had peed on his favorite pair of shoes."

"He's upset because I am trying to find out what really happened the night Annie was killed," Jack said.

"Touchy subject," Joshua responded.

"Yes," Jack said, "Isn't it, though? I seem to recall that you and Annie were chummy in high school."

"Hardly chummy," the photographer said, looking Jack straight in the eye. "I took some pictures to illustrate a poetry book she was writing, but we didn't see each other socially." He turned and started toward another group that hadn't been photographed.

"Wait a second," Jack said, to stall Joshua's departure. He quickstepped to grab the photographer's arm. "Let me comb my hair and pose for a good picture." Jack wanted information, but his attempts to engage Sterling and Joshua in conversation about Annie weren't getting results. "Give me just a second," he said, gesturing for the photographer to stay put. He took his comb out of his back pocket and stepped toward a nearby column that had a mirror on one side. He gave his hair a quick swipe with his comb.

"How's that?" he asked Joshua, as he walked back to where the photographer was waiting.

"Fine," Joshua said. "I do take my work seriously."

"Then I'll look dead serious for you," Jack said, standing up a little straighter and tilting his head back in a pose suggesting a noble birthright. "You said that people all around the world coveted your work. Do you travel outside the US very much?"

"Occasionally," Joshua said, lifting the camera to his face. "But not very often compared to someone like Jessie Dalton. She travels all the time."

A bright flash momentarily blinded Jack as Joshua's camera went to work. Joshua half-turned as if ready to leave. Jack's artificial grin grew wider. "Take a couple more, will you?" he said, attempting to coax Joshua to stay. "You do such great work. I'd like to talk to you about doing a portrait for Mollie and me."

Joshua paused and looked down at his camera. "I don't think you can afford me," he said, turning back toward Jack. "But I'll take a few more of you now. Stand over by the window."

"So how do you know that Jessie travels out of the country a lot?" Jack said, as he moved toward the window.

"Didn't she tell you what she does?" Joshua said, aiming the camera and taking some more pictures of Jack.

"She said she was a secretary," Jack said.

"Hardly," Joshua said. "She is the executive assistant to P.D. Newhouse."

"The guy who writes all those travel books?" Jack said.

"Affirmative," the photographer said, taking aim for another shot.

A flash of light from Joshua's camera once again left Jack struggling to see. "Interesting," he said, as he blinked his eyes in an attempt to restore his vision. "So she probably follows him around on his trips then," he said, as Joshua turned to walk away again.

"It's my understanding that *she* does all the traveling and research," Joshua said, slowing his pace toward his next photo subject.

Jack again hurried to Joshua's side to keep him from escaping. "She's just as shy now as she was in high school," he said. "Doesn't seem the type to wander all over the world by herself."

Joshua stopped and leaned toward Jack. "Don't let that 'shy' routine fool you," he said, then patted Jack on the shoulder and disappeared into a huddle of classmates.

Jack stood in the middle of the room by himself. The implications of what Joshua had just told him, if true, meant that Jessie could be connected to both Annie's death and the work of Magellan, at least from an opportunity standpoint. But how did Joshua know so much about Jessie? He needed to find out more about both of them.

Bruno grabbed Jack's arm from behind and started to drag him toward a table near the front of the room. "Come on, Jack," he said, with a twinge of anxiety. "We need to get a good seat. This lunch should be fun."

Jack, somewhat startled by the big man, lost his balance for a moment and then fell in step with his host. Bruno looked back at him with a "why are you moving so slow?" look. The lovable giant was acting like a teenager sneaking off to look at his first *Playboy* magazine.

Jack figured that if anyone had more information about Sterling, Joshua, and Jessie, it would be Bruno. Bruno would share all he knew with Jack, without giving it a second thought. He didn't seem to look beyond the surface of Jack's questions, nor did he show concern about the consequences of sharing what he knew. The only exception was confidential information about guests at the inn. Even his friendship with Jack didn't seem to unlock that door.

"What's the big hurry?" Jack said, as the two men plopped down at an unoccupied table.

"Buxom Betty is going to be the emcee of this thing," Bruno said, with a huge grin. "I've been waiting to see her ever since her name showed up on the attendee list last year."

"Isn't she staying here at the inn?" Jack said.

"No," Bruno said. "She just got into town yesterday, and she's staying at her aunt's house. I even drove by last night to catch a glimpse of her."

"Hackett, you're pathetic," Jack said, mocking his friend's zeal. "You're worse now than you were in high school."

The big man turned toward Jack and blocked out the sun that was covering Jack's part of the table. "Look, Jack," he said, the smile now absent from his face, "my wife left me three years ago, and I've been in love with Betty Hendricks since the third grade—since before she grew breasts."

Jack looked away for a moment, searching for the right words to confess that he felt like a jerk for making fun of his friend. "Sorry, big guy," he said. "You never said anything about your wife leaving you. I should have asked you how you were doing, been a better friend."

"No," Bruno said, looking wistful. "You had no way of knowing. I try not to let it bother me, but . . . ." He paused for a moment, then waved his hand as if brushing away the bad memory.

Jack remained silent. He didn't know what to say, but his lawyer instincts told him that Bruno needed someone to listen.

"When Margie left me," Bruno said, "she said she was tired of living in the past. She never understood what this place means to me. My grandfather built the original building with his own hands. My dad expanded it and created the style and feel of the place. Who am I to change that?"

Jack patted Bruno on the back. "Must have been tough," he said.

"Yes," Bruno said, "it was demoralizing. But when I heard that Betty was coming to the reunion, I decided to get on with my life."

"I don't remember you drooling over her in high school," Jack said.

"When Betty hit puberty and turned into a living legend," Bruno confessed, "I just kind of gave up, ya know? I figured she would never go for a guy like me. She hung around with the country club crowd."

Bruno paused for a moment, then the smile reappeared on his face. "But Betty is back, and now I belong to the country club. This might be my chance to get her attention. Darren Smith is on the reunion committee, and he told me she registered as *single*."

"Okay," Jack said. "But if your goal is to get her attention, we'd better sit closer." With that comment, Jack rose and motioned for Bruno to follow. The two men walked past the entrance and grabbed their nametags on the way to a half-full table beside the podium. Jack patted the back of one of the chairs to prompt Bruno to sit down. It had a direct line of sight to the podium. Jack positioned his own chair so he could observe the rest of the room. Bruno fidgeted with the place setting and rattled the utensils while he searched the room for Betty.

After exchanging greetings with the other class members and spouses at the table, Jack leaned in and motioned for Bruno to do the same. "So what do you know about Jessie Dalton's professional life?" he said in a low voice.

"She's an admin type for a writer, from what I hear," Bruno responded in an equally low voice. "And like most admins, she does all the work and he gets all the credit."

"So she travels a lot, right?" Jack said.

Bruno raised his head and did an abrupt ninety-degree turn in his chair. "Oh, there she is."

"Jessie?" Jack responded.

"No, Betty," Bruno said, as his eyes glazed over and his large frame melted back into the chair.

Jack felt a hand on his left arm. He turned to find that a woman seated two chairs away from him had leaned way over and was staring at him.

"I couldn't help but overhear that you were asking about Jessie," the woman said.

Jack glanced at the woman's nametag. "Carol (Miller) Eagleton," it read. The name didn't sound familiar and neither did the picture on the tag, nor the live face before him.

"Carol," Jack said, pretending to recognize her. "Yes, I did ask about Jessie. Just eager for a little gossip about classmates."

Carol straightened up, slid over to the chair next to Jack, and then leaned over again to get even closer. "Well," she began, "I happened to be in the business center at the inn yesterday, changing my airline reservations, and I overheard her talking to someone about doing a job in some city in Spain. And she seemed quite familiar with how to make travel arrangements, so I suspect that the answer to your question is yes, she probably travels a lot."

"Thank you for sharing that information," Jack said. He paused for a second, trying to figure out how to disguise his motive for asking about Jessie. "Any other interesting gossip you want to pass along?" he said.

Carol looked around, to make sure no one was watching her, and then spent ten minutes recounting one information tidbit after another to a disinterested and impatient Jack McCall. The flow of irrelevant hearsay was finally interrupted by Jack's cell phone, buzzing and shaking in his pocket.

The caller ID on the phone read "Mollie." "Excuse me for a minute, Carol," Jack said. "I have to take this call. Thanks for the update."

Carol flashed an offended frown at the cell phone being raised to Jack's ear and shifted her posture upright, slid back to her own chair, and reentered the conversation to her left.

Jack headed for the hallway outside the room as he poked the "answer" icon on his smartphone. "What's up, Mollie?" he said. He turned and glanced at Bruno as he walked away from the table, checking for a "where are you going?" look. But Bruno was fixated on Betty, who was now issuing the formal welcome speech, so Jack continued out the door at a casual pace, to be as inconspicuous as possible.

"How's the luncheon going?" Mollie said.

"Typical stuff," Jack responded. "I was going to try to extract some info about Jessie and Joshua from Bruno, but he's off in la-la land, pining over one of our classmates."

"So what's your plan, McCall?" Mollie said.

"I need to find Peter," Jack said. "This may have started with Annie, but it's beginning to look like her death may be just the snow cone on top of a giant Slurpee of murders."

"Cute metaphor, McCall," Mollie said. "What the hell does it mean?"

Jack stopped at a deserted spot in the main hall outside the ballroom. "I'll tell you later," he said. "But right now I need you to do a little online research."

"I can do that," Mollie said.

"Are you still at Henry and Jennifer's place?" Jack said.

"Yes," Mollie said.

"Find out everything you can about Sterling Whitehurst, Joshua Pitts, and Jessie Dalton," Jack instructed.

"Okay," Mollie said.

"And if Henry's there, have him look over all the stuff you dig up," Jack continued. "Maybe the good doctor will spot something that doesn't look right. I'll be out after I visit with Peter."

"Who's Peter?" Mollie shouted into her phone, just as Jack moved his phone away from his ear and pushed the "end call" icon on the screen.

He heard Mollie's question as his finger touched the screen on the phone, but Jack decided not to call her back. He didn't want to take time to explain, so he made his way to the parking lot, hopped in the Mustang, and headed to the police station to find Peter.

When Jack arrived at the station, he took out his Department of Justice ID badge, attached it to his shirt, waited until two smokers finished their break, and then followed them in the side door. He wanted to talk to Peter, but he didn't want to talk to Frank Kirby. He got a few second looks from police personnel, but no one stopped him as he made his way to the office where Peter was working.

Peter was signing some documents when Jack opened the side door to the office and went in.

"Jack," Peter said, looking up from the stack of papers on the desk. "I haven't heard from the teams following the suspects yet, if that's what you're here for."

"Among other things, yes," Jack said. "This whole Magellan business hasn't helped me solve the puzzle I'm working on. Instead, it has given me two puzzles to work on simultaneously, which may or may not have common pieces."

Peter laid his pen down on the desk. "How can I help you?"

Jack sat down in the chair in front of the desk. "I have four questions I need to answer," he said. "One, was Annie's death an accident or a murder? Two, if it was murder, who killed her? Three, who tried to kill me? And four, is this Magellan character involved?"

Peter pursed his lips and tapped his fingers against the desk in a manner that Jack recognized, from their time as roommates, as an outward sign of his internal thought process.

"I have two questions to answer," Peter said, after a few moments. "One, is the attempt on your life the work of Magellan? And two, who is he here to kill, other than you?"

"How do you know he or she is here to kill someone?" Jack said. "Other than me?"

"Trust me," Peter said. "Magellan is here to kill someone other than you."

"It seems to me, then," Jack said, "that the first step in solving this convoluted equation, with all its variables, is to determine whether Magellan is one of the reunion participants. Is it safe to assume you are already working on that?"

Peter grabbed one of the documents on his desk and turned it around so Jack could read it. "This is a request for a court order," he said. "We are asking to search all travel-related records for every reunion participant, to see if one or more will correlate with the unsolved homicide cases we suspect were committed by Magellan."

Jack picked up the document and leafed through the attached list of classmates attending the reunion. "Check Whitehurst, Pitts, and Dalton first," he said. "That will speed up the resolution of my questions."

"Sounds like a plan," Peter said. "We should have some information by tomorrow. Be here first thing in the morning, and we can compare notes."

"What are you doing here, McCall?" a voice echoed from the hallway. Jack turned and looked through the office window that adjoined the hallway. He saw the back of Frank Kirby's head moving toward the office door. His index finger flew up to his lips to signal Peter to remain silent about their discussion.

"I thought I told you to check with me if you had any relevant input for the investigation," Frank said, as he entered the room.

Jack nodded. "And that is my intention, Chief," he said. "But Peter mentioned that he had some pictures of an old girlfriend of mine that he wanted to show me."

Frank looked at Peter.

"Yes," Peter said. "Her name is Laura." He reached into his coat, extracted a black leather wallet, and put it on the desk. "Jack and I had the hots for the same girl," he said, as he pulled out several pictures from his wallet and put them on the desk. "But she ended up marrying me."

Frank glared at Jack, then at Peter. "She chose you over Joe College here?" he said, pointing to Jack without looking at him. He picked up the top picture and studied it. "Pretty—and smart." He put the picture down on the desk and walked out of the office.

"Told you I had your back," Peter said to Jack, as he gathered the pictures and put them back in his wallet.

"Thanks," Jack said. He got up from his chair, walked toward the door, and then turned back toward Peter. "Speaking of Laura, whatever happened to Laura Dingman, that girl we both actually dated?"

Peter took the picture back out of his wallet and held it up. "I married her," he said. "You don't think I'd lie to a police chief, do you?"

Jack did a double take, then shook his head. "You sly devil," he said. "You told me she was going to marry that no-neck guy from the wrestling team after graduation."

"She did," Peter said. "But she divorced his ass two years later, then called me."

"Kids?' Jack said.

"One," Peter said.

"Well done," Jack said, giving a thumbs-up as he left the room.

The interior of the Mustang was an oven when Jack climbed in, so he opened the windows and headed for Henry's farm. The wind cooled the black upholstery and sent his mind flashing back to his youth: an image of riding in Bruno's convertible, wind in his hair and a Winston cigarette between his fingers. The boy in the image coughed and gagged on the cigarette, which made the man chuckle at the recollection. He had tried to be cool and act like a sophisticated urbanite, but his lungs had betrayed him. Good thing too, the man thought. Otherwise he might have actually taken up the nasty habit.

Upon reaching Henry's house, Jack headed for the back deck, where he suspected the intelligence-gathering team would be taking advantage of the shade and the cool afternoon breeze that was blowing in from the coast. Henry was alone on the deck, huddled over his laptop, and gave a startled twitch when Jack rounded the corner of the house.

"Damn, Jack," Henry said. "You might at least honk the horn or something to let us know you're here."

Jack laughed, taking pleasure in rattling his friend. "You always did have a tendency to retreat into your own world when you were studying," he said, as he moved a chair next to Henry and sat down. "Did Mollie find anything interesting?"

"Very interesting," Henry said, focusing back on his computer screen. "But Mollie didn't find it—I did. It appears that there might have been a connection between Mr. Whitehurst and Ms. Ridgeway after all."

Jack slid forward in his chair and leaned over to view the computer screen. "Whatcha got?" he said.

"It occurred to me that if Sterling didn't want an investigation," Henry said, "it might be that he didn't want anyone investigating her birth, not her death. So I used my medical clearance to access the county's medical database, to find the record of her birth."

"Is that legal?" Jack said.

The doctor turned his head and looked at Jack over the top rim of his reading glasses. "For me, yes."

"Whatever we find has to stand up in court if it leads anywhere," Jack said.

"Sometimes," the farmer responded, "you have to test the soil to find the best place to start digging."

Jack just rolled his eyes and shook his head. "Okay," he said. "What did you find?"

"The certificate lists Annie's father as Herman Alexander," Henry said.

"Wasn't he the butler at the Whitehurst estate?" Jack said.

"Yes," Henry said.

"He was some kind of war hero, wasn't he?" Jack said. "Can you check his medical records? Check his blood type to see if it fits with Annie's."

Henry took off his reading glasses and set them on the table. "It's one thing to look up a birth certificate, Jack. It's another to dig into someone's personal medical files. I will do everything

I can to help you get a court order," Henry continued. "But I won't access private medical records. Not sure I can, anyway."

Jack leaned back in his chair. "I understand," he said, but his body language and sad facial expression contradicted his words. He stared at Henry, trying to stimulate a lethal dose of guilt.

"Let's see if there's another way to find the information we need to solve this puzzle," Henry said, in apparent response to Jack's sorrowful face. "Maybe I can get Frank to help. Or what about your friend Peter, the FBI guy?"

"That's a possibility," Jack said. "I have a meeting set up with Peter in the morning, and you can talk to Frank. Then let's get together at The Shed for lunch to compare notes."

Henry rose from his chair. "Sounds like a plan."

Jack followed Henry into the house to find Mollie, and then, after some social banter, he and Mollie headed back to the inn. Jack was looking forward to a good night's sleep, and he suspected Mollie was as well. He didn't have all the answers yet, but he had a plan and a way forward, which always allowed him to sleep a little better.

CHAPTER 11

JACK AWOKE THE NEXT MORNING and hopped out of bed. Mollie was still motionless, so he did his best ninja walk to the bathroom and eased the door closed. A ten minute shower left him feeling sharp, focused, and determined to find answers to the mystery of Annie's parentage and her possible links to the Whitehurst family.

When he opened the bathroom door, Mollie was hugging her pillow with her eyes open, watching him. "How are you feeling?" he said.

"I feel better," she mumbled. "I think I'm going to live."

Jack smiled in response, then got dressed while Mollie inched her way out of bed and into the bathroom.

"I need you to work your magic on the computer this morning," Jack said, in a voice loud enough to be heard through the half-closed bathroom doorway. "We need to meet Henry and Jennifer at The Shed for lunch, and I want to have some answers before then."

Mollie poked her head out of the bathroom. "Am I going to land in jail for this?"

"Don't get caught," Jack said. "But if you do get caught, I'm a damned good lawyer, so I think I can get you off with a light sentence."

"Oh," Mollie said, "that makes me feel better. Give me a few minutes."

Jack took his laptop out of its carrying case. He powered it up and then connected the power cord, anticipating a long run time for the mission at hand.

Mollie exited the bathroom in her thin summer robe and walked over to the desk, ready to work her Internet magic.

"What are you staring at?" she said.

"I like the way you jiggle in that robe," he said.

"You'd get turned on by a pile of Jell-O under a napkin," she said, as she pushed him out of his chair and sat down on the warm seat. "What am I looking for?"

"Caldwell General Hospital's medical records for one Herman Alexander," Jack said.

Mollie leaned back in the chair and twisted around to stare at her husband. "I knew I was going to end up in jail," she said. "Do you know how much HIPAA cybersecurity they have around medical records these days?"

"Are you saying you can't get in?" Jack said, smiling in anticipation of the answer he knew was coming.

"Of course I can get in," Mollie said, as she turned around and began tapping on the keyboard.

Jack put his hands on her shoulders and then moved his right hand down to explore the cleavage exposed at the front of her robe.

"Stop it, you pervert," she said. "How do you expect me to load this penetration test program with you playing with my boobs?"

Jack's hand completely disappeared under the lapel of the garment. "You made the task sound so easy," he said. "I thought I'd throw in a pleasant distraction to make it—harder."

She slapped his arm, and his hand withdrew from its hiding place.

"So what's your plan to hack into this hillbilly hospital's database?" Jack said.

"You don't want to know," the cyber-sleuth said.

Mollie hit the "enter" key and swiveled her chair around toward Jack. She raised her right leg and braced her foot against his thigh.

"How much time do you have?" she said. She raised her foot higher on his leg, and the bottom flap of the robe slid off her leg, leaving the right side of her lower torso completely naked.

Jack's eyes opened wider.

"First I have to run a special script to look for common vulnerabilities on the subnetwork for the website computer," she said. She reached up and pulled the robe off her right shoulder, exposing her breast.

Jack smiled. "I hope there's more to this explanation."

"Then," Mollie continued, "I'll search the subsystems for any holes, like unpatched systems or unprotected files with security data." Her left hand reached out and pulled the bottom left portion of her robe up her left thigh. The excess material draped between her legs.

"Please continue," Jack said.

Mollie laughed. "Hopefully, I'll find something to give me root access or at least a login ID that I can use." She reached up and pushed the robe just far enough off her left shoulder that her left nipple was peeking out from the lapel of the robe.

Jack grabbed Mollie's ankles and spread her legs apart. "How much time do we have before that pentest program finishes?" he said, as he eased her feet down to the floor and lifted her up by the waist.

Mollie snuggled up to his chest. "You'll finish long before it does."

"What?" Jack said. He set her back down in the chair. "You certainly know how to inspire a guy."

"What do you mean?" she said. "It was an honest answer."

"You make it sound like I'm a fourteen-year-old virgin who fires off a volley while he's unzipping his pants," Jack said.

Mollie reached up and grabbed his pants at the belt buckle. "You're too sensitive for my own good," she said, pulling him toward her. "I don't care how long it lasts," she whispered into his mouth. "It's always the best."

Jack put his arms back around her and lifted her up again. She wrapped her arms and legs around his body and squeezed as she kissed him. His ego took a back seat to Mother Nature, and he matched her passion and aggression.

Just as Jack decided to take this moment of intimacy to the next level, his smartphone started beeping and vibrating across the surface of the desk. It was headed for the edge and an uncertain ending on the tile floor below the table. *"Damn,"* he said, and moved over to rescue the device, with Mollie still clinging to his torso. He grabbed the phone and turned off the alarm.

"What the hell was that about?" his wife said.

He held on to her even tighter, as he pivoted again to set the phone in a chair so it wouldn't move if the alarm went off again. "Damn," he said. "I have to meet Peter in fifteen minutes."

Mollie let her feet drop to the floor. "You owe me, McCall."

Jack nodded to acknowledge the debt and grabbed a shirt and the car keys on his way out the door. "Call me when you get something." He took the back stairs to get to his car and headed toward the police station, where Peter was expecting him.

Jack had only traveled ten blocks when the Bluetooth feature on the car stereo notified him of an incoming call. He looked at the display. It was Mollie, so he picked up.

"Do you know an 'R Meekam'?" Mollie said.

"No."

"How about 'B Smathers'?"

"No."

"'A Hamlin'?"

"Yes," Jack said. "He's one of the kids I grew up with, if 'A Hamlin' is Arthur Hamlin. Why do you ask?"

"Some lazy IT tech left copies of the VPN log files lying around," she said. "I was able to poach his user ID from them."

"Excellent work, Mrs. McCall," Jack said. "I'll cut my usual legal fees in half if you get caught."

"Very generous, Mr. McCall," Mollie said. "And I'll cut my usual fees in half if you want to get laid tonight."

"Sounds fair," Jack said. "At least I don't have to get naked to represent you in court."

"Enough," Mollie said. "I need to know more about your friend Arthur so I can figure out his password."

"Log into the class website and look at his bio," Jack said. "Maybe that will give you a clue."

"Okay," Mollie said, and disconnected the call.

Jack continued his journey to the police station, but he was soon following a small fleet of hay balers that he guessed were heading for a harvest cleanup assignment at a field north of town. His usual impatience with slow-moving vehicles was, in this case, tempered by the fact that he needed information that would connect Annie's death directly with Magellan, and he was counting on Mollie to find something in Herman Alexander's medical file that would be intriguing enough to provoke Peter to help him. The slow traffic would give her time to work her magic, so he squelched the urge to take off down a side street. Besides, there were enough new streets and structures that he figured he might get lost, and he didn't want to be too late or Peter might be gone.

The procession weaved its way through town, with Jack one of the few followers who didn't peel off and find another route to their destination. When the group reached the street where Jack had to turn to reach City Hall, Mollie still hadn't called, and Jack began to thump the steering wheel with his right hand to vent his anxiety. The thumping was interrupted by the need to turn, so he grasped the steering wheel and guided the Mustang onto the side street and into the City Hall parking lot.

Jack wanted to make his way to Peter's temporary office without sparking an interrogation session in the chief's office, so he parked the Mustang behind a dumpster at the back of the parking lot. He did a quick scan of the area and then got out of the car. No sooner had he stepped out of the car than his smartphone began to ring. So much for being stealthy. He retrieved the noisy device from his pocket and tapped its face to accept the call and silence the ring. It was Mollie.

"Tell me you found something," he said, while scanning the parking lot from behind the dumpster.

"*Something* is an understatement," Mollie said. "Alexander couldn't have been Annie's father," Mollie said. "He was in the Vietnam War, and his injuries left him impotent."

"Ouch," Jack said. "Why would he have been listed as the father?"

"I didn't find anything else in the records that might give a clue," Mollie said.

"Well, it's a cinch that Frank won't care," Jack said. "I need to get Peter and his FBI people curious. They have the resources to dig into this."

Jack paused for a moment and looked around for a low-profile path into the building. "Thanks, honey," he said. "We'll pick up where we left off when I get back to the inn."

He looked around once more and then headed toward the building via a covert route behind several large trucks. Once inside, he waited until the lobby was clear and Trina, the Goth gatekeeper, was distracted by filing chores that kept her looking in the opposite direction. He headed across the lobby to where Peter was working.

"I've got some interesting stuff," Jack said, as he entered the room where his friend's head was buried in a stack of documents.

Peter jerked his head up. "Damn, McCall. You could at least make a little noise as you enter the room."

"Sorry," Jack said, glancing back toward the lobby and closing the door.

"You're lucky I didn't draw my gun and shoot you," Peter said, turning his attention back to the papers on his desk.

"You invited me," Jack said. "Besides, think of all those forms you'd have to fill out if you shot me,"

"Good point," Peter said. "So, what's so interesting?"

Jack sat down in the oak chair in front of Peter's desk. He paused for a moment to plan how he was going to phrase his request. He had to explain how he had obtained the information Peter would need to get the answers Jack wanted.

"The girl who died twenty years ago . . . ," he began. "There are some significant incongruities in that investigation." Jack squirmed a little in his chair and looked out the window. "Plus, the person listed as her father on her birth certificate couldn't have been her father."

"And how is that relevant to me and my investigation of Magellan?" Peter said.

Jack put both feet on the floor and leaned forward toward Peter. "Because," he said, "current events that you attribute to Magellan appear to have been sparked by my investigation into Annie's death. And the lie I discovered on her birth certificate could have been a factor in her death."

"Weak," Peter said, without looking up from his pile of papers.

"The present and the past have to be linked," Jack said. "Why else would Magellan try to kill me?"

"Still weak," Peter said.

Jack got up from his chair and walked to the window. "You need to help me out here, Peter," he said, as he stared out the window.

Peter put down his pen, rose from his chair, and walked to the window. He put his hand on Jack's shoulder. "Jack," he said, "I am more than willing to give you the benefit of the doubt if you can get me close to a scenario that I can defend."

Jack nodded to acknowledge his friend's explanation.

"But no judge is going to give me a warrant to start digging into the personal lives of our three persons of interest, based solely on your belief that the death of your friend is connected to my ongoing investigation of Magellan," Peter said.

"Damn," Jack said, as he moved away from the window and started toward the door. "Any results on the travel patterns of Whitehurst, Pitts, and Dalton?"

"Yes," Peter said. "Each of them has traveled out of the country frequently, but we haven't finished comparing their travel destinations and dates to the suspected activity of Magellan. That should be completed in a couple of hours."

"Will you call me when you finish the analysis?" Jack said.

"Yes," Peter said.

"Thank you," Jack said, exiting the room.

When he reached his car, behind the dumpster, Jack grabbed his cell phone and called Mollie. "Another roadblock. Henry wouldn't bend the rules a little, and now Peter is giving me more of the same."

"Sounds like I'm the only shady character you know," Mollie said. "Come on back to the inn, and we'll see what else we can dig up."

Jack hopped in the car and headed back to the inn. When he arrived, he went up to the room via the back stairs, since there were bound to be classmates milling around the lobby, and he didn't want to get into a nostalgia-fest at that moment. Mollie was waiting in the room with the laptop hooked up to the portable printer, and she greeted him with a hug and a kiss when he entered.

"Let's start with Herman Alexander," he said, as he slid into the chair next to Mollie. "Check the newspaper records for anything on him."

Mollie weaved her way through the windows and lists from the *Caldwell Gazette*. The portable printer she had borrowed from Bruno periodically spit out a page or two.

Jack read each document as soon as it was ejected from the printer. "I'm disappointed in Peter," he said, as he completed a document and stacked it on top of the ones he had finished reading. "I thought he would see the connection between Annie's death and his current case, but he just said 'weak' to every point I made."

"Maybe it's obvious to you because you want them to be connected," Mollie said.

Jack mumbled and picked up another document from the printer. He wasn't getting much cooperation from the resources at hand. Frank wanted to lock him up, and Henry would only bend his ethics so far to help. Peter wanted hard evidence before he'd take any action, and even Mollie was playing devil's advocate in response to his conclusions.

Something on the page he was scanning caught his eye. "You're not going to believe this."

Mollie stopped typing. "What?" she said.

"When Whitehurst Senior died, Alexander received a significant bequest," Jack said.

"How significant?" Mollie said.

Jack finished his reading and then flashed a broad grin at his partner. "The old man left the dry cleaning business to Alexander. Now that is weird, bequeathing a valuable family asset to the hired help."

"What was the family's reaction?" Mollie said.

"They immediately bought it back from him, and he retired to Palm Springs," Jack said.

Mollie took the document from Jack's hands and began to read. "That is strange," she said.

Jack looked at his watch. "Time to head to The Shed," he said.

Mollie gathered the newspaper articles she had printed about the Whitehurst funeral and subsequent business transactions, and stuffed them into her purse. "You going to feed me sometime today?"

"No," Jack said. "You've got to condition yourself for what you'll encounter during your impending jail time for hacking into the hospital database."

"Thought you were going to help me beat that rap," Mollie said, as she exited the room.

"Always be prepared for the worst-case scenario," Jack said, closing the door as he entered the hallway.

******

Henry and Jennifer were just getting out of their car when Jack and Mollie arrived at The O'Toole Shed. They joined up on the wood-plank porch at the front of the building, and Jack pushed on the rustic wooden door at the entrance, holding it open so Mollie, Jennifer, and Henry could enter. The first thing he noticed was a noise meter on the wall by the front door. A sign next to the meter read "ENTER AT YOUR OWN RISK."

"What is that for?" Jack asked Henry.

"Spike got hit with a lawsuit from one of his frequent flyers who lost his hearing," Henry said. "He won the case but put this up as a deterrent to future claims."

The two couples found a suitable table as far away from the speaker system as possible, even though the decibel level was moderate. They exchanged small talk as they ordered their food. When the waiter departed for the kitchen, Jack took the newspaper articles out of Mollie's purse and set them on the table in front of Henry.

"Take a look at these," Jack said.

The waiter returned with a round of drinks while Henry was skimming over the material Jack had given him. "Help me understand their relevance."

"Simple," Jack said. "Herman Alexander was impotent, so he couldn't have been Annie's father."

"And you know this how?" Henry said.

"You don't want to know," Jack said. "But trust me. It's true."

"And how does the Alexander bequest described in these stories relate to your message from the spirit world informing you that Alexander wasn't her father?" Henry said.

Jack sucked on the straw rising from the bottom of his glass of Diet Coke. "What if . . . ," he said, dribbling some soda on the table in his haste to answer, "what if old man Whitehurst was the father and used the bequest to pay Alexander so he'd take the rap for getting Annie's mom pregnant?"

"That would make Sterling Annie's half-brother," Henry said. "And it would be a reason for Sterling to stifle any inquiries into Annie's past."

"Exactly," Jack said.

"But the question remains," Mollie interjected, "is a family secret like that motive enough for murder? And Sterling would have to have known that Annie was his half-sister for that to be a motive."

"Do you suppose Annie found out that old man Whitehurst was her dad, and was going to blackmail the Whitehursts after she graduated?" Jack said. "She could have been planning to take the money and leave town to start a new life somewhere else. She did say that she had just figured out a way to pay for college."

Henry stared at Jack. "When did she say that?"

"It was in a letter that her mother kept," Jack said. "Frank showed it to me. Blackmail is a strong motive."

Mollie shook her head. "Sterling's such a wimp," she said, contradicting the notion that anything would provoke him. "He'd have to ask Victoria for permission to kill someone."

Henry nodded in agreement and siphoned some more Diet Coke while pondering the conundrum.

Jennifer took out her iPad and hit the power button.

She typed out a message:

Haven't you ever heard of The Scarlet Pimpernel?

"Of course," Mollie said.

Jack looked at Henry, whose leathery face was contorted, as if he were having difficulty trying to extrude a thought.

Jennifer continued to type:

He was a literary British nobleman, who pretended to be a foppish airhead to hide the fact that he was an accomplished swordsman and who rescued French noblemen from the guillotine.

"He certainly plays the airhead part well," Mollie said.

"He wasn't stupid in high school," Henry said. "He got good grades and was offered scholarships to some pretty good schools."

"So he could be a psycho killer pulling a 'Scarlet Pimp' act to fool everyone," Mollie said, which elicited an attempted laugh from Jennifer.

"And why has he stayed away until now?" Henry added. He looked at Jack. "When your mom moved back east to be near you, it was understandable that you might not have reasons to come back to Caldwell. But Sterling has always had family here, and he only came back to Caldwell for his father's funeral.

"Strange," Jack said. "Why would he leave a comfortable life behind him?"

"He landed a pretty good deal in Louisiana," Henry said.

"True," Jack said, "But considering the worth of his family holdings here, you would think he would at least stay connected.

It sounds more like he was driven away by some extraordinary event."

Jennifer put her hands back on the keyboard:

Were Annie's crash and Sterling's departure the result of a common extraordinary event?

"Good question," Jack said, "but Frank will just laugh it off, and I know what Peter is going to say if I present him with our theory."

"Weak?" Mollie said.

"You got it," Jack said.

"But you don't have a motive for either Pitts or Dalton, do you?" Mollie said. "The only thing that connects them to Annie's death is the fact that they knew we were going flying the other day. And they both made comments to discourage you from asking questions. So, one of them could have been the person who spiked my coffee with that deadly South American Kool-Aid."

As Mollie finished her thought, the waiter showed up and dealt out the entrées. Conversation temporarily turned to an assessment of culinary artistry, while the team began to ingest their food and digest the facts they had uncovered.

"So let's assume that Sterling is a wimp and didn't kill Annie," Jack said, breaking the silence. "Our next step would be to find a motive for Joshua or Jessie to have killed her." His dining companions nodded and kept chewing. "We know that neither Jessie nor Joshua wanted me to investigate Annie's death, right?" The detective team mumbled agreement. "And both had knowledge of our sightseeing flight and probably had opportunity to spike our coffee. And both travel a great deal, which means either one could be the international hit man that Peter is looking for."

"Apparently," Henry said, between bites.

"Does Whitehurst travel internationally?" Mollie said.

"Yes," Jack said. "Peter is in the process of comparing their past trips to the work of Magellan."

"Why don't we just wait for him to finish?" Henry said. "Won't that tell us who the killer is?"

182

"Not necessarily," Jack said. "Even if one of them is Magellan, it doesn't automatically follow that Magellan was responsible for killing Annie, so *we* need to focus on Annie's death and let Peter focus on Magellan."

"Makes sense to me," Henry said. "What's next?"

Jack grabbed the stack of newspaper articles on the corner of the table and shuffled through them. "Here," he said, handing several to Henry. "See if you can find something in these articles that I missed."

"I'll work on Jessie," Mollie said. "She opened up to me once already, so I'll dig a little deeper."

Jack glared at his wife. "I don't want you in the line of fire again," he said.

"I'm probably the only person in this burg who can get close to her without setting off an alarm," Mollie said in rebuttal.

Jack ruminated for a moment on her plan. "Okay," he said, "but if you get even a hint that she might be involved, you back off. I'll see what I can dig up on Pitts. We will meet up at the reunion dinner tonight and fill in as many pieces of this puzzle as we can. Peter should have the travel information completed on Magellan by then."

Henry put on his sunglasses. "I can do more than just read through newspaper articles, you know," he said, as he rose from the table.

"I know you can," Jack said, "but considering the potential for danger, I will feel better if the three of you stay in the background."

The team paid for lunch and then headed out to work on their respective assignments.

Jack and Mollie slid into the seats of the Mustang, and Jack hit the switch to put the top down. "Call Jessie and make a date for cocktails prior to dinner tonight," Jack said, as the convertible top settled into place behind the back seat. "A little alcohol might lower some of the barriers between her brain and her mouth."

"I'll bet your next paycheck that she's not a killer," Mollie said.

Jack put the car in gear and pulled out on Highway 99, heading for the inn. "I hope you're right," he said.

The two sleuths rode in silence back to the inn. Jack stopped the car at the front entrance and gave his wife a kiss as she got out and headed into the building. He watched her as she walked away. He liked the way she walked. He was tempted to park the car and follow her upstairs. A vision of her walking toward him in her thin robe that morning flashed into his brain. The urge to follow her got stronger. As she disappeared into the lobby, he put the car in gear and cranked the steering wheel sharply to the left. He needed to find the nearest parking spot.

The car jolted as Jack headed down the nearest section of the lot, scanning for an empty space as he went. Finding nowhere to park in the first row, he circled the landscaped island at the end of the row and started down the next section. He saw something odd about halfway down the row of cars, so he slowed the Mustang to a crawl. Behind one of the cars, sitting on the pavement, were what looked like travel cases for some kind of equipment, and a tripod. The trunk of the car was open. *That has to be Joshua Pitts's camera gear. But the reunion function scheduled for the evening was at the inn. Why would he be loading his camera gear into a car at this time of day?*

Since it was Jack's responsibility to investigate Pitts as a possible suspect, he circled the car around to the next row and parked where he could watch the car with the camera gear. With the engine off, he slouched down in his seat and waited to see what would happen.

He hadn't waited long before someone he recognized walked up to the car, carrying another travel case. But it wasn't Pitts; it was Blondie.

He felt a sense of disappointment that he wasn't going to be able to follow Pitts. At the same time, he felt some relief that he wasn't going to have to explain to Mollie why he kept bumping into Blondie at odd moments. He watched her load all the baggage into her car and head out to the highway. *Thank God, one less issue to deal with.*

Jack opened the car door and stepped out. At that moment, he saw Joshua Pitts walk out of the building. He ducked down so Pitts wouldn't see him. Pitts walked to a car parked two rows away and got in. Jack decided to follow him. Pitts was in a white mid-size rental car, so Jack figured the rental car couldn't outrun the Mustang, if he spotted Jack following him. The sporty black Mustang, however, stuck out like a sore thumb cruising down the street. He had to stay far enough behind Pitts to avoid detection.

Pitts pulled out of the parking lot and headed toward the center of town, with Jack following five cars back. Jack wasn't particularly practiced or skilled at tailing suspects, but he had been on enough ride-alongs with the FBI that he knew the basics, the first of which was to use an inconspicuous vehicle. The Mustang violated that rule, but he didn't have a choice. Pitts didn't seem to be in a hurry, so Jack stayed well back and kept an eye on traffic to make sure he didn't get boxed in or unable to change lanes quickly, if needed. The white rental car made several unhurried turns, using proper turn signals, and even slowed to allow another vehicle to merge. If Pitts suspected Jack was following him, he wasn't showing any panic about it.

Pitts made a right turn onto a one-way street and mingled with a string of vehicles headed toward the Caldwell Mall. The herd slowed somewhat and then stopped at a stoplight. Pitts was about a half block ahead of Jack, in the right lane. When the light turned green, Pitts went straight ahead at the intersection, but the cars between him and the Mustang all turned right, leaving no buffer zone between Jack and Pitts. Jack couldn't remember a rule for what to do in this situation, so he slowed to a cautious pace and tried not to get too close to Pitts. The white rental car made a right turn onto a four-lane, two-way street, but when Jack turned right to follow, there were still no cars between him and Pitts. Pitts signaled and moved over one lane to his left. There was another vehicle in that lane, so Jack waited a moment and then pulled in behind the other car. *Finally, some cover. Maybe he hasn't noticed me.*

Jack's cell phone rang, and a second later it rang through the Bluetooth connection on the car stereo system. *Not now.* He looked at the screen on the car stereo; it read "FBI." *Shit.* He pressed the phone button on the stereo to pick up the call. "McCall," he said.

"What the hell do you think you're doing?" Peter's voice boomed through the car sound system.

"What?" Jack said. "Peter? How did you get my number?"

"What are you doing tailing Pitts?" Peter said.

"How did you know I was tailing Pitts?" Jack said, looking in his mirrors as if he might see Peter's face in a nearby car. Jack glanced ahead to make sure Pitts hadn't changed lanes. He saw red railroad crossing lights start to flash. "Hold on," he said. "Pitts is stopping at a rail crossing."

"I know," Peter said.

Pitts's car stopped right in front of the crossing barrier that pivoted down from the right side of the street. There was a car between Jack and Pitts, so Jack hoped that Pitts didn't see him. He heard the train horn sounding, but his view of the track to his right was blocked by a large industrial warehouse that adjoined the track, and there was no train to his left.

"I have two cars tailing Pitts," Peter said. "And they spotted you the second you pulled out of the parking lot at the inn."

Jack looked back at Pitts's car. The brake lights went off, and the tires began to spin and smoke as the white sedan jumped forward, weaved around the crossing barriers, and disappeared behind the train engine that emerged from behind the warehouse.

"Damn," Jack said. "Peter, he spotted me. He dodged the barrier just in front of the train, and he's gone."

"Nice work," Peter's sarcastic voice blared from the car speakers. "Leave it to an attorney to screw up an investigation."

Jack sat helpless in the Mustang. "What do we do now?" he said, as he sat watching boxcars and lumber cars creep across the intersection.

"Come back to the police station," Peter said, "We've got a few more pieces to the puzzle. We have reason to believe Pitts is Magellan."

"I'll be there as soon as the train passes," Jack said. He pushed the "disconnect" button on the steering wheel, ending the call. He couldn't go anywhere, so he called Mollie. "Peter thinks Pitts is Magellan," he told her. "Which means he probably was the one who tried to kill us, but I'm not sure that means he killed Annie."

"So what do you want me to do?" she said.

"Keep your date with Jessie, and see what you can coax out of her," Jack said.

"Okay," Mollie said, then hung up.

Jack went through everything again in his mind, trying to connect all the dots. If Pitts was Magellan, why would he try to kill Mollie and Jack? And did Pitts put the snake in his chest of drawers? And blow up the golf cart? Even if Peter had figured out the "who" of this puzzle, Jack still didn't know the "why." And he needed to connect current events to Annie's death.

Jack put the car in gear as the last train car passed through the intersection and the crossing barriers lifted. He headed toward the police station and called Henry from the car as he drove. "Henry, this is Jack," he said. "I've got an update for you."

"What do you have?" Henry said.

"The FBI thinks that Pitts is Magellan," Jack said, "which means he was the one who tried to kill me and Mollie with the nerve agent from South America. But that doesn't directly tie him to Annie's death."

Henry didn't respond immediately.

"You still there?" Jack said.

"What if Annie's death really was an accident?" Henry said.

"My gut tells me that it wasn't," Jack said, as he stepped on the accelerator to beat a red light.

"Your gut tells you," Henry said, "or your guilt tells you."

"Why else would Pitts try to kill me?" Jack said. The tires on the Mustang screeched as it drifted around a corner.

"Do you still want me to investigate Whitehurst?" Henry said.

"Yes," Jack said. "There's a remote chance that I'm wrong, and we can't afford a delay if we hit a dead end on Pitts. If Pitts didn't kill Annie, we can let the FBI deal with him, but they're not going to investigate Annie's death, even if Pitts did kill her. It's up to us to find out if and why Annie was murdered."

"I'll call you in one hour," Henry said.

Jack pushed down on the accelerator in the Mustang and hastened his travel to the police station. He could feel the adrenaline affecting his muscles and his mind. Finally he had something concrete to work with. It was only a small ray of sunlight peeking through the clouds that had hovered over his conscience for decades, but it was his best hope to be free of the guilt that tainted his life. He pushed down even harder on the accelerator.

The Mustang jumped the corner of the curb as it turned into the police station parking lot. It bounced up and down several times, then jolted to a stop when Jack hit the brakes. In a flash, Jack was out of the car and halfway to the back door of the station. When he reached the door, he grabbed the handle and pulled. The door didn't budge. It was locked, and he didn't have the access code, so he sprinted around to the front entrance and ran past Trina, the receptionist.

"They're expecting you in the conference room, Mr. McCall," Trina shouted, as Jack passed by.

Jack's shoes slipped and made a screeching sound as he changed direction and headed down a side hall. He saw Peter, Kate, and Frank through the conference room picture window adjoining the hall as he approached the doorway at the far corner of the room. They saw him. They weren't smiling.

"I thought I told you to leave the investigation to me," Frank said, as Jack entered the room.

"And you screwed up our tail on Pitts," Peter said, raising his hands in the air as if surrendering to Jack's incompetence.

Kate just gave him a half grin, and a slightly-tilted-head expression that Jack interpreted as a "what did you expect?" comment. Kate was seated at the conference table, which was strewn with papers and a few pictures. "Over here, McCall," she said, inviting Jack to view the display from her side of the table. "I'll go over the new information we have."

Frank mumbled a few words, then walked over to the window and lit a cigarette.

"Isn't that against the law?" Kate said, flashing a disapproving stare at the chief.

"So, who's going to arrest me?" Frank said, then opened the window and exhaled the smoke in the direction of a nearby tree.

Peter grabbed a pile of documents and passed it to Jack. "Here's the travel itinerary report we received. As you can see, Pitts is the only one who comes close to matching up with the assassinations we have attributed to Magellan."

Jack examined the list. "But his itinerary only aligns with seventy percent of the killings," Jack said.

"True," Kate said, "but Dalton only matches up with five percent, and Whitehurst doesn't match up with any."

"Seventy percent was enough to get us a warrant," Peter said, taking the travel report from Jack's hands. "We've got a team heading for Pitts's condo in Chicago now. We should hear from them sometime tonight."

Frank dropped his cigarette into a half-full coffee cup, creating a hissing sound and a small burst of steam. "And if Pitts shows up anywhere in the state, we'll pick him up—and lock him up."

Peter's cell phone rang. "Wilder," he said. The agent picked up a pen off the conference table and wrote some notes on a pad of paper. "Okay, check the flights out of Portland and see if he's booked on any of them."

Peter tapped the face of his smartphone to disconnect the call and then stowed it in his pocket. "Pitts turned in his rental car at the local Enterprise lot about twenty minutes ago," he said.

"That's odd," Jack said. "If he's an international assassin on the run, why would he bother to turn in his rental car? Why not just abandon it somewhere remote?"

Kate took off her glasses and put them on the table. "Did the rental agent see anyone pick him up?" she said.

"Yes," Peter said. "The agent said that Pitts walked out the door and stood at the curb in front of the lot, trying to hitch a ride."

"So who picked him up?" Jack said.

"A West Coast Freight tractor-trailer rig picked him up and headed north," Peter said.

"I'll find him," Frank said. "There can't be that many West Coast trucks on I-5 or Highway 99. I'm going to get the county sheriff and the state troopers to set up roadblocks." He walked out of the room and headed down the hall, shouting orders to unseen personnel in distant workspaces.

"I still think he came here for a contract hit," Peter said. "And I don't think he's going to leave until he's done the deed." He picked up his phone again and poked at the screen.

Jack sat down in the side chair by Peter's desk. He could hear the ringtone from Peter's phone as the agent raised it to his ear. His brain was starting to slow down to a pace that helped him concentrate on the big picture.

A voice mumbled a response to Peter's call.

"Bob," Peter said. "The Oregon State Police are going to initiate a BOLO on a West Coast Freight semi that might be carrying Joshua Pitts."

Peter paused while Bob rattled off a comment.

"Yes," Peter continued, "looks like he may be our guy. Call the OSP and give them all the details so they don't underestimate the danger."

Jack rose out of his chair and headed out the door.

"Where you goin'?" Kate said, as Jack passed by her chair.

Peter disconnected his call to Bob and repeated the question. "Where are you going, McCall?"

Jack stopped at the door and turned to face the inquiring minds of the FBI. "You think Pitts is here to kill someone," he said. "Right?"

Both Kate and Peter nodded their heads.

"Well," Jack said, "I'm willing to bet that the West Coast truck is a red herring and that his target has something to do with the reunion. The dinner-dance is tonight. So I'm betting that he is going to be at, or near, the inn tonight."

"Do you think he's that stupid?" Peter said.

"I think he's that smart," Jack said, and turned to walk out the door.

"Wait," Peter said, prompting Jack to stop again. "What are you going to do if he *is* there, ask him to dance?"

A short chuckle from Jack's mouth evolved into fully committed laughter. The question caused him to pause, and the laughter allowed him to think of a response. "Maybe you should tag along," he said, looking in Peter's direction.

Peter crumpled up his face and shook his head. "No way."

Jack looked at Peter's rumpled suit and the half-completed knot on his tie, which tried in vain to cover the unbuttoned collar of his shirt. "Maybe not."

"But someone should be there to keep a watchful eye on things," Peter said. His eyes wandered around the room, and his gaze landed on Kate. "Did you bring a prom dress with you, Agent Simpson?"

Kate snapped her head around and glared at him. "You're kidding," she said.

Peter just smiled at her.

"Why me?" she said. "There are plenty of local law enforcement people that can go dancing."

"I want someone there," Peter said, shaking his head, "and I want someone who Pitts won't recognize."

"Get her a dress and a date, McCall," Peter said.

"How am I supposed to get her a date?" Jack complained. "I haven't lived here in twenty years, and I have no idea who's in town as a single."

Peter walked to the door and got in Jack's face. "Then find someone who does know."

"You guys are nuts," Kate said, flapping her arms in disgust.

Jack took out his cell phone and poked at the face. "Hackett," he said. "I have a friend in town, and she needs a date for the dance tonight. Any guys attending the dance alone?" He listened for a moment. "No, not him," he responded to Bruno's first offering. "No," he said to the second. "Hell, no," he said to the third. Finally, he nodded up and down and a broad grin flashed onto his face. "Excellent," he said. "Set it up, and don't let him say no." He tapped the face of his phone and stuffed it back into his pocket.

By this time, Kate was red faced and flinging obscene gestures in Jack's direction. "You can just forget it," she said to the collective group of matchmakers.

"You're going," Peter insisted.

Jack ignored her complaints and directed a quick text message to Jennifer Coleman, asking for her assistance in finding a suitable dress for the protesting federal agent. "You'll have fun," he said, after he finished his message. "Jenny Coleman is going to meet you at Macy's, at the mall, to make sure they give you good service."

Kate walked up to Jack and looked him in the eye. "If Pitts shows up and people start shooting, a stray bullet just might end up in your ass."

She started to walk out the door and then stopped and looked back at Jack. "So who'd you find to be my date?" she said. "Some bozo with no teeth?"

The broad grin returned to Jack's face. "Oh, he has teeth," he said. "You're going with Dakota Douglas."

Kate's glare turned to laser beams as her jaw dropped. "*The* Dakota Douglas?" she said.

Jack nodded.

"Oh, no," she said. "I'm not going to spend the evening with an over-inflated ego with capped teeth."

Jack took Kate's arm. "This should be fun," he said, as he led her out the door.

CHAPTER 12

MUSIC WAS BLARING from an expansive sound system when Jack and Mollie entered the ballroom at the inn. The party was well in progress, and the room was three-quarters full. All three of the portable bars set up around the room were ten deep with eager consumers.

Jack scanned the crowd in an attempt to identify groups to avoid. The anxiety that had kept him on the other side of the country for so long was welling up from his stomach. He began to feel trapped.

Mollie snuggled up to his side. "Buy me a drink, big boy," she said. She took his hand and moved forward into the room.

Jack followed at arm's length and continued to scan the room. When his gaze settled back on his wife, he was almost startled by how beautiful she looked. For a moment, her long red hair and the trim white floor-length dress that hugged the shape of her body caused him to forget where he was. Then he realized that he wasn't the only man in the room staring at her. Even some of the women were watching. He tightened his grip on her hand and eased her back to his side as they walked.

A flash of light hit the right side of Jack's face. In the millisecond it took for his brain to realize that it was a photo flash, his hand dove under his coat lapel and settled onto the 9 mm pistol hugging his left side. *Pitts.* The name flashed through his mind as bright as the photo flash that triggered his reaction. He turned and saw an unfamiliar face appear from behind a camera. The pistol, which instinct had extracted from its holster, settled back in place. Jack's hand rubbed against his side, as if he were attending to a mild muscle irritation. He hoped no one had noticed his reaction.

It was Mollie's turn to tighten her grip on his hand. "Easy, Jack," she said, caressing his bicep. "Our felonious photographer is probably a hundred miles away by now."

"Don't bet on it," Jack said, continuing his journey toward the nearest bar. He once again scanned the room as he walked. Most of the "beautiful people" from high school were there. Time blurred the memory of his aspirations to be one of them. Now that he probably qualified, from a money and power standpoint, he struggled to recall why his longing for acceptance by this crowd had been so strong. The longing had dissolved into apathy. Now the "beautiful people" were just people.

"Heard you had an interesting afternoon," Henry said, as he stepped out of a crowd with Jennifer in tow. "Frank's temper was still percolating when I arrived."

Jack put his unencumbered arm around Henry's shoulders and gave him a squeeze.

"Easy, Jack," Henry said. "Does Frank know you're packing a pistol around town?"

Jack reached under his coat and adjusted the holster. "Like you said, it's been an interesting afternoon."

Mollie took Jennifer's hand and then tipped her head toward the bar. "Let's get some refreshments," she said. Jennifer smiled to accept the invitation and fell in step with Mollie.

"Did Frank fill you in on everything?" Jack said.

Henry nodded. "You don't think Pitts will show his face here, do you?"

Jack didn't answer. Once more he scanned the crowd, but now anxiety about the past was replaced with anticipation of the future, and his eyes were searching for the unexpected instead of the unwanted.

A rumble of voices bubbled up from the entrance area, and almost half of the people in the room turned and moved toward the commotion. The number of camera flashes tripled as the din of voices grew louder.

"Who is that?" Henry said, as he grabbed Jack's arm and turned him back to face the main entrance.

A smile erupted from Jack's face. "That, my dear doctor, is the FBI."

Dakota Douglas was walking into the room—all eyes turning to watch. The movie star arrived with a transformed

Kate Simpson on his arm. The crisp and neat FBI agent wore a soft floor-length pale-orange dress, a modest string of pearls around her neck. Her blonde hair brushed across her shoulders as she turned her head from side to side, smiling at people who were greeting her escort. The couple ended their grand entrance at the bar, where Jennifer and Mollie were waiting in line.

Jack moved toward the bar and motioned for Henry to follow.

"Who's your guest?" Jack asked Dakota Douglas, as he walked up to the crowd that hovered around the celebrity. Kate's eyes were shooting darts at Jack, but her mouth managed to maintain its obligatory smile.

"Jack," Dakota said, shaking his classmate's hand. "Good to see you again. And Henry."

"Dakota," Henry said, returning the greeting.

The movie star pulled Jack aside. "My date—you know, the one you and Hackett conned me into bring to this event—she has a gun under her dress!"

Jack laughed.

"I'm not kidding," the actor continued. "She showed it to me."

Jack forced a serious look onto his face.

"It's in a holster, strapped to her right leg," Dakota said, patting his right rear pocket. "Almost up to her butt cheek."

Jack wrinkled his face in order to look even more serious. "You mean she showed you her bare leg all the way up to her butt cheek?"

"Yes," Dakota said. "And then she said she was an expert in self-defense and could render a man impotent for life without leaving a scar."

Jack turned his head to hide the laughter-induced contortions erupting onto his face.

"It's not funny," Dakota said. "This woman could hurt me."

Jack took several deep breaths and then turned back to the frightened actor. "She could also save your life," he said. He grabbed the actor and coaxed him back to the side of his date.

Kate still had the plastic grin on her face as she took Dakota by the arm and dragged him up to the bar.

"Who's the bimbo with Dakota Douglas?" an already inebriated Victoria Whitehurst shouted, from behind a huddle of men.

Jack waited a moment until the wobbly southern belle peered out from the crowd. He shrugged his shoulders, wanting to maintain at least a modest amount of anonymity for the unhappy undercover FBI agent.

"Probably some guard dog from the studio," Victoria said, "here to make sure he doesn't back out of his next picture."

"Now, Victoria," Sterling said, stepping out of the group and taking her by the arm. "Sharing tabloid gossip isn't polite, even at a reunion."

"Well, it's probably true," Victoria insisted, tugging to escape her husband's grasp. "He backed out of the last one, and it cost 'em a bundle."

The noise level in the room once again spiked, but the cameras weren't quite as active. The crowd near the main door parted, and Stewart Ramsey strolled into the room like a king reviewing his court. He was followed by a much taller grey-haired man in a black suit.

Henry leaned closer to Jack. "In case you don't recognize him," Henry said, "that's US Senator Bob Mason."

"I thought he wasn't showing up until tomorrow," Jack said.

The senator and the candidate started working the crowd, on their way to one of the bars at the back of the room. Jack watched until Sterling and Victoria approached the campaign procession. He motioned for Henry to follow him and then headed for the gathering.

"Introduce me to the senator, Stewart," Jack said, injecting himself into the group. He put one hand on Stewart's shoulder and extended the other to greet the senator.

"Certainly, Jack," Stewart responded. "Senator Mason, I'd like you to meet United States Attorney Jack McCall."

The senator's grip was tight on Jack's hand as the two men exchanged greetings. "Do you work out of the Eugene office or the Portland office?" the senator said.

"Out of the Hartford office, Senator," Jack said. "I haven't been back to Caldwell since I left for college on the East Coast."

"You'll have to excuse us, Jack," Stewart said, as he tugged at the senator's arm to coax him toward another group. "The senator and I don't have much time, and we need to meet with as many local voters as possible."

"I thought your big campaign launch was tomorrow," Jack said.

Stewart stopped and leaned back toward Jack. "Frank told me that the FBI wanted to cancel the senator's appearance because of the attempts on your life and the possible connection to some hired killer."

"Sounds reasonable," Jack said.

"The senator and I insisted that he participate, but the FBI made us change the schedule to reduce the predictability of the event," Stewart said. "So we're doing the campaign announcement tonight, and the senator is going to leave immediately afterward."

Jack began a slow nod of the head as he contemplated the schedule change and its impact on the current situation. He watched as Stewart and the senator moved from group to group, shaking hands and discussing politics.

Henry interrupted Jack's thought process by handing him a diet soda. "What do you think?" he said.

"What do I think?" Jack said. "I think that when the senator leaves, Peter is going to pack up and leave Caldwell faster than a boy beagle after a bitch." He took a big gulp of soda, then threw the plastic cup and the remainder of the drink in the general direction of a nearby trash can. The container, and most of the drink, didn't find their mark.

"Hackett isn't going to be happy about you trashing his carpet," Henry pointed out to the disgruntled lawyer.

Jack stared at the cup on the floor and then looked around the room. He spotted Bruno, with Betty Hendricks on his arm, at a small gathering near one of the bars. Bruno looked in his direction and shook his head in disapproval, but he was smiling as he did so. The proprietor motioned for an attendant to clean up the spill, then turned his attention back to his companion and the rest of the group.

"What's up with Bruno?" Jack asked Henry.

"He's in love, you dunce," Henry said.

A man wearing a white wait-staff jacket arrived on site to clean up Jack's mess. The man leaned over and began soaking up the spilled soda, using a white bar towel. When he rose up, Jack caught sight of a shoulder holster and handgun through a gap in the coat. Jack's eyes darted around the room to find Frank Kirby. He spotted the policeman and walked over to him with as much casual demeanor as he could affect, considering what he'd seen. He grabbed Frank by the arm.

"The waiter over there cleaning up the spill has a gun," Jack said in a quiet voice.

Frank looked in the direction of the culprit, then back at Jack. "He's supposed to have one. He's a state trooper."

"Yes," Jack said, trying to sound unsurprised. "That makes sense." He looked around the room. "How many of the staff are undercover officers?"

Frank didn't answer. He just grinned, in a manner that Jack interpreted as the policeman enjoying Jack's anxiety. Frustrated, Jack looked around for Kate Simpson and spotted her on the dance floor with her date. He walked over to Mollie and took her hand.

"Excuse us for a few minutes, Jennifer," Jack said, as he coaxed Mollie toward the dance floor. "I feel the need to dance."

Mollie followed, and the couple made a gradual circle around the dance floor, ending up next to the movie star and the FBI agent.

"Dakota, this is my wife, Mollie," Jack said. He took Mollie's hand and put it on Dakota's arm. "She's just dyin' to dance with you." He took Kate's hand off the actor's shoulder and pulled her away, requiring the befuddled actor to resume the dance with Mollie.

"What the hell are you doing?" Kate said, as she assumed the dance position with Jack and moved away from the group.

"How many law officers are here tonight?" Jack said. "And why didn't you and Peter tell me this event was going to be heavily guarded?"

Kate looked around and flashed her plastic smile at a couple as they strolled by. "Your friend the police chief didn't tell *us*, either," she said, after the couple was out of hearing range.

"Okay," Jack said. He stopped dancing and moved his head closer to Kate. "Did you know that Bob Mason was going to be here tonight instead of tomorrow?"

Kate nudged him to start dancing again, but Jack didn't move.

"Of course we knew," Kate said, as she continued to coax him into motion. "Changing the schedule is standard operating procedure when we can't convince one of these congressional clowns to give up a high-risk public appearance."

Jack started to move again. "And what happens if Pitts doesn't show up tonight?"

"You'll have to ask Peter," Kate said.

Jack picked up the dance pace and moved his partner to a less-populated part of the dance floor. "Call him," he said.

"Listen, Perry Mason," Kate said, going face-to-face with Jack. "You and Inspector Clouseau forced me to attend this function with that self-absorbed actor, so I'm here and doing my job. But if you two want to get into a pissing contest like a couple of neighborhood cocker spaniels, you can pee on someone else's leg." She flashed her plastic smile and walked off toward her assigned escort.

Jack stood there for a minute, surprised by her reaction and puzzled about what to do next. If nothing happened tonight and Bob Mason left town, then Peter would probably pack up and leave in the morning. The FBI would still be after Pitts, but they wouldn't be around to help him solve the mystery of Annie's death, even if Pitts had been responsible. He was running out of time, so he decided to shake things up and see what happened. With alcohol flowing freely in the room, he might get lucky.

He spotted Mollie, turning custody of Dakota Douglas over to Kate, and headed in her direction. "Where's Jessie?" he said, as he arrived at her side.

"She's at that bar with the Whitehursts, Stewart Ramsey, and the senator," Mollie said, pointing toward a small gathering on the other side of the room.

Jack studied the group for a moment. "Let's shake a few trees and see if anything falls out."

They walked arm in arm at a slow pace around the room. Several classmates greeted Jack, but he kept moving while he returned their greetings.

"Were you able to meet with Jessie this afternoon?" Jack said.

"No," Mollie said. "I left a message for her, but she never returned my call."

"Well, I think the time for being subtle has passed," Jack said, as they arrived at the bar where the campaign group was huddled.

"McCall," Stewart said. "Come on over. We were just talking about you."

"Something nice, I hope," Jack said.

Stewart laughed and flicked cigar ashes toward a tray cluttered with mostly empty glasses. "I was telling the senator here how you saved my boy's life by landing your airplane on the street in front of the hospital."

"You must be one hell of a pilot," the senator said.

Jack sensed an opening to do a little tree shaking. "It's amazing what you can do when your life is on the line," he said to the senator. "Someone was trying to kill me because I was asking too many questions about one of our classmates, a girl who died the night we graduated from high school. Right, Sterling?"

Sterling did a double-take, seeming to be startled that the conversation was directed at him.

"What do you mean?" he said. "How would I know anything about that?"

"Excuse me for a minute," Jessie said. "I need another drink." She stepped away from the group and headed toward the bar, pulling some cash out of her clutch purse as she walked. A few words and a laugh with the bartender later, she returned with a very tall drink.

"You'd better go easy on that stuff, Jessie," Stewart said.

Jessie snarled at Stewart, then looked straight at Sterling. "I'm just getting started," she said, and downed half of the drink.

Stewart took the senator by the arm. "Come on, Bob," he said. "We need to circulate some more before you give your speech." The two men left.

"I don't know why everyone keeps looking at me when they mention Annie," Sterling said.

Victoria, having remained silent and at her husband's side up to that point, raised her drink glass. "Well, here's to Annie," she said. "Still dead after all these years. And still on everyone's mind, evidently."

Jessie started to laugh. "That's ironic," she said. "I thought you Southerners were all about family values and such."

Mollie looked at Jack and whispered, "She knows, doesn't she?"

Jack didn't say anything but kept his eyes on Sterling.

"This has gone far enough," Sterling said, taking his wife's drink from her hand and placing it on a nearby tray. "Come on, Victoria. We're leaving."

"Don't you want to drink a toast to dear departed family members?" Jessie said, raising her glass.

Sterling turned and tried to take the glass from Jessie's hand. "You need to sober up and shut up," he said.

Henry and Jennifer walked up to join the group. "You folks are drawing a lot of stares from the rest of the crowd," Henry said.

Jessie jerked her hand away from Sterling. "I don't care," she said. "I don't care anymore." She tipped her head back and finished off her drink. "I'm through hiding the fact that I loved Annie."

Mollie stepped close to Jessie and put her arm around her waist. "It's okay," she said. "You don't have to do this."

"Yes, I do," Jessie said. "And I'm through keeping secrets."

Victoria laughed. "And what secrets could you possibly have that would interest anyone else?" she said.

The tall, blonde-haired Jessie stepped closer to the short, dark-haired Victoria and looked down into her face.

"They should interest you," Jessie said, her eyes and mouth twitching in apparent anticipation—either of what she was about to say or of the reaction she was about to extract from Victoria. "They're about your sister-in-law."

Victoria laughed and looked at Sterling. "She wants to tell me something about Gloria or Grace," she said.

Sterling sat down in a chair and buried his face in his hands.

Jessie placed her hand under Victoria's chin and rotated her face so the two women were staring into each other's eyes.

"Annie was his sister," Jessie said.

Several classmates who were eavesdropping on the conversation mumbled and pointed at Sterling.

Jack put his hand on Jessie's arm and coaxed her hand away from Victoria's face.

Once free from Jessie's grip, Victoria turned her attention to Sterling. "Is that true?" she said.

Sterling didn't lift his head or say anything. His head just moved up and down twice to confirm the fact.

"How long have you known?" Jack asked Jessie.

Jessie grabbed a drink off the tray of a waiter passing by. "Rosemary Poole said she saw someone in the car with Annie the night she died," she said. She downed half the drink in one swallow. "It was me."

"You couldn't have been in the car with her when she went over the cliff," Jack said. "You didn't have a mark on you the next day. I remember."

Jessie drained her glass and shook her head. "We drove around awhile that night and got into a big argument," she said.

"What was the argument about?" Jack said.

"Her mother had told her who her real father was," Jessie said.

Jack interrupted her. "That old man Whitehurst was her father, and that Sterling was her half-brother?" Jack said.

Jessie looked over at Sterling and glared. "Tell 'em, Whitehurst, you weasel," she shouted, drawing more attention from the crowd.

Sterling stood and put his arm around his wife, who was standing silent, with her mouth open. "I'm sorry I've kept this from you, Victoria," he said. He looked at Jessie. "What she wants me to tell you, Jack, is that Annie and I had the same father *and* mother—we were twins."

Jack's eyes opened a little wider at this unexpected declaration; then he got into Sterling's face. "Did that motivate you to arrange for her to have a fatal accident that night?"

"Easy, counselor," Mollie said, tugging on her husband's arm.

Sterling shook his head. "I didn't know anything about it at the time of Annie's death," he continued. "After my father died, my mother told me that Annie was my twin sister. Father paid the doctor to falsify our birth records so no one would know. The doctor also falsified Annie's birth record to make it appear that our butler was her father. Father paid out a lot of money to keep everything quiet."

"Why?" Jack said.

"Simple," Sterling said, flashing a brief smile. "He had two daughters. His wife could no longer bear children, and he wanted a son."

"He paid Annie's mother a lot of money to bear a child," Jessie interjected. "But when he found out that he had sired twins and that one was a girl, he paid her a monthly support allowance to keep the girl."

"So Annie's mother's pregnancy wasn't a fling or an affair," Jack said.

"No," Sterling said. "The whole thing was planned, purchased, and delivered to the front door, making his wife an angry and bitter woman."

Jessie started to cry. "That's what we fought about that night," she said. "I didn't want her to take any money from them. I told her that I could take care of her."

"So Annie was blackmailing the Whitehursts?" Jack said.

Jessie shook her head. "No—yes—sort of. She wanted to feel whole and complete for the first time in her life. I guess she thought that provoking them to part with the one thing the Whitehursts valued most, money, would be symbolic recognition of her place in the world." She reached out and put her hand on Sterling's arm. "And she wanted to be with her brother. That's why she was on the mountain road that night; she was trying to find you. She wanted to tell you that she was your twin sister."

Frank Kirby barged into the group. "What's all the commotion about?" he said. No one spoke, so he tried to stare a response from Jack.

Henry watched the contest for a few moments, then ended it. "Frank," he said. "I'm glad you're here. Jack and I have eliminated Sterling as a suspect."

Sterling flashed an annoyed look at Henry.

"Suspect for what?" Frank said.

"For my sister's death," Sterling said.

"Gloria's sick, but she's not dead," Frank said. "I saw her yesterday." He looked around at the group. "Is Grace dead?"

Jessie stepped over to Frank and put her arms around his neck, giving him a gentle hug. "Annie, Frank," she said. "Annie was also Sterling's sister."

Frank pushed Jessie away. "What do you mean?" he said. "Sister?"

"It's true, Frank," Henry said. "But Sterling didn't know until years later."

"So he says," Jessie mumbled.

"Yes," Henry responded. "And I believe him."

Stewart Ramsey was the next person to barge into the conversation. "Can you folks hold down the noise?" he said. "Senator Mason is about to deliver his speech."

Again, no one said anything. Stewart looked around the group. "Frank, can you keep this crowd quiet for me, please?" he said.

Frank was still trying to digest the new information about Annie, so he mumbled a response and pushed Stewart back toward the podium.

"I've had enough fun for one evening," Sterling said. "Come on, Victoria, let's get out of here."

"Not so fast," Frank said. "I have some questions for you."

Sterling stopped and glared at Frank. After a few moments, he turned and continued to walk away.

Frank grabbed him by the arm. "I'm not done with you, Whitehurst," he said.

Sterling whirled around and pushed the policeman away. "Well, I'm done with you—and this town," he said. He took his wife by the hand and headed toward the door.

Frank started to reach for Sterling again.

"Let him go, Frank," Henry said. "He doesn't have the answers you want."

"No one has the answers you want," Jack said. "There is no answer. Annie's dead, and we may never know why or how."

Frank stood motionless for a moment and then smiled. "Perhaps you're right," he said. He started to walk away, then stopped and turned back toward Jack. "So there's no reason for you to be here after tomorrow, McCall," he said. He pointed toward the stage, where Senator Mason was well into his speech. "The senator will be gone tonight, your FBI buddies will be gone in the morning, and Hackett and Coleman are the only friends you have left around here."

"How do you know the FBI will be gone in the morning?" Jack said, wanting to pick a fight.

Frank chuckled and shook his head. "Pitts is probably 300 miles away from here by now," he said.

"He could be hiding out, waiting to complete the contract that brought him here," Jack said.

Frank walked back to where Jack was standing. "I don't think a contract brought him here," he said. "And the FBI don't think so either. They found a coded list of names at Pitts's condo in Chicago. Your friend Agent Wilder, he and I both reviewed the list. No one connected with this event or city was on it."

Frank turned and walked toward the door. "So it's time for you to leave again, McCall," he said over his shoulder. "And don't come back so soon next time."

Jack's knees became weak, and he wobbled a little, causing him to bump up against Mollie.

Mollie tightened her grip on his arm to steady him. "You okay?" she said.

Jack nodded, but he wasn't confident in his response. All the energy and tension that had been driving him since he had arrived in Caldwell flushed out of his mind and body. Fate brought Rosemary Poole to this place and time to taunt him with a resolution to the mystery of Annie's death. Pitts tried to scare him and then tried to kill him. Then the resolution dissolved when faced with facts and logic. All the possible motives of all the possible suspects made no sense. There seemed to be no reason for anyone to have wanted to kill Annie. Sterling didn't know that Annie was his sister, Jessie was in love with her, and old man Whitehurst seemed to be willing to buy his way out of any conflicts. He couldn't even speculate as to a motive for Pitts to have killed her. He was left with only the underlying guilt he had been carrying around since the night she died. She wouldn't have been there—looking for her brother, as he now knew—if Jack hadn't picked the lock and opened the gate on the road to the park.

"Why don't we sit down for a few minutes?" Henry said, pointing toward an empty table.

Mollie tugged at Jack to break his trance, and they followed Henry and the rest of the group to the table. No one spoke. To fend off questions, Jack pretended to listen to the senator's speech while he ruminated on everything that had just happened. Mollie stood and excused herself and headed for the ladies restroom, and Jennifer followed. When the senator finished speaking, Stewart Ramsey made a short speech announcing his run for the state senate. Then the music started again, and people queued up at the bars to continue the celebration. The senator was escorted out of the room, and Ramsey started working the crowd.

Jack rose and wandered toward the large patio doors. He weaved in and out of clusters of classmates and tried to smile, even though his gut was churning and his mind was dropping into an abyss of depression with every step he took. Reality was setting in; he would never escape his quilt for Annie's death. It would weigh him down the rest of his life. A dense crowd blocked the exit to the patio, so he stood next to the wall and tried the breath fresh air. The crowd flexed and someone nudged him to his left, causing him to bump into a tray. He looked down—a drink tray with some empty glasses and two full margarita glasses. He stared a moment and then pick up one the full glasses. He stared at the drink again and then raised it up to his lips. It was salty and wet with a tangy smell that he knew all too well. He started to tip it further to drain the contents into his mouth, but a hand settled on top of his and prevented the glass from tipping. He stared at the hand. He knew that hand.

"Don't do it," a voice said.

Jack heard the voice but he continued to stare at the hand and the drink.

"I didn't stop you when we were young," the voice said, "but I won't let it happen again."

Jack turned—it was Henry.

"Put it down, Jack," Henry said. He pressed down on Jack's hand and put his other hand on Jack's shoulder.

Jack lowered the drink to the tray but his hand continued to grip the stem of the glass.

"Come on Jack," Henry said. "Let's go find Mollie. I think she needs you."

Jack's fingers release the glass, and then he and Henry walked side-by-side back to the table where Jennifer and Mollie were waiting.

"You okay," Mollie said, rising to take his arm.

Jack looked at Henry. "Yeah, I'm okay."

Someone tapped Jack on the shoulder. He turned around—it was Dakota Douglas and Kate Simpson.

"Peter wants to talk to you in the morning," Kate said, and then she turned and headed out the door with a smiling Dakota Douglas in tow.

"Well, that's surprising," Henry said.

"Surprising?" Jack said. "That the FBI would want to see me?"

"No," Henry said. "Surprising that our actor seems to be smitten by your FBI agent."

Mollie tugged on Jack's arm. "You and I have some unfinished business from this morning," she said.

Jack followed her out of the room.

CHAPTER 13

WHEN JACK AWOKE UP the next morning, his feet were hanging off the end of the bed. Mollie's naked body was lying across the head of the bed, her butt wedged between several pillows and the headboard. *A good night*. And then he wondered whether the neighbors had complained. He rolled over and looked at the room phone. No message light, so he assumed there wasn't anyone in the room next door who had found the night noises anything but entertaining.

He got up and went to close the curtains. When he reached the doorway, his mind flashed back to the naked blonde who had been lounging on the balcony adjacent to his room the second day of his stay at the inn. He peered between the curtains toward the adjacent balcony before remembering he had changed rooms. Then he recalled seeing Blondie loading luggage into her car. *Just as well*.

Mollie rolled over and covered her head with a pillow, so Jack pulled the curtains closed, blocking the light that was shining on the bed. He crawled back under the sheet and nuzzled his head up against her bare stomach.

"You awake?" he said.

Mollie answered with a grunt.

"Maybe we should just leave," he said. "Nobody seems to give a damn whether I'm here or not."

Mollie raised her head. "Henry gives a damn," she said. "And so does Bruno."

Jack laughed. "Bruno gave a damn until Betty showed up." He shifted his position so he was lying across the bed, parallel to and facing his wife. "But you're right. Henry has been a great friend this week. Like he was in grade school."

His recollection of his childhood friend sparked an image of the drink he held in his hand the night before—with Henry's hand on top of his, blocking the flow of alcohol into his mouth.

"I think we should leave now."

"Well," Mollie said, "if you leave with that one solid connection reestablished, that will be a pretty worthwhile outcome."

Jack mumbled his agreement and ran his hand up her arms to her bare shoulder. His cell phone started ringing and vibrating on the nightstand next to the bed. He reached over and tilted it to read the caller ID. "Ugh," he said. "It's the FBI." He propped his upper body up on one elbow and poked the face of the phone to answer the call. "A little early, isn't it, Peter?"

"We're packing up to move our team to Portland," Peter said. "The director wants you to contribute to the report on the events here, so I've left a sealed copy of my report with attachments in the safe at your hotel."

"Oh, great," Jack said. "I'm on vacation and I end up helping you do paperwork." An avalanche of laughter pounded Jack's ear, causing him to jerk the phone away from his head.

"Some friend you are," he said, as he brought the device back to his ear.

"Just get your part to me when you get back to your office in Hartford," Peter said. "I'll keep you updated on the case—off the record, of course."

"Is Simpson leaving too?" Jack said.

"No," Peter said. "She's staying here in case we need follow-up work. Besides, I think she and your actor friend hit it off last night."

"Really?" Jack said. "What makes you say that?"

"Douglas called me this morning and insisted that she remain here to protect him," Peter said. "Just in case Pitts comes back."

Jack looked down at Mollie, who was in the process of rolling her nude body over onto her back. "You're probably right," he said to Peter, as he stared at his wife's bare breasts. "It's amazing how a beautiful woman can affect a man's mind."

"I assured him that Pitts is long gone," Peter said.

"You're sure about that." Jack said.

"Pitts knows that we know who he's Magellan," Peter said. "And since Senator Mason left last night and there's no one tied to Caldwell on Pitts's hit list, smart money says he's going to try to disappear—forever."

"You checked out everyone on the list, then?' Jack said.

Peter hesitated. "Well—there were a few names we couldn't identify," he said. "But Kirby didn't recognize any names as being local."

"Okay," Jack said. "Just catch the bastard."

He disconnected the call, then rested his head on Mollie's pillow. He draped his arm over her and coaxed her to roll up against his body, a movement that ended with her opening her eyes and brushing her lips against his. It was more of a "nuzzle" than a kiss. She moved her face back and forth against his.

His pulse slowed and his muscles relaxed, but even the softness of her touch and the aroma of her skin couldn't remove the image Henry's hand blocking his reunion with the euphoria and subsequent downward spiral of alcoholism from his mind. Drinking to excess and a large amount of time in psychotherapy hadn't been enough to purge his guilt. Even the safe haven of Mollie's arms couldn't shield him from the reality that his hope for redemption had slipped away.

"I have a confession to make," Jack said.

Mollie lifted her head off the mattress and propped it up with her elbow.

Jack fidgeted with his pillow and looked away from her for a moment to assemble the words, then looked straight into her beautiful green eyes. "I almost took a drink last night."

Mollie didn't flinch.

"I'm sorry," he said.

Mollie reached over and massaged the back of his neck. "I saw you—and I saw Henry stop you."

The couple stared at each other while Mollie continued to massage Jack's neck until his cell phone rang again.

"Throw that damn thing in the trash," Mollie said, dropping her head back down to the mattress.

Jack looked at the caller ID.

"It's Henry," he said. "I need to answer this."

Mollie mumbled and covered her head with a pillow again.

Jack poked the screen to accept the call. "Good morning, Henry."

"Good morning," Henry said. "I'm headed to the stadium for the barbecue. Where shall I meet you?"

"Stadium?" Jack said. "Ramsey made his big announcement last night. Why are we still going to the stadium?"

"Do you think he'd pass up the opportunity to prance around in front of a couple thousand people?" Henry said. "And before you ask, he has already invited the entire population of the county to attend a barbecue lunch at the stadium, so he's going to make his big announcement again, without Bob Mason."

"Why doesn't that surprise me?" Jack said. "Okay, I'll meet you at the stadium, behind the home team bench."

Mollie jabbed an elbow into Jack's leg as he disconnected the call and put the cell phone on the nightstand. "You're going to leave me to do all the packing, aren't you?" she said. Her remark was punctuated with a pillow flung at Jack's head.

"You said yourself that Henry's been a great friend since I've been back," Jack said. "He wants me to come to the barbecue."

Jack crawled off the bed and stood up next to where Mollie's feet were hanging over the side. She kicked him in the leg.

"Do you want to come to Ramsey's big barbecue—campaign launch?" Jack said.

Mollie raised her head and glared at her husband. "No," she said. "I'm tired of his cigars."

Jack nodded and headed for the bathroom. "I didn't think so," he said, closing the door behind him.

When he finished his morning routine, he put on some khaki shorts and a T-shirt and headed down to the front desk of the inn. Bruno was at the counter, along with a couple of his customer service staff.

"Morning, big guy," Jack said. "How did your date with Betty turn out?"

A wide grin appeared on Bruno's face. "Can't give you a complete report," he said. "It hasn't ended yet."

"You realize, of course," Jack said, "that you've answered my next question."

Bruno grinned again and nodded.

"A friend of mine left an envelope for me," Jack said. "He said you put it in your safe."

"Yes," Bruno said. "He said it was highly confidential, so I put it in my personal safe. I'll get it for you."

Bruno disappeared through his office door behind the front desk, so Jack turned around and leaned his back against the counter. It was mid-morning, and the lobby of the inn was busy with people checking out or heading for the day's activities. The room was crowded, but he felt alone and empty, as if he were standing in a courtroom and had just lost an important case. He was home, but the experience he had envisioned when he arrived, the closure he had sought, hadn't materialized. Maybe an accident was just an accident, he thought. And maybe it was partly his fault.

"Here's your envelope," Bruno said, dropping the package onto the front counter behind Jack.

Jack turned around and picked up the envelope. "Thanks, buddy," he said. "Are you going to Ramsey's barbecue at the stadium?"

"Probably," Bruno said, but his body language, including a gentle shake of the head and raised eyebrows, said "begrudgingly."

"I'm heading over to join Henry," Jack said. "Maybe I'll see you there. And maybe I'll see Betty?"

Bruno smiled again. "If you don't see her, you won't see me."

Jack gave Bruno a thumbs-up and headed out of the inn toward the parking lot. As he left the building, he spotted Kate exiting through a side door, wearing her orange formal dress from the night before and carrying her shoes. "Kate," he hollered. Kate glanced in his direction, smiled, and kept on moving. *Someone else had a good night.*

The Mustang was sluggish when he got in and tried to start the engine. *Just my luck.* He turned the key to the off position, waited for a few moments, and then tried again. After an extended effort, the engine roared to life, and Jack guided the car out of the parking lot. When he stopped the car at the entrance to the highway, he hesitated. A thought flashed into his brain that pulled at him like the gravity of a black hole in space and terrified the little boy inside of him. The man wanted to turn the car toward the cemetery where his father and Annie were buried, but the little boy resisted. It's over, the little boy said. Just go back to Hartford and live your life. The man felt compelled to face the failures of the past and the present. A car horn, coming from an ancient Buick land yacht behind him, brought him back to the present. The man turned the steering wheel to the left and headed toward the cemetery. The little boy made his presence known by releasing 10,000 butterflies into his gut.

Mollie had asked to be with him if he decided to go visit his father's gravesite. But Jack was glad he was alone. He wasn't sure how he was going to react. A vision of the markers around Annie's grave flashed into his mind. Headstones are very final, he thought. They are an entrance to the past for anyone standing before them, a barricade to the future for anyone buried beneath. He took several deep breaths, trying to clear his mind, but the vision remained. The black hole kept sucking him in.

After a short journey through the city, the Mustang turned and passed through the entrance to Oak Hill Cemetery. Jack guided the car along a narrow roadway through a maze of headstones and trees on the hillside property. The older gravesites were near the entrance, on the uphill side of the grounds, and the downhill end was still undeveloped. Jack stopped the Mustang about midway down the road, near a group of headstones in an open area framed by several large oak trees. He sat for a few moments, recalling his father's funeral. His mother had been very calm during the service, projecting (he later decided) a sense of relief. She hadn't cried or wailed. She seemed to be focused on him, her young son. It wasn't until he had started to come to grips with his own drinking that he finally understood his father's condition—and his mother's burden. She didn't want to end up in this place, so before she died she instructed Jack to cremate her remains and spread her ashes among the redwoods in Northern California, near where she was born. He had done so, and he was comforted in the knowledge that she was at peace.

He got out of the car and wandered among the headstones, searching for his father's grave. Blades of freshly cut and watered grass clung to his shoes. He recognized a few of the names on the markers as he walked, some invoking memories of a face, others not. He paused for a moment and looked down the hill to the valley beyond. He remembered standing in this spot as he watched six large men lower his father's casket into the ground. His eyes lowered, and he saw the headstone he came to find. He walked over and placed his hand on it.

"How you doin', Dad?" he said, and then patted the marker as if to comfort the man buried beneath. His father wasn't a bad man, just a happy drunk. He managed to hold down a job and provide a good middle-class life for his family. The car wreck, on a lonely back road that took his life, involved only him. No one else was harmed. As Jack lifted his hand off the headstone, he noticed that his fingers were shaking and twitching. He still had butterflies in his stomach. He had hoped that visiting his father's grave would calm his anxiety, but he had been wrong. The black hole was still drawing him in. It was Annie.

Jack had gone to Annie's funeral, which was a graveside ceremony in this cemetery, but his memory of the location of the site was vague. He started walking and reading grave markers. He didn't know how he was going to find it. Maybe the black hole would do the work for him, draw him to it. He crossed the narrow road several times as he traversed the hillside. After twenty minutes, his pace increased, and he still had a lot of markers to search. As he crossed the road once more, an old man, wearing green coveralls and a green Oak Hill cap and driving a golf cart, pulled up next to him and stopped.

"You look like you're searching for someone," the old man said, as he got out of the cart.

"Yes, sir," Jack said. "I'm looking for Ann Ridgeway's grave."

The old man reached under the seat and pulled out a binder.

"I think I know where she is," he said, "but let's look her up, just to be sure."

He thumbed through the pages and then tracked down one page with his index finger.

"Yup, there she is," he said. "Hop in, I'll drive you over to her."

Jack walked around to the passenger side of the machine and slid into the seat. The old man climbed into the driver's seat and piloted the cart to the opposite side of the property and back up the hill a short distance.

"She's over here," the old man said, as he pulled off the pavement and stopped the cart. He got out and headed down a row of headstones, with Jack following. When he arrived at Annie's gravesite, he bent over and pulled two weeds that were beginning to sprout around the base of her monument.

"How are you doing today, Miss Annie?"

Jack stood back and watched the old man tidy up around the site.

"Do you talk to all the people buried here or just Annie?" he said.

The old man smiled and walked back to where Jack was standing. "I talk to all of them," he said. "And if they start talking back to me, I'll know it's time to retire." He chuckled and headed back to his golf cart. "Let me know if you need to find anyone else."

Jack turned around and looked at the grave and headstone. The little boy inside him released the butterflies again as he stepped up to the side of her grave. Tears began to flow down his cheeks. "I'm sorry," he said.

He stood beside her for a while, letting all the emotion drain out of his body. He cried for her, for his dad, for his mom, and for himself. His legs began to feel weak, so he sat down in

216

the grass. When the tears stopped, he read the inscription on the monument: "A LIFE WELL LIVED." He recalled several memories: his pushing her in a swing when they were in grade school; her attacking one of the school bullies who was picking on a younger kid in middle school; and her standing knee-deep in mud as she struggled to pull an old tire out of a local creek, during a high school environmental cleanup project. *Yes, indeed, a life well lived.*

His cell phone rang, jolting his mind back to the present. He removed the phone from his pocket and looked at the screen. It was Henry. He poked the face of the phone to accept the call.

"Henry," he said.

"Where are you?" Henry said.

Jack hesitated as he thought about how to answer the question. Henry had shared his life as a boy, and Annie was a big part of their shared experience. He wanted to share this moment with Henry, but at the same time he felt it was very personal.

"I stopped to see a friend," he said, not wanting to lie to Henry. "I'll be there in about fifteen minutes."

"Okay," Henry said. "Just wanted to make sure you were all right."

"I'm fine," Jack said. "See you in a few minutes."

Jack disconnected the call and stuffed the phone back in his pocket. He sat for a few more moments looking at Annie's monument, then stood and stepped over beside it, placing his hand on top as he had at his father's grave. "I'm sorry," he said once more, and then walked back to his car.

When he slid into the driver's seat of the Mustang, Jack unlatched the convertible top and flipped the toggle switch that retracted the top back behind the seats. The sun felt good on his face, and the air was filled with the familiar scent of harvested grass seed from a field at the bottom of the hill, below the cemetery. He brought the engine to life and followed the road through the grounds and back to the street. Henry was waiting for him.

CHAPTER 14

WHEN HE ARRIVED at the Caldwell High School football stadium, Jack parked the car in the shade created by one of the trees at the edge of the parking lot. The school building looked pretty much the same, but the grounds and sidewalks, he observed, had been remodeled. The stadium was behind the three-story brick school building, and there was a rather large landscaped outdoor classroom area, along with a park-like sitting area, between the school and the stadium. Jack could see smoke, probably from barbecue trailers, rising from inside the stadium, and banners, balloons, and a swarm of people congregated at the outdoor classroom area. He grabbed Peter's case report from the passenger seat of the Mustang, in case the speeches got boring, and headed toward the banners and balloons.

As he approached the gathering, Jack was greeted by Stewart Ramsey, who was dressed in white from head to toe.

"McCall," the candidate shouted, extending a hand in greeting. "Glad to see you could make it."

"What's with the white outfit?" Jack said. "Trying to convince the voters you're still a virgin?"

Ramsey demonstrated his amusement with a raucous laugh. He pulled a cigar out of his pocket and thrust it at Jack.

"No, thanks," Jack said. "Save them for the registered voters."

Frank Kirby walked up and took the cigar out of Stewart's hand. "I'll take that one," he said. "I'm a registered voter." He glared at Jack. "Are you still here, McCall?"

"On guard duty today, Frank?" Jack said.

Frank smiled at Jack's taunt. He lit the cigar. "Not much need for guards today, McCall," he said. "Your pal Pitts is probably halfway to Mexico by now, and everyone you thought might have a motive to kill Annie actually had a motive to keep her alive."

"What about Pitts?" Jack said. "He's a professional killer. He might have killed her—and he surely came here to kill someone connected to the reunion or this campaign."

"What possible motive could he have had to kill Annie?" Frank said. "He was eighteen years old and graduating from high school when she died. And as for a current contract to kill someone here, there wasn't a single name on his hit list connected to this event."

"You're sure of that, are you?" Jack said.

"I checked the list myself," Frank said, blowing a cloud of cigar smoke in Jack's direction.

Jack didn't have a response, so he gave Frank a one finger salute and walked off toward the stadium, leaving Frank and Stewart both laughing at him.

Joe Ramsey was manning the registration table at the entrance to the stadium.

"How are you feeling?" Jack said, as he stopped at the table.

"Good, Mr. McCall," the boy said.

"And how is Carrie?" Jack said.

The boy's face morphed into a sad-clown expression. "Well . . . ," he hesitated, "I think she's okay. She hasn't wanted to see me since we went flying."

"Sorry to hear that," Jack said. "And I'm sorry that my troubles endangered your life and hers."

The boy's expression perked up a little. "That's okay," he said. "The upside is that I'm somewhat of a celebrity around town now. Lots of girls want to hang out with me."

"Hang in there, partner," Jack said. "Life can be great fun."

Joe handed Jack a "Ramsey for State Senate" button, and Jack clipped it to his shirt as he walked into the stadium. The smoke from three barbecue trailers obscured part of the stadium, but a warm wave of nostalgia flowed through his body as he entered. Some of his finest high school memories were rooted in this stadium. He stopped at the top of the steps and looked around. The turnout was pretty impressive, he thought, considering that Ramsey hadn't run for office before. He guessed that the home team side of the stadium was about sixty percent filled. People seemed to be enjoying the food and the atmosphere of the event; a few kids were having an impromptu game of football on the field. There was a speaker's stand set up just shy of center field, with a twenty-yard-wide "Ramsey for State Senate" banner as a backdrop.

Jack spotted Henry in the bleachers right behind the south end of the home team bench, so he made his way over to where his friend was sitting. "How's the food?"

Henry finished chewing a mouthful of pulled pork sandwich and then wiped the sauce off his mouth. "Pretty good," he said. "It ought to get Stewart at least fifteen percent of the votes he needs."

"A good investment," Jack said, as he sat down beside his friend. "Who's giving the big endorsement and introduction speech, now that Mason's left town?"

"Virgil," Henry said with a snicker. "Nothing like a little star power to get people's attention."

Jack set the report envelope down on the bench beside Henry and stood up. "Watch that for me, will you? I'm going to get something to eat."

Henry looked at the envelope. "What's in that envelope that's so important it has to be guarded?"

"If I told you," Jack said, "I'd have to . . ."

"Kill me?" Henry finished.

Jack laughed. "Yes," he said, and headed down the steps to the food line.

As he stepped onto the track that encircled the field, Jack spotted Dakota and Kate, chatting with some of the classmates. He decided to find out how their evening had gone, so he walked over to the group and stood next to Kate.

"Guess you're glad you weren't a target last night, aren't you?" he said, addressing the actor. "And I hear you are going to give the endorsement speech for Ramsey today."

The actor rolled his eyes and took a drink of beer. "I have to," he said. "Seems I promised him an 'anytime favor' when he helped me pass a math class our junior year. He reminded me of it last night."

"You seem relaxed today, Ms. Simpson," Jack said, turning his attention to the undercover FBI agent.

Agent Simpson just nodded and took a sip from her wine glass.

Jack leaned his head close to her ear. "How 'undercover' did you get last night?" he said in a low voice.

Kate smiled and raised her plastic cup in the manner of a toast, then downed the rest of the contents. "He's a nice guy, underneath all that Hollywood-hype BS," she said.

"Yes, he is," Jack said. "Sounds like you got to meet Virgil."

Kate flashed a bewildered look at Jack. "Huh?" she said.

"Ask Dakota about Virgil," Jack said, and headed for the end of the food line.

The line was moving at a snail's pace, in part because there was a lot to choose from, but also because the candidate had parked himself at the end of the string of tables and was making a campaign speech to everyone who passed. Jack took the opportunity to look around the stadium and check out the crowd. As his gaze came around to where Dakota and Kate were standing, he saw something that surprised him. It was Blondie, from the hotel. She had a tablet and pen in her hands and appeared to be talking with Dakota, so when Jack finished his food selection he walked back over to where they were standing.

"Who's your friend, Dakota?" Jack said, looking at Blondie.

"Oh," Dakota said, "This is Barbara Dahl, an entertainment reporter for the *LA Times*."

"We've met," Jack said, "Informally, that is, though I didn't know her name. Barbara Dahl? Do your friends call you Barbie?"

Blondie flashed a pouty, annoyed look at Jack. "My mother had a sense of humor—I don't."

"Ms. Dahl is here to do a story on me and my classmates," Dakota said, in an apparent attempt to appease the reporter. "She's been doing background for several days."

"I thought I saw you packing your gear into your car yesterday," Jack said, "yet here you are today."

"I had to run up to Portland yesterday to cover a premiere," Barbara said. "I drove back down this morning."

"Well, nice to meet you again, Ms. Dahl," Jack said. "I'll look forward to reading your article about our class celebrity."

Jack joined Henry in the bleachers and prepared to eat his lunch and listen to the speeches.

"Who's the blonde?" Henry said.

"Do you remember me telling you about the naked girl lounging on the balcony at the inn?" Jack said.

Henry mumbled and nodded.

"Well, that's her," Jack continued. "Turns out she's a reporter for the *LA Times* who covers the world of entertainment."

"Here to see our movie star?" Henry said.

"Yup," Jack said. He stared in her direction for a moment. "Does she look familiar to you?"

Henry leaned forward and watched as the reporter and Dakota walked around the speaker's stand. "Not from this distance," he said. "Why?"

"I'm not sure," Jack said. "I just saw her for the first time without her sunglasses."

Jack shook his head and started to eat his sandwich just as the background music stopped and the mayor stepped onto the speaker's platform. He and Henry listened to the first speech and then a second speech by another local celebrity. After giving a rousing endorsement of Stewart Ramsey, a state official introduced Dakota Douglas. Kate followed him up to the speaker's platform.

Dakota started his speech, which Jack assumed was written by one of Ramsey's minions, so he decided to pass the time by browsing through Peter's report on Joshua Pitts. He had thumbed through the description, identification, and some of the details before two boys, running along the seats, bumped into him, causing him to drop the document into the footwell of the bleachers. As he picked up the papers from the ground, one of the documents caught Jack's eye. It was a copy of the hit list the FBI had found at Pitts's condo in Chicago. He glanced at the list and began to slide it back into the envelope, when a name on the list caused him to stop. His heart started beating faster, and his hands started to shake.

"Oh, *shit*," he said.

"What?" Henry said, directing his attention away from Dakota's speech.

"Look," Jack said, pointing to a name on the list.

Henry read the name. "Oh, shit," he said. "Pitts wasn't here to kill Bob Mason, he was here to kill Virgil."

Jack stood up and scanned the crowd. "Yes," he said, "and I bet he's not on his way to Mexico."

Henry stood up and looked around. "Where's Frank? You need to tell him what you found."

"You need to tell him," Jack said. "If I tell him, he'll laugh in my face and then throw me in jail."

Henry took his cell phone out of his pocket and punched at the keys. "Why didn't Frank recognize the name Virgil Critchman on the list?" he said.

"Because," Jack said, "Frank didn't move to Caldwell until he was in middle school. Virgil's mom changed his name to Dakota Douglas when he started doing local commercials. He was nine years old, and that was long before Frank hit town."

"You need to get Virgil out of here," Henry said. "I'll find Frank and get some security set up for him."

"Yes," Jack said. "If we can get him out of the stadium, then everyone else should be safe." He paused a minute to develop a quick plan. He scanned the stadium again, looking for anything out of place. "Try to act casual," he instructed Henry. "If Pitts is here and he sees us panic, he'll know we're onto him. You go down first, and then I'll go out to the speaker's platform and alert Kate."

Henry nodded as he walked to the end of the row of seats and down to the track. As soon he disappeared into the exit tunnel, Jack walked down to the track and made a circuitous route to the back of the speaker's platform. Kate was sitting in a chair at the back of the platform, which put the seat of her chair at Jack's shoulder height.

"Kate," Jack said.

Kate turned her head and looked down at Jack. "What are you doing?" she said.

"You need to act calm," Jack said. "Pitts came here to kill Dakota. We need to get him off the stage."

Kate stood up, went to Dakota's side, and whispered in his ear.

The actor's eyes got very large, and he turned back toward the audience. "My friend tells me that if I tell you any more great things about my longtime friend Stewart Ramsey, you are going to think he paid me to be here—which he didn't, unless you count his buying me a pizza after a football game during our senior year in high school."

The comment produced a modest laugh track from the crowd.

"So without further ado," Dakota continued, "I am proud to introduce to you . . . my friend Stewart Ramsey."

Kate took Dakota by the arm and started to lead him off the platform. Jack moved to the bottom of the steps, where several people, including the seductive *LA Times* reporter, were standing. When Kate and Dakota reached the bottom step, Kate pushed the actor toward Jack just as Jack heard a swishing sound and a thud. Kate flew backwards against the steps. In an instant, Jack heard the report of a rifle, and people in the stadium started running in all directions and screaming in terror. He stepped up to Kate and threw her over his shoulder.

"Move," he shouted to the group.

Dakota and the rest of the group made a dash for the cover of the concrete field-access tunnel. Another swish and thud dropped a campaign worker to the track. Dakota and the reporter picked the man up off the track and helped him to the tunnel under the stands.

"Kate," Jack shouted, as he set her on the concrete floor of the tunnel. "Kate!" Blood was gushing out of the wound on her left shoulder.

Dakota took off his shirt and handed it to Jack. "You've got to get her out of here," he said.

Jack pressed the shirt against Kate's wound, then took off his belt and secured the bandage while continuing to scan the area for Pitts.

"My weapon," Kate said. "Take my weapon and get Dakota out of here." She reached under her vest with her right arm and extracted her service revolver.

"I'm not leaving you," Dakota said.

Jack took the weapon from her hand and looked around for an escape route, then looked Dakota in the eye. "We need to get you out of here," he said. "Pitts is after you—not her. When you're gone, she and the rest of these people will be safe."

A man walking in a crouched position, holding up a badge in one hand and a pistol in the other, approached the group from the entrance to the tunnel.

"I'm a deputy sheriff," he said. "You folks need to lie low until help arrives."

"Deputy," Jack said, "The lady bleeding here is FBI Agent Kate Simpson, and the man holding her hand is the person the sniper is shooting at. Based on the way she fell when the bullet struck her, I think the shooter is in the building just outside the school grounds to the north. I am going to take our target away from the rest of the group to minimize the risk to them. Can you stay here and protect them, just in case?"

The deputy looked the group over and then glanced at both ends of the tunnel. "Okay," he said. "I'll see if I can help Agent Simpson."

Jack checked both ends of the tunnel and then grabbed Dakota by the arm. "Come on," he said, "time to go."

Dakota hesitated and stared at Kate, still holding her hand.

"Go," Kate said. "I'll be okay."

Jack pulled harder on Dakota's arm, and the actor stood up and followed Jack as he started for the entrance to the tunnel. "Stay against the wall," Jack said.

As the two men moved toward the entrance, Jack heard a clatter of footsteps from behind and looked back. Barbara the reporter was following them. Jack stopped. "Get back to the group," he said in a low voice, so as not to broadcast their movement.

The girl kept coming. "If you think I'm going to miss a story like this," she said, "you're crazy."

Jack crumpled his face to a menacing look. "You get the hell back or I'll shoot you myself," he said, as firmly as his muffled voice could muster. The girl stopped, so Jack coaxed Dakota forward and headed for the entrance to the tunnel.

At the entrance Jack stopped and peered around the corner of the concrete wall. Most of the crowd were running out the south end of the stadium toward the parking area. A few people were huddled behind the concrete benches and trash bins. He needed to get Dakota away from the crowd. He looked at the school building. It was the width of a football field away, but there was some good cover between them and the school building.

"We're heading for the school," Jack said. "When we go, stay crouched down to make as small a target as possible, okay?" He looked around again. "We're going to that brick wall first."

Dakota nodded, and the two men sprinted toward their first cover. When they reached the brick wall, they crouched behind it and looked around.

"Thank God he didn't take a shot at us," Dakota said, gasping for air.

"Yes," Jack said, "and that bothers me. Where is the bastard?"

Jack heard a clatter of footsteps again and looked back toward the tunnel. It was the reporter again. She was following them. "What the hell does she think she's doing?" he said.

"Never underestimate the commitment of the press to follow a good story," Dakota said, followed by a very nervous laugh.

Jack watched the girl stop behind one of the concrete garbage bins. "She's going to get herself killed," he said. Then it dawned on him that she was hiding on the wrong side of the bin. Pitts would have an open shot at her.

"Get back to the tunnel," Jack shouted at the girl.

Her head popped up from behind the bin, followed by an arm, and a hand with a pistol in it. Jack watched the pistol rotate from a vertical position to a horizontal one and point straight at him and Dakota. He lifted Kate's 9 mm pistol and fired in the girl's general direction, causing her shot to strike the top of the wall just above Dakota's head. She ducked down behind the bin again.

A startled Dakota Douglas pressed himself hard against the brick wall. "What the hell is going on here?"

Jack was in survival mode and didn't answer. In two beats of his racing heart, he scanned the girl's position and saw her reflection in the glass window of the concession stand built into the stadium behind her. She started to rise up for another shot. Jack took aim just over the top of the bin. Her head appeared. He fired. Her body lurched backward onto the concrete, and the gun flew out of her hand, landing back by the entrance to the tunnel.

Jack did a 360 scan of the area to see if there were any other immediate threats and then looked back where the girl was sprawled out on the concrete. She wasn't moving. The deputy appeared at the tunnel entrance and kicked the girl's gun backwards.

"Your FBI agent is okay," the deputy said. "Another off-duty deputy and a nurse are with her." He scanned the area north of the stadium and then dashed to the trash bin where the girl was lying. "I'll keep an eye on this one."

Jack nodded and turned back toward Dakota, who was still huddled as close to the brick wall as he could get. "Why didn't Pitts shoot at us?" he said. He peered over the top of the wall, scanning the building to the north. "That bathroom complex is our next stop."

Dakota nodded.

"Go," Jack said, and the two men sprinted for the small brick building between them and the school building. Their movement seemed to inspire bystanders to get away from the shooting. Several people left their cover position and were running toward the parking lot. When Jack and Dakota reached the complex, they crouched down in case an attack came from an unexpected direction again.

"Why is Pitts trying to kill me?" Dakota said, with a quiver in his voice.

"Pitts is a contract killer," Jack said. "You must have pissed off somebody big-time."

"I'm a movie star," the actor said. "All I've ever done is pretend to be other people all my life."

"This is not the time to speculate about motives," Jack said. "We need to get to the school building." He pointed to the stadium side of their current cover building. "Go to that corner and keep an eye out for anything that moves," he said. "I'm going to check the other side. If you hear me holler 'run,' I want you to head for the nearest concrete structure as fast as you can. Got that?"

Dakota nodded, then walked in a stooped position to the west corner of the small building, while Jack went to the other corner, next to the entrance to one of the toilet areas. He peered around the corner. He didn't see any sign of Pitts, but then again, he hadn't really expected the gunman to be standing in the open with a weapon in his hand. *Where is he?*

He glanced back to check on Dakota and saw what appeared to be reflected light shining on the actor's shirt. Then he saw the barrel of a gun protrude from the entrance of the toilet area between him and Dakota. His heart stopped for a moment and then started to race. In a matter of milliseconds, his brain determined that if he shot at the barrel of the gun he would hit Dakota.

"Run," Jack shouted, as he leaped forward toward the arm with the gun.

Dakota bolted away from the wall just as a shot was fired. The shot ricocheted off the concrete, and Dakota sprinted in the direction of the parking lot to the south. As the hand holding the pistol extended further out of the building and swung around, tracking the moving target, Jack reached the edge of the entrance and knocked the gun out of the hand. As he stopped in front of the entrance, a body lunged at him, knocking him to the ground. The two bodies hit the concrete walk, and Jack lost his grip on Kate's gun, causing it to slide across the concrete out of his reach. The two men wrestled and rolled on the walkway until Jack ended up on his back and the other man was able to reach his gun and point it at Jack. Jack finally got a good look at his face.

"Pitts," he said.

"You're a hard man to kill, McCall," Pitts said. "But I don't think I can miss from this range."

Pitts raised up to his knees and extended his arm, pointing the pistol at Jack's head. Pitts started to grin as if he were about to experience a moment of great pleasure, his eyes partially closed. Then, in what appeared to Jack to be slow motion, a hand reached out from above and grasped Pitts's gun, pulling it up and backward. At the same time, an arm wrapped itself around Pitts's neck and pulled him backward as well. Jack, still flat on his back on the ground, rolled his head to the right. It was Henry.

Henry and Pitts stumbled backwards until Henry tripped over a shrub and both men fell down. Henry's head slammed into the concrete, and the gun flew out of Pitts's hand when he landed on the walkway next to Henry. Henry was dazed, so both Jack and Pitts scrambled for their weapons. Pitts reached his gun first. He turned and fired, striking Henry in the arm as he was staggering to his feet. Jack picked up Kate's gun and fired at Pitts as he ran toward the school building. Jack then ran over to check on Henry, who was back on the ground.

"You hit bad?" Jack said, shifting his gaze between Henry and the school building.

"I'll be okay," Henry said, with a grimace. "My head hurts worse than my arm."

Jack stood up. "I need to stop this guy now," he said.

"Go," Henry said.

Jack ran toward the school building.

When he reached the main doors, he was torn between being cautious and not wanting Pitts to escape. He entered with his pistol at the ready and heard footsteps echoing from down the main hall, so he started running toward the echo.

The black linoleum squares in the main hallway didn't provide much traction for Jack's leather-soled shoes, as he rounded the left-hand corner full-throttle in pursuit of Pitts. His left arm flailed in the air to maintain his balance. His right arm was fully extended, to keep Kate's 9 mm pistol pointed straight ahead. Light was scarce in the hallway of the empty building, but the gray plaster walls amplified the small amount of illumination provided by the windows in the main entry doors at the base of the stairs ahead and to his right. The rhythmic clatter of his shoes striking the floor echoed down the corridor, disguising any sounds that might have revealed the location or direction of flight taken by his quarry.

Slowing his pace, Jack scanned each door as he passed, searching for anything that didn't look right. *The auditorium door, did it move? Yes.* He saw it close. Moving at a swift and quiet pace, Jack turned to look down the main stairwell as he passed, to make sure the movement of the auditorium door across the hall from the stairs hadn't been a decoy. The stairwell was clear. He crossed the hall to the auditorium's double doors, checking up and down the hall as he moved. He stopped with his back to the wall, just to the right of the doors. He listened. All he could hear were the thumping of his own heart and the gasping of his own oxygen-starved lungs. *Relax. You can't hear anything with your heart pounding like this. Relax.* He leaned over, putting his right ear against the door, while forcing his internal noises into the background. Through the cold, painted metal door he heard footsteps. Footsteps in a hurry. They sounded like they were pretty far away from the door, probably at the front of the auditorium. He knew that there were double doors on each side of the auditorium down by the stage. Each set of doors opened to the outside of the building. *But they're locked and chained in the summer. That was twenty years ago, dummy. Are they still chained, or could Pitts just walk out and walk away?*

Jack pulled out his cell phone to call for help. *No service. Great.*

He had to go in. He couldn't let Pitts get away. *If Pitts is at the front of the auditorium, I can open the door and leap behind the back row of seats.* He backed away a couple of steps from the doors and examined them carefully. They opened outward. That would make his task more dangerous. They wouldn't provide cover as he opened them. He would have to move quickly — very quickly. *The room will be dark; why would he turn on the lights?* The open doorway would be the only source of light. He would have to pass right through the lighted area. But once he was inside, the door would close, and the two adversaries would be on equal ground. With his pistol in his right hand, he grabbed the door handle with his left, took two deep breaths, and pulled.

The door flew open, squeaking and rattling in unwelcome announcement of Jack's entrance. He lunged headfirst toward the seats on the right side of the aisle, landing on his side behind the metal-framed auditorium seats. *Perfect.* He was in position. He looked back at the light coming in from the door, which was inching its way closed. He moved away from the light and listened as the door continued to close. Clunk. Clunk. Pitts was trying to open the doors at the front of the room. *Chains* — he heard the sound of chains. The doors were all chained closed. The only way out was the door Jack had just come through.

"Stupid move, McCall," Pitts said. His voice came from the front of the acoustical chamber, but Jack couldn't gain a sense of positioning from the sound, since the room was designed to make all sound heard equally from every seat.

"You should have stayed out in the hall and waited for me to come out," Pitts continued.

Jack looked back at the large double doors. The door he came through wasn't closed yet. It was stuck open about a foot. He could see the scuff marks on the floor where the door had documented its misalignment over time. If he stayed in the back of the room, he would be at a disadvantage. Pitts might find a position on the stage to get a shot at him. If he went back through the door, Pitts would definitely get a shot at him. *You're right, Pitts, stupid move on my part.*

Jack pondered his next move. Had anyone seen him and Pitts come into the school building? How long would it be before anyone arrived to help him subdue this sociopathic killer? Lots of questions, but no answers. The one thing he knew for sure was that the man he had trapped in this auditorium was dangerous. Ice-cold, unfeeling dangerous. He had watched Pitts smile as he prepared to pull the trigger on the revolver pointed directly at his head. It was a sick, demonic smile. Now he, Jack McCall, was all that stood between Pitts and his next kill. He couldn't let Pitts out of this room to kill again. It had to end here.

He had to get that door closed. Once it was closed, he would have an advantage: time. With the room completely dark, he could wait. If Pitts tried to force open any of the doors, Jack could use the sound as a target for his 9 mm pistol. All he had to do was sit at the back of the auditorium and guard the main doors. He could wait for Frank to show up. Simple, except for getting the door closed. When he had bolted into the auditorium, he had the element of surprise to protect him. This next maneuver would be a lot more risky. His knees were beginning to ache from being in this awkward, cramped position behind the seats. He wondered if they would have enough strength left to propel him toward the door and then carry him to the other side of the aisle, where he could hide again.

Jack got on his hands and knees and crept toward the aisle. The linoleum tiles were cold and slick from their own fresh coat of wax. His sweaty right hand grabbed the back leg of the end seat, and his right foot braced itself against a convenient seat leg to give him the traction he would need to get to the door and then cross the aisle safely. He had to go. Now.

Jack bolted into the lighted area and toward the door, with his left arm extended to reach the bar. His left foot hit the linoleum, but it slipped on the waxed floor and he hit the floor face down in the lighted aisle. In one motion, he bounced off the floor and continued toward the door, his brain adjusting his stride to compensate for the slippery floor. He reached the door bar and gave it a quick jerk. As he pulled against the door bar, he changed directions and lunged toward the seats on the other side of the aisle. In midair, something hit his calf muscle, sending his left leg out from under him, and he hit the floor as the room resonated with the high-pitched silencer whine of a bullet from Pitts's gun. He crawled face down to the cover behind the seats on the other side of the aisle, breathing even harder than before.

"Second stupid move in a row, McCall," Pitts's voice proclaimed.

Not stupid, just clumsy. The burning sensation in his leg increased as Jack rolled over onto his back and pushed himself up to a sitting position. Unable to see in the darkened room, he grasped his leg at the point of the pain. It was wet. Very wet. He put his hand on the floor. A pool of blood was beginning to form around his leg. He put his gun down and took off his T-shirt. He rolled it up and tied it tightly around his leg to stop the flow of blood.

"If you were aiming for my head, you hit the wrong end."

"Shot you in the ass, did I, McCall?"

Jack picked up his pistol and slid further away from the door. The pain in his leg was becoming more intense. Burning, stabbing waves of pain shot up his body as he moved backward. His inoperative left foot followed his leg as it slid across the floor. The sole of his shoe caught on even the smallest gap between the tiles, aggravating the injured limb. He had to keep moving despite the pain. Pitts knew approximately where Jack was hiding. Jack had no idea where Pitts was hiding.

"I'm coming for you, McCall; you can't hide from me."

"Why did you try to kill me?" Jack said, "Was it because you killed Annie and I was getting too close to the truth?" He waited. Pitts said nothing.

Jack continued to move toward the wall of the darkened auditorium, where he hoped to find some reference point to get his bearings. If he could orient himself in the room, then wait and listen, maybe he could gain an advantage on his adversary. His arms were shaking from fatigue and shock by the time he reached the side wall.

In the dark, he could visualize the rest of the room. If there was any advantage he could gain in this face-off, his sense of space and distance was it. He rose up slowly and peered over the back of the seat in front of him. He couldn't see a thing.

Jack sat with his back against the auditorium wall, waiting for Pitts to answer. *Where is he? Where could he be hiding?*

Jack turned his head toward the front of the room and then rested it against the wall. The textured concrete was cold against his ear. Squeak. He heard a noise being carried through the wall. Squeak—squeak. He heard it again. *What is it?* It sounded like metal rubbing against metal. He leaned his head away from the wall and listened. *Nothing.* He put his ear to the wall again. Squeak. Something was making that noise.

"Goodbye, McCall," Pitts said, his voice muffled as if facing away from Jack.

Jack closed his eyes and grimaced, as a wave of pain shot up his wounded leg. The bleeding had slowed, but the pain was beginning to intensify. His mind raced. Did Pitts know a way out of the building?

Jack heard several clinking sounds like metal hitting metal. With his ear to the wall, Jack visualized himself standing on the stage. *What would I see if I looked up? Curtains. Lighting. The lighting catwalk.* Jack raised his head, looking for an outline of anything on the stage, his eyes again straining to acclimate to the dark room. *The roof hatch. Students used to climb on the roof through the access hatch above the catwalk.*

Jack put his ear against the wall again to verify that Pitts was still on the platform. Nothing. He kept his ear to the wall and waited. Squeak. *If he gets out onto the roof, he'll get away.*

Jack draped his forearms over the seatback in front of him and pulled himself up to a kneeling position. His leg throbbed and his head spun around a little, compelling him to rest a few seconds before proceeding. Putting his left arm straight out, he inched sideways until he was against the wall. Again he rested a moment. He put his right arm straight out, parallel and level with the left, his pistol in his right hand. In his mind he could visualize the front of the auditorium, the stage, and the curtains.

Keeping his left arm against the wall, he raised his right arm and moved it slightly to the right, aiming toward the platform where he suspected Pitts was waiting. Jack pulled the trigger.

BOOM. The sound of his pistol filled the auditorium. It was a sharp, tinny roar that was immediately sucked up by the acoustical panels in the room. Jack didn't know how many times he fired the weapon. The recoil of the pistol and his weakened condition caused him to fall backwards to the floor. He heard the rattle of metal structures above the stage and then a loud THUD that sounded like a body hitting the stage floor. Jack listened, holding his breath. No sound. He blacked out.

CHAPTER 15

JACK OPENED HIS EYES. Mollie, her image a bit blurry, was sitting by the window of the hospital room reading a book. "If that story is about the 'afterlife,'" he said, rubbing his eyes to clear his vision, "I can tell you how it starts."

Mollie closed the book and stood up. "I'm glad you can't tell me how it ends," she said. She leaned in and kissed him on the lips.

"Maybe there is a heaven," he said. "I think I just got a taste."

"That wasn't heaven you tasted," Mollie said, giving him another kiss on the lips. "It was a Hershey Bar."

Jack smiled. "Close," he said.

Frank Kirby walked into the room.

A smile appeared on Jack's face and then disappeared. "Speak of the devil."

"Relax, McCall," Frank said. "I'm here for your official statement, not your hide." He reached into his sports coat and extracted a notepad. "Nice shooting, by the way." He pulled a chair over toward the bed and sat down. "How'd you manage to hit him in the dark from where you were?"

"He has supernatural abilities," Mollie said, giving Jack a love-pat on the cheek.

Frank rolled his eyes, with a hint of a grin on his face.

"How many bullets hit their mark?" Jack said.

Frank laughed at the question. "One, but it went through his left eye."

"That's not good," Jack said, closing his eyes and shaking his head to feign disappointment.

Frank stared at him for a moment. "Okay, I'll bite. Why isn't that good?"

"I was aiming for his right eye," Jack said, as he reached over to the bed controls and raised his head.

Frank put on a fake grin. "Statement from Smart-Ass Lawyer," he said, as he jotted the same on his notepad.

"How're Kate and Henry?" Jack said.

Peter Wilder knocked on the open door and paused. "Kate lost a lot of blood, but she should be okay," he said.

"Good," Jack said. "You shouldn't have gone to Portland—you missed all the fun."

Peter walked into the room and stood next to Mollie. "Pitts was the one who had the least amount of fun. How'd you manage a shot like that?"

"I used 'The Force,' Luke."

"Pure dumb luck, if you ask me," Frank said.

Jack chuckled. "That too."

Peter sat down and scooted the chair closer to Jack's bed. "You'll be glad to know that the girl you shot is very much alive and talking like a parrot on speed."

"Rebekah Pitts," Jack said.

"Yes," Peter said. "I convinced her that if she could help us tie her brother to killings here in the US, we would do our best to block any requests from foreign jurisdictions trying to extradite her as an accessory to crimes he committed offshore."

"You're going to overlook her trying to shoot me?" Jack said, looking at Frank.

Frank smiled, cocked his head as if considering the topic from all perspectives, and then said, "Right now that's the *only* crime she's committed, that we know of."

Jack straightened his body. "Well, thank heavens she didn't do anything serious," he said, as he grabbed the hospital water jug on the tray next to his bed. "Let's give her two weeks of community service and send her home."

"Don't be rude," Mollie said. "Your friends came here to comfort you and make you feel better."

Jack looked at Frank. "So did you come here to make me feel better?"

Frank tried to squelch a laugh, but it escaped anyway.

Mollie walked over and put a hand on Frank's shoulder. "Jack, the paramedics told me that Frank pulled you from inside the auditorium out to the hallway where he could see better, and was using his handkerchief to compress the wound in your leg by the time they arrived."

Everyone in the room stared at Frank.

"He was bleeding all over the floor," Frank said, looking around at the group. "Do you know how hard it is to get blood out of linoleum?"

"Thank you," Jack said.

Frank grumbled and stood up. "I used that handkerchief to clean the windshield on my cruiser this morning." He laughed again.

"Did you ask Rebekah about Annie's death?" Jack said to Peter.

Peter shook his head. "Frank asked her."

Jack looked at Frank. "Did Joshua kill her?"

"Yes," Frank said. "Turns out mom and dad did more than just run a photo studio. They had a pretty lucrative business making people dead."

"That's why we seldom saw people going into their studio," Jack said. "The studio wasn't their real business."

Frank nodded. "Mom and dad trained Joshua in the family arts, and when Constance Whitehurst paid old man Pitts to kill Annie, Joshua was assigned the kill as sort of a 'graduation' exercise."

"Ooooh," Mollie said, contorting her face as if she smelled a skunk. "That's sick."

"Murder generally is," Peter said. "Little sister also told us that Joshua tried to kill you and Jack because he was afraid your snooping would expose the family business."

"Mrs. Whitehurst must have really hated Annie," Mollie said. She looked at Jack. "Remember what Sterling said? His mother even hated *him*."

"Yeah," Jack said, nodding in agreement. "But the old man probably would have personally strangled his wife if she'd messed with his son.

"So she had Annie killed instead?" Mollie said"

"Then Joshua and Rebekah carried on in the family business," Jack said.

"Well, to hear Rebekah tell it," Peter said, "Joshua carried on in the business alone but forced her to help him on a few jobs. She was just an innocent wedding photographer from Florida—most of the time."

"Bullshit," Mollie said, drawing stares from all in the room.

"Undoubtedly," Peter said.

"Didn't you tell me," Jack said, "that Joshua's travel matched up with only seventy percent of his suspected kills?"

"Yes," Peter said.

"Smart money says that if you check Rebekah's travel," Jack said, "it will match the remaining thirty percent."

Peter nodded and started to stand up, but Jack grabbed his arm, prompting him to remain seated.

Jack rolled over closer to Peter. "Did you ask her who paid them to assassinate Dakota?"

"Of course I asked her," Peter answered. "She claims the only thing Joshua told her was 'H-Two-O.' "

Jack and Mollie looked at each other. "Water rights," they said, as if one mind.

Frank's face sprouted a confused look. "Water rights? What the hell are you talking about?"

"California water rights for his ranch," Mollie said.

"You should probably pass this along to the California attorney general," Jack said. "They should be able to give you a list of people, or companies, who wanted Dakota's water rights."

"Water rights," Frank said, rising to his feet and pushing his chair back to the wall. "Don't have those issues in the Willamette Valley." He left the room.

"We'll follow the money," Peter said, "once we get access to Joshua's accounts and records."

"I'll bet it leads straight to the San Joaquin Valley," Jack said. He grabbed the bed control and pushed the down arrow until he was lying flat. "Thanks, Peter, for helping me catch Annie's killer."

"Just doing my job, buddy," Peter said. "Listen, call me when you get back to work in Hartford. I'll fly up to do a final interview for my report, and maybe the four of us can have dinner."

"Yes," Jack said. "Love to."

******

Jack lay flat on his back on the lawn outside the main terminal at Caldwell Airport, his face drenched in sunlight. He was waiting for Mollie and the flight service ground crew to get everything loaded into the Aero Commander so they could depart for home. The warmth felt good; it took his mind back to summer days when he was a boy. He would lie on the freshly mowed grass with his eyes closed and listen to the sounds of the airplanes flying overhead, imagining that he was a pilot and could fly off to any destination he chose.

"Jack," Mollie's voice called from a distance. "Look who I found."

Jack did a slow, cautious roll onto his side so he wouldn't aggravate his wounded leg. Heading toward him were Mollie, Henry, and Jessie, arm in arm. The three were smiling and laughing like lifelong friends. He started to stand up, but his efforts proved insufficient.

"Don't get up, silly," Jessie said, as the trio arrived at his resting place. "I just came over to thank you again and say goodbye."

Jack abandoned his effort to stand up. He could only manage to struggle to a sitting position, prompting the three healthy bodies to join him by sitting on the ground. Mollie brushed the grass off his shirt and skin and out of his hair.

"I'm glad everything turned out well, Jessie," Jack said. "You deserve to have some good things happen in your life."

Mollie gave Jessie's arm a squeeze and jumped into the conversation with an enthusiastic "I should hope so."

The recipient of this outpouring of goodwill displayed a huge white, toothy grin that immediately aimed itself toward the ground and was shrouded by a curtain of blonde hair.

Henry added his voice to the chorus of encouragement. "Jessie, I've always been proud to call you my friend."

"Thank you, Henry," she said, raising her head. "All three of you, thank you." She scattered her smile generously to each of them. "I'd forgotten what it was like to have friends," she said. "I've spent the last twenty years hiding." She sat up a little straighter.

"What are you going to do now?" Jack said.

Jessie closed her eyes for a moment, as if to imagine the future. "It's time I stopped hiding behind P.D. Newhouse," she said. "I'm not sure how my readers will react, but I am willing to risk it. I'm going to live dangerously from now on."

"Too bad Jack's not the one flying us home," Mollie said, "or you could really live dangerously and fly with us."

Jack feigned emotional trauma by emitting a mock whimper. "Yeah," he said, "Why don't you?"

Jessie looked puzzled for a moment, as if waiting for Mollie to confirm that her husband's offer was a joke. "Really?" she said, after some hesitation.

Mollie rose to her feet and held out her hand. "Let's go cancel your reservation and grab your bags," she said. "We can stop in Indianapolis to drop you off on our way home."

Jessie grabbed Mollie's hand and pulled herself to her feet. "That sounds crazy—let's do it."

Mollie aimed an index finger at her wounded husband. "Henry, you can help 'peg leg' here out to the airplane while Jessie and I get her stuff," she said.

"Come on, Peg," Henry said, draping Jack's arm around his neck. "Let me help you." He lifted Jack to a standing position.

"You've been helping me for as long as I can remember," Jack said, shifting his weight to the crutches his friend held in place for him. "We damned near learned to walk together, ride a bike together, swim, read, write—everything. Then, when we reached high school, it was like we just stopped being friends. Why did that happen?"

The two men ambled their way across the lawn, neither one answering the question. The snail's pace amplified the silence and added to Jack's discomfort, especially since he hadn't thanked Henry for stopping him from falling off the wagon the night before. As they arrived at the gate that led to the parking apron, Dakota came out of the flight service lobby and jogged toward them.

"Hold up a minute," Jack said. "I want to say goodbye to him."

Dakota slowed to a walk when he saw the two men waiting. "I never got the chance to thank you for saving my life," he said to Jack, as he arrived at the gate. He gave Jack a hug.

"Hey," Henry said. "I got shot too—saving your life."

Dakota gave Henry a hug as well.

"Was that hug from Dakota or Virgil?" Henry said.

"That was from me—Virgil Douglas," the actor said.

"Virgil Douglas?" Jack said. "That's kind of a hybrid identity, isn't it?"

Dakota nodded and smiled. "Dakota Douglas has a lot of money, guys," he said. "And Virgil's not stupid."

The three childhood friends laughed and had another round of hugs.

"So, Virgil," Jack said. "Are you heading out on the next flight?"

Virgil shook his head. "Heading out in my Gulfstream," he said, pointing to a private jet being fueled for departure on the parking apron. "Like I said, Dakota Douglas has a lot of money. I'm just waiting for Kate to get here."

"Kate's going with you?" Jack said.

Virgil took a deep breath and seemed to fight off a tear. "Every day of my glamorous life," he said, "I'm surrounded by people who would dump me in a heartbeat if there's even a hint of a box office hiccup. Do you know how endearing it is to be with someone who is actually willing to give up her life for me?" The tear made a last-second appearance.

Jack looked at Henry and put a hand on his shoulder. "Yes," he said. "I know what it's like."

"Besides," Virgil said, as he started to walk toward his airplane, "she said if I ever left her, she would render me impotent, without …"

"Leaving a scar?" Jack finished.

A medical transporter pulled up to the Gulfstream. Medics unloaded Kate and wheeled her to the aircraft's steps. Dakota sprinted over to the plane while Kate eased her way out of the wheelchair and stood up. The smitten actor lifted his guardian angel into his arms and carried her up the stairs. She gave a wave to Jack and Henry as the couple disappeared into the executive jet.

Henry and Jack walked through the gate and out onto the parking apron. When they reached the airplane parked at the edge of the ramp, Henry turned to Jack and reached out, putting his hands on Jack's shoulders. "You asked why we stopped being friends," he said. "You were a drunk, Jack. And I'm ashamed to say that I couldn't stand watching your life go down the drain. I convinced myself that there was nothing I could do about it, so I stopped watching."

"Can't blame you, I guess," Jack said, turning toward the Aero Commander and shuffling through his pants pocket for the door key.

"I can blame me," Henry said. "You needed me then, and I avoided you. I'm sorry."

Jack hugged his friend. "You more than made up for it last night," he said. "Thank you so much."

"Are you okay today?" Henry asked.

"One day at a time," Jack said, and then started toward the door of the airplane. He stopped and looked at Henry. "When we were at your house the other day, you said that plants don't commit suicide," he said. "What did you mean?"

Henry was silent for a moment. "The comment was about Jennifer," Henry finally said. "She was a patient."

Jack nodded. "So moving back to the farm was …"

"She's safe and happy there," Henry said.

Mollie and Jessie arrived at the opposite side of the airplane and started to load Jessie's baggage, their efforts resulting in a flurry of giggles and groans. Jack unlocked the passenger door to allow his traveling companions to climb on board, after a momentary stop to give Henry a hug and say goodbye. Mollie strapped herself into the pilot seat, with Jessie in the copilot seat, leaving the rest of the cabin for Jack to find a comfortable seating position to accommodate his wounded leg. He inched back into the rear seat of the cabin and placed the tender limb on a pillow Mollie had placed on a middle seat.

"Did you find what you came looking for, Jack?" Henry said through the open doorway.

"Yes," Jack said.

"What was it?" Henry said.

Jack paused for a moment to reflect on everything that had happened over the past five days. "Forgiveness," he said.

"Who forgave you?" Henry said, backing away in preparation for closing the cabin door.

"I did," Jack said.

Henry smiled and nodded as he closed the door.

"Clear," Mollie yelled out the window of the Commander. She started the engines, received taxi instructions from the tower, and taxied the airplane out to the runway.

"Caldwell Tower, Six-two-seven-eight-Bravo for takeoff, runway one-seven, over," she said, when she had brought the airplane to a halt short of the runway.

"Seven-eight-Bravo, Caldwell Tower, altimeter two-niner-niner-five, wind calm, cleared for takeoff, runway one-seven."

"Roger, Caldwell Tower, Seven-eight-Bravo, cleared for takeoff." Mollie eased the aircraft forward and then turned when it reached the centerline. Full throttle sent the Aero Commander roaring down the runway.

Jack watched the ground fall away as the aircraft rose into the air. The boy had never tired of the sensation he felt during the first moments of flight. The man cherished the memory.

LETTER TO THE READER

Dear Reader:

Thank you for purchasing *The Dead Girl Reunion*, the first of my Jack McCall mysteries. I hope you enjoyed the story.

As an independent author, I don't have a big (*or even a small*) publishing company promoting my book. The best marketing tool I have is you. Please consider writing a review on the website where you purchased this book or, if you purchased the book at an independent bookstore, tell the store staff and your friends about your reading experience with this story. It would be very helpful and very much appreciated.

If you would like to learn more about me and my writing, you can go to my website: www.pkross.com.

Thank you again.

P.K. Ross

ABOUT THE AUTHOR

P.K. Ross is a former Human Resources Director and Senior Professional in Human Resources who lives in Corvallis, Oregon, with his wife, Elizabeth. He returned to his hometown in 2012 to get away from the "big city" and concentrate on writing. This book is his first novel, after honing his writing skills on corporate communication and marketing materials. The author's formal training in writing fiction was acquired through professional instruction from author Elizabeth Engstrom, and professional association workshops. He is a member of Mystery Writers of America, Willamette Writers, Oregon Writers Colony, and Northwest Independent Writers Association. P.K. is currently working on the second book in the Jack McCall series, titled The Deadly Sunday Drive.

More information about the author is available at http://www.pkross.com/.